$3.⌐

c2

D1557170

NEBULA AWARD STORIES ELEVEN

Nebula Award Stories Eleven

EDITED BY URSULA K. LE GUIN

HARPER & ROW, PUBLISHERS

NEW YORK
HAGERSTOWN
SAN FRANCISCO
LONDON

Acknowledgment is made for permission to reprint the following material:

"Catch that Zeppelin!" by Fritz Leiber. Copyright © 1975 by Mercury Press, Inc., first published in *The Magazine of Fantasy and Science Fiction*, March, 1975; reprinted by permission of the author and the author's agent, Robert P. Mills, Ltd.

"End Game," by Joe Haldeman. Copyright © 1974 by The Condé Nast Publications Inc., first published in *Analog Science Fiction/Science Fact*, Jan., 1975; reprinted by permission of the author and his agent, Robert P. Mills, Ltd.

"Home is the Hangman," by Roger Zelazny. Copyright © 1975 by Roger Zelazny, first published in *Analog Science Fiction/Science Fact*, Nov., 1975; reprinted by permission of the author and his agents, Henry Morrison, Inc.

"Child of All Ages," by P. J. Plauger. Copyright © 1975 by The Condé Nast Publications Inc., first published in *Analog Science Fiction/Science Fact*, March, 1975; reprinted by permission of the author.

"Shatterday," by Harlan Ellison. Copyright © 1975 by Harlan Ellison, first published in *Gallery*, Sept., 1975; reprinted by permission of the author and his agent, Robert P. Mills, Ltd.

"San Diego Lightfoot Sue," by Tom Reamy. Copyright © 1975 by Mercury Press, Inc., first published in *The Magazine of Fantasy and Science Fiction*, Aug., 1975; reprinted by permission of the author and his agent, Virginia Kidd.

"Time Deer," by Craig Strete. Copyright © 1974 by UPD Publishing Corporation, first published in *Worlds of If*, Nov.-Dec., 1974; reprinted by permission of the author.

Contents

v

To James Blish   1921–1975
Analyst and catalyst of science fiction,
creator mirabilis.

Acknowledgments

As I have been living this past year in England, where the science fiction scene is as lively as in the States, and as I had three totally science-fictional weeks in Australia around the World Science Fiction Convention in Melbourne in August of 1975, I had a strong wish to get the view from Overseas and Down Under represented in this volume. I was very fortunate in being able to catch both in the person of Mr. Peter Nicholls, administrator of the Science Fiction Foundation, editor of *Foundation* magazine, an Australian living in England, a hopeless fan, and a superb critic. For the home view—so that we remember that not all subversives are foreigners—Ms. Vonda McIntyre consented to write an article, to my great pleasure and, I think, yours.

To Ms. McIntyre, Mr. C. L. Grant, Mr. Dean McLaughlin, and all others who helped get this book together and keep it flying back and forth across the Atlantic Ocean, my most cordial thanks and praise. As for Ms. Virginia Kidd, who wrote the headnotes and who did all the hard and hidden work, no thanks are adequate, no praise sufficient.

Ursula K. Le Guin

Introduction

The Nebula Award is an object—a lovely cube of lucite and rock crystal. The Nebula Awards are also a process, which works like this: throughout the year the members of the Science Fiction Writers of America nominate for the Award works of science fiction printed in the United States during that year, and early in the following year they vote on the nominated works in four categories, novel, novella, novelette, and short story. This procedure, like most democratic procedures and the flight of the bumblebee, seems, to the analytic eye and logical mind, impossible. The list of works nominated gets so long that only a superspeed full-time bookworm could possibly read them all. What the members do is vote for the ones they like best from those they have read. This is not perfect justice. But then, perfection seems not to be a human province; and anyhow, it works. The bumblebee gets off the ground. A fine work may now and then be missed, but the Nebula Award has never yet been given to trash, and year after year the Awards reliably signify excellence.

Therefore the job of the editor of a Nebula Awards volume is a heartbreaker: all those grand also-rans that can't be squeezed in, not to mention the novels, which can't be represented at all. We were fortunate this year in obtaining a story by Joe Haldeman which is actually a part of his Award-winning novel, *The Forever*

War. But I can only mention the names of the top runner-up novels—*The Mote in God's Eye* by Larry Niven and Jerry Pournelle, Samuel R. Delany's *Dhalgren,* Joanna Russ's *Female Man.* The variety in style, subject, scope, intent of just these four novels is shining proof of the versatility and venturesomeness of the sf novel today.

A Nebula Award in drama (intended for the *writer* of a script, play, opera, et cetera) was added a couple of years ago, and this year was given to *Young Frankenstein.* We can't get that into the book either, since no one has yet invented a process for reproducing Gene Wilder in print. But thinking about that funny and curiously tender movie got me to thinking about Old Frankenstein, and about monsters and creators.

I agree with Brian Aldiss that probably the first person you can usefully call a science fiction writer was Mary Shelley. She made our first myth. And the first myth, properly, is the Creation Myth.

The creators of sf, the writers, are a kind of composite Frankenstein; and they have, like him, created a composite being, which is both more and less than human.

The creature Frankenstein made was superhuman in his strength, his physical capacities; and that will do nicely as a metaphor for the potentialities of sf as a fiction form—its limitless flexibility as to subject matter and style. One is free, writing sf, with a heady kind of freedom—"I can do anything!"—such as a person of great physical strength or the manipulator of a building crane or an advanced computer must feel.

Where Frankenstein's creature was less than human, properly a monster, was in the ethical mode. Frankenstein evaded his responsibility as creator, failing to give his creation either love or instruction. And so it went wrong, wasting its strength on revenge, destruction, and stupid violence.

The metaphor still holds. Where sf has most often failed as literature, as good writing or good work by any definition, is in the ethical mode. It is inventive, intellectually ingenious, but morally trivial, and therefore blunders senselessly from act to act, from violence to violence. What might have been dramatic is merely theatrical; what might have been imaginative is stereotyped fantasizing. Rock and iron, flesh and blood become plastic toys, and Spacetime itself, the great theme, shrinks to the pettiness of a TV stage set.

I think that this characteristic irresponsibility will always be a besetting danger to sf; and I think more and more sf writers are conscious of it. The profound change in sf during the last couple of decades may come down to just that: an intensification of moral consciousness, of conscience. The stories in this volume, in all their variety, show it. There is a kind of sensitivity, a vulnerability, about most of them, whether, like Joe Haldeman's and Roger Zelazny's novellas, they are full of action and "hardware," or whether like Tom Reamy's prize-winning novelette and most of the short stories, their action is psychological and their imagery more related to the dream. If we could have included the novella and novelette runners-up, notably Lisa Tuttle and George R. R. Martin's "Storms of Windhaven," Randall Garrett's "Final Fighting of Fionn Mac-Cumhaill," Richard Cowper's "The Custodians," William K. Carlson's "Sunrise West," and James Tiptree Jr.'s magnificent "A Momentary Taste of Being," this mood or quality would be still clearer.

It does not, of course, involve any one particular moral stance. Still less does it involve the enunciation of moralisings and ethical directives. Just the opposite. It is a refusal of the closed, the rigid, the ready answer, the final solution; it is a quality of openness.

To be open is to be vulnerable. Nothing in sf used to hurt. Solar systems went poof, vast stellar empires perished painlessly. These days, things hurt.

To be open is to be uncertain. The lines used to be so clear between Human and Alien, Man and Woman, Now and the Future. These days, the distinctions vanish and reappear where least expected. Barriers become connections, and vice versa. Which is Us and which is Them? Time is no longer a line along which history, past or future, lies neatly arranged, but a field of great mystery and complexity, in the contemplation of which the mind perceives an immense terror, and an indestructible hope.

For to be open is to admit hope, along with pain, uncertainty, and fear. That's why, although there's a good deal of sadness in some of these stories, and considerable wrath, the effect they finally give as a whole is not depressing, as so much of the old Man-Conquers-Cosmos sf was. When you've conquered the cosmos all that's left to do is sit down, like Alexander the Great, and cry. But these writers are after greater game than a mere galaxy or two. They are looking, in their various and peculiar ways, for the truth. Nobody knows if any of them found it, but that doesn't matter. What matters is the wit and strength and beauty of these minds, these words. "The journey, not the arrival, matters." I confidently wish you a good journey.

Ursula K. Le Guin

London, England
April, 1975

NEBULA AWARD STORIES

FRITZ LEIBER

Catch That Zeppelin!

Fritz Leiber has been writing and selling science-fiction, supernatural-horror, and heroic-fantasy stories for thirty-seven years. During some of that time he was a resident of Chicago, New York and Los Angeles. For the past six years, however, he has lived in San Francisco in a small downtown apartment building, from the seventh-story roof of which he observes the stars through a three-inch refracting telescope. What with San Francisco's fogs, lights, highrises and other aerial apparitions (seagulls, he says, like shooting stars before dawn and aircraft seeming UFO's in sunset glow) this viewing has led to an equal interest in meteorology and the roofscapes and general anatomy and ecology of large cities—one thing leading to another. Afternoons he spends in walks about the romantic hilly city.

His growing engrossment in San Francisco has led him to write his first full-scale supernatural-horror novel since 1943's *Conjure Wife*. It concerns Thibaut de Castries, a modern black magician who has created a new brand of the occult based on the malign influences and "black music" generated by tall buildings and large cities. *Our Lady of Darkness* (the full-length novel to be published later in 1977 by Putnam's/Berkley after the appearance of a two-part excerpt, "The Pale Brown Thing," earlier in the year in the pages of *The Magazine of Fantasy and Science Fiction*) will involve not only the influences of

3

large cities but also real-life characters such as Jack London, Ambrose
Bierce, Isadora Duncan, Dashiell Hammett and Clark Ashton Smith.
Nor will his new novel be the first example of Fritz Leiber's fascination
with real-live real-dead personae. Read on:

This year on a trip to New York City to visit my son, who is a social historian at a leading municipal university there, I had a very unsettling experience. At black moments, of which at my age I have quite a few, it still makes me distrust profoundly those absolute boundaries in Space and Time which are our sole protection against Chaos, and fear that my mind—no, my entire individual existence—may at any moment at all and without any warning whatsoever be blown by a sudden gust of Cosmic Wind to an entirely different spot in a Universe of Infinite Possibilities. Or, rather, into another Universe altogether. And that my mind and individuality will be changed to fit.

But at other moments, which are still in the majority, I believe that my unsettling experience was only one of those remarkably vivid waking dreams to which old people become increasingly susceptible, generally waking dreams about the past, and especially waking dreams about a past in which at some crucial point one made an entirely different and braver choice than one actually did, or in which the whole world made such a decision, with a completely different future resulting. Golden glowing might-have-beens nag increasingly at the minds of some older people.

In line with this interpretation I must admit that my whole unsettling experience was structured very much like a dream. It

5

began with startling flashes of a changed world. It continued into a longer period when I completely accepted the changed world and delighted in it and, despite fleeting quivers of uneasiness, wished I could bask in its glow forever. And it ended in horrors, or nightmares, which I hate to mention, let alone discuss, until I must.

Opposing this dream notion, there are times when I am completely convinced that what happened to me in Manhattan and in a certain famous building there was no dream at all, but absolutely real, and that I did indeed visit another Time Stream.

Finally, I must point out that what I am about to tell you I am necessarily describing in retrospect, highly aware of several transitions involved and, whether I want to or not, commenting on them and making deductions that never once occurred to me at the time.

No, at the time it happened to me—and now at this moment of writing I am convinced that it did happen and was absolutely real—one instant simply succeeded another in the most natural way possible. I questioned nothing.

As to why it all happened to me, and what particular mechanism was involved, well, I am convinced that every man or woman has rare, brief moments of extreme sensitivity, or rather vulnerability, when his mind and entire being may be blown by the Change Winds to Somewhere Else. And then, by what I call the Law of the Conservation of Reality, blown back again.

I was walking down Broadway somewhere near 34th Street. It was a chilly day, sunny despite the smog—a bracing day—and I suddenly began to stride along more briskly than is my cautious habit, throwing my feet ahead of me with a faint suggestion of the goose step. I also threw back my shoulders and took deep breaths, ignoring the fumes which tickled my nostrils. Beside me, traffic growled and snarled, rising at times to a machine-gun rata-tat-tat, while pedestrians were scuttling about with that desperate ratlike urgency characteristic of all big American cities, but which reaches its ultimate in New York. I cheerfully ignored that too. I even smiled at the sight of a ragged bum and a fur-coated gray-haired society lady both independently dodging across the street through the hurtling traffic with a cool practiced skill one sees only in America's biggest metropolis.

Just then I noticed a dark, wide shadow athwart the street ahead of me. It could not be that of a cloud, for it did not move. I craned my neck sharply and looked straight up like the veriest yokel, a regular *Hans-Kopf-in-die-Luft* (Hans-Head-in-the-Air, a German figure of comedy).

My gaze had to climb up the giddy 102 stories of the tallest building in the world, the Empire State. My gaze was strangely accompanied by the vision of a gigantic, long-fanged ape making the same ascent with a beautiful girl in one paw—oh, yes, I was recollecting the charming American fantasy-film *King Kong*, or as they name it in Sweden, *Kong King.*

And then my gaze clambered higher still, up the 222-foot sturdy tower, to the top of which was moored the nose of the vast, breathtakingly beautiful, streamlined, silvery shape which was making the shadow.

Now here is a most important point. I was not at the time in the least startled by what I saw. I knew at once that it was simply the bow section of the German zeppelin *Ostwald,* named for the great German pioneer of physical chemistry and electrochemistry, and queen of the mighty passenger and light-freight fleet of luxury airliners working out of Berlin, Baden-Baden, and Bremerhaven. That matchless Armada of Peace, each titanic airship named for a world-famous German scientist—the *Mach,* the *Nernst,* the *Humboldt,* the *Fritz Haber,* the French-named *Antoine Henri Becquerel,* the American-named *Edison,* the Polish-named *T. Sklodowska Edison,* and even the Jewish-named *Einstein!* The great humanitarian navy in which I held a not unimportant position as international sales consultant and *Fachmann*—I mean expert. My chest swelled with justified pride at this *edel*—noble—achievement of *der Vaterland.*

I knew also without any mind-searching or surprise that the length of the *Ostwald* was more than one half the 1,472-foot height of the Empire State Building plus its mooring tower, thick enough to hold an elevator. And my heart swelled again with the thought that the Berlin *Zeppelinturm* (dirigible tower) was only a few meters less high. Germany, I told myself, need not strain for mere numerical records—her sweeping scientific and technical achievements speak for themselves to the entire planet.

All this literally took little more than a second, and I never broke my snappy stride. As my gaze descended, I cheerfully hummed under my breath *Deutschland, Deutschland uber Alles.*

The Broadway I saw was utterly transformed, though at the time this seemed every bit as natural as the serene presence of the *Ostwald* high overhead, vast ellipsoid held aloft by helium. Silvery electric trucks and buses and private cars innumerable purred along far more evenly and quietly, and almost as swiftly, as had the noisy, stenchful, jerky gasoline-powered vehicles only moments before, though to me now the latter were completely forgotten. About two blocks ahead, an occasional gleaming electric car smoothly swung into the wide silver arch of a quick-battery-change station, while others emerged from under the arch to rejoin the almost dreamlike stream of traffic.

The air I gratefully inhaled was fresh and clean, without trace of smog.

The somewhat fewer pedestrians around me still moved quite swiftly, but with a dignity and courtesy largely absent before, with the numerous blackamoors among them quite as well dressed and exuding the same quiet confidence as the Caucasians.

The only slightly jarring note was struck by a tall, pale, rather emaciated man in black dress and with unmistakably Hebraic features. His somber clothing was somewhat shabby, though well kept, and his thin shoulders were hunched. I got the impression he had been looking closely at me, and then instantly glancing away as my eyes sought his. For some reason I recalled what my son had told me about the City College of New York—CCNY—being referred to surreptitiously and jokingly as Christian College Now Yiddish. I couldn't help chuckling a bit at that witticism, though I am glad to say it was a genial little guffaw rather than a

malicious snicker. Germany in her well-known tolerance and no-
ble-mindedness has completely outgrown her old, disfiguring anti-
Semitism—after all, we must admit in all fairness that perhaps a
third of our great men are Jews or carry Jewish genes, Haber and
Einstein among them—despite what dark and, yes, wicked memories may lurk in the subconscious minds of oldsters like myself and
occasionally briefly surface into awareness like submarines bent on
ship murder.

My happily self-satisfied mood immediately reasserted itself,
and with a smart, almost military gesture I brushed to either side
with a thumbnail the short, horizontal black mustache which
decorates my upper lip, and I automatically swept back into place
the thick comma of black hair (I confess I dye it) which tends to
fall down across my forehead.

I stole another glance up at the *Ostwald,* which made me think
of the matchless amenities of that wondrous deluxe airliner: the
softly purring motors that powered its propellers—electric motors, naturally, energized by banks of lightweight TSE batteries
and as safe as its helium; the Grand Corridor running the length
of the passenger deck from the Bow Observatory to the stern's
like-windowed Games Room, which becomes the Grand Ballroom
at night; the other peerless rooms letting off that corridor—the
Gesellschaftsraum der Kapitän (Captain's Lounge) with its dark
woodwork, manly cigar smoke and *Damentische* (Tables for Ladies), the Premier Dining Room with its linen napery and silver-
plated aluminum dining service, the Ladies' Retiring Room always
set out profusely with fresh flowers, the Schwartzwald bar, the
gambling casino with its roulette, baccarat, chemmy, blackjack
(vingt-et-un), its tables for skat and bridge and dominoes and
sixty-six, its chess tables presided over by the delightfully eccentric
world's champion Nimzowitch, who would defeat you blindfold,
but always brilliantly, simultaneously or one at a time, in charm-
ingly baroque brief games for only two gold pieces per person per
game (one gold piece to nutsy Nimzy, one to the DLG), and the
supremely luxurious staterooms with costly veneers of mahogany
over balsa; the hosts of attentive stewards, either as short and

skinny as jockeys or else actual dwarfs, both types chosen to save weight; and the titanium elevator rising through the countless bags of helium to the two-decked Zenith Observatory, the sun deck wind-screened but roofless to let in the ever-changing clouds, the mysterious fog, the rays of the stars and good old Sol, and all the heavens. Ah, where else on land or sea could you buy such high living?

I called to mind in detail the single cabin which was always mine when I sailed on the *Ostwald—meine Stammkabine.* I visualized the Grand Corridor thronged with wealthy passengers in evening dress, the handsome officers, the unobtrusive, ever-attentive stewards, the gleam of white shirt fronts, the glow of bare shoulders, the muted dazzle of jewels, the music of conversations like string quartets, the lilting low laughter that traveled along.

Exactly on time I did a neat *"Links, marschieren!"* ("To the left, march!") and passed through the impressive portals of the Empire State and across its towering lobby to the mutedly silver-doored banks of elevators. On my way I noted the silver-glowing date: 6 May 1937 and the time of day: 1:07 P.M. Good!—since the *Ostwald* did not cast off until the tick of 3:00 P.M., I would be left plenty of time for a leisurely lunch and good talk with my son, if he had remembered to meet me—and there was actually no doubt of that, since he is the most considerate and orderly minded of sons, a real German mentality, though I say it myself.

I headed for the express bank, enjoying my passage through the clusters of high-class people who thronged the lobby without any unseemly crowding, and placed myself before the doors designated "Dirigible Departure Lounge" and in briefer German *"Zum Zeppelin."*

The elevator hostess was an attractive Japanese girl in skirt of dull silver with the DLG, Double Eagle and Dirigible insignia of the German Airship Union emblazoned in small on the left breast of her mutedly silver jacket. I noted with unvoiced approval that she appeared to have an excellent command of both German and English and was uniformly courteous to the passengers in her smiling but unemotional Nipponese fashion, which is so like our

German scientific precision of speech, though without the latter's warm underlying passion. How good that our two federations, at opposite sides of the globe, have strong commercial and behavioral ties!

My fellow passengers in the lift, chiefly Americans and Germans, were of the finest type, very well dressed—except that just as the doors were about to close, there pressed in my doleful Jew in black. He seemed ill at ease, perhaps because of his shabby clothing. I was surprised, but made a point of being particularly polite toward him, giving him a slight bow and brief but friendly smile, while flashing my eyes. Jews have as much right to the acme of luxury travel as any other people on the planet, if they have the money—and most of them do.

During our uninterrupted and infinitely smooth passage upward, I touched my outside left breast pocket to reassure myself that my ticket—first class on the *Ostwald!*—and my papers were there. But actually I got far more reassurance and even secret joy from the feel and thought of the documents in my tightly zippered inside left breast pocket: the signed preliminary agreements that would launch America herself into the manufacture of passenger zeppelins. Modern Germany is always generous in sharing her great technical achievements with responsible sister nations, supremely confident that the genius of her scientists and engineers will continue to keep her well ahead of all other lands; and after all, the genius of two Americans, father and son, had made vital though indirect contributions to the development of safe airship travel (and not forgetting the part played by the Polish-born wife of the one and mother of the other).

The obtaining of those documents had been the chief and official reason for my trip to New York City, though I had been able to combine it most pleasurably with a long overdue visit with my son, the social historian, and with his charming wife.

These happy reflections were cut short by the jarless arrival of our elevator at its lofty terminus on the one hundredth floor. The journey old love-smitten King Kong had made only after exhausting exertion we had accomplished effortlessly. The silvery doors spread wide. My fellow passengers hung back for a moment in awe and perhaps a little trepidation at the thought of the awesome journey ahead of them, and I—seasoned airship traveler that I am —was the first to step out, favoring with a smile and nod of approval my pert yet cool Japanese fellow employee of the lower echelons.

Hardly sparing a glance toward the great, fleckless window confronting the doors and showing a matchless view of Manhattan from an elevation of 1,250 feet minus two stories, I briskly turned, not right to the portals of the Departure Lounge and tower elevator, but left to those of the superb German restaurant *Krähenest* ("Crow's Nest").

I passed between the flanking three-foot-high bronze statuettes of Thomas Edison and Marie Sklodowska Edison niched in one wall and those of Count von Zeppelin and Thomas Sklodowska Edison facing them from the other, and entered the select precincts of the finest German dining place outside the Fatherland. I paused while my eyes traveled searchingly around the room with its restful dark wood paneling deeply carved with beautiful representations of the Black Forest and its grotesque supernatural denizens—kobolds, elves, gnomes, dryads (tastefully sexy), and the like. They interested me since I am what Americans call a Sunday painter, though almost my sole subject matter is zeppelins seen against blue sky and airy, soaring clouds.

The *Oberkellner* came hurrying toward me with menu tucked under his left elbow and saying, *"Mein Herr!* Charmed to see you once more! I have a perfect table-for-one with porthole looking out across the Hudson."

But just then a youthful figure rose springily from behind a table set against the far wall, and a dear and familiar voice rang out to me with *"Hier, Papa!"*

"Nein, Herr Ober," I smilingly told the headwaiter as I walked past him, *"heute hab ich ein Gesellschafter, Mein Sohn."*

I confidently made my way between tables occupied by well-dressed folk, both white and black.

My son wrung my hand with fierce family affection, though we had last parted only that morning. He insisted that I take the wide, dark, leather-upholstered seat against the wall, which gave me a fine view of the entire restaurant, while he took the facing chair. "Because during this meal I wish to look only on you, Papa," he assured me with manly tenderness. "And we have at least an hour and a half together, Papa—I have checked your luggage through, and it is likely already aboard the *Ostwald.*" Thoughtful, dependable boy!

"And now, Papa, what shall it be?" he continued after we had settled ourselves. "I see that today's special is *Sauerbraten mit Spatzel* and sweet-sour red cabbage. But there is also *Paprikahuhn* and—"

"Leave the chicken to flaunt her paprika in lonely red splendor today," I interrupted him. "*Sauerbraten* sounds fine."

Ordered by my Herr Ober, the aged wine waiter had already approached our table. I was about to give him direction when my son took upon himself that task with an authority and a hostfulness that warmed my heart. He scanned the wine menu rapidly but thoroughly.

"The Zinfandel 1933," he ordered with decision, though glancing my way to see if I concurred with his judgment. I smiled and nodded.

"And perhaps *ein Tropfchen Schnapps* to begin with?" he suggested.

"A brandy?—yes!" I replied. "And not just a drop, either. Make it a double. It is not every day I lunch with that distinguished scholar, my son."

"Oh, Papa," he protested, dropping his eyes and almost blushing. Then firmly to the bent-backed, white-haired wine waiter, "*Schnapps* also. *Doppel.*" The old waiter nodded his approval and hurried off.

We gazed fondly at each other for a few blissful seconds. Then I said, "Now tell me more fully about your achievements as a social historian on an exchange professorship in the New World. I know we have spoken about this several times, but only rather briefly and generally when various of your friends were present, or at least your lovely wife. Now I would like a more leisurely man-to-man account of your great work. Incidentally, do you find the scholarly apparatus—books, *und so weiter* ("et cetera")—of the Municipal Universities of New York City adequate to your needs after having enjoyed those of Baden-Baden University and the institutions of high learning in the German Federation?"

"In some respects they are lacking," he admitted. "However, for my purposes they have proved completely adequate." Then once more he dropped his eyes and almost blushed. "But, Papa, you praise my small efforts far too highly." He lowered his voice. "They do not compare with the victory for international industrial relations you yourself have won in a fortnight."

"All in a day's work for the DLG," I said self-deprecatingly, though once again lightly touching my left chest to establish contact with those most important documents safely stowed in my inside left breast pocket. "But now, no more polite fencing!" I went on briskly. "Tell me all about those 'small efforts,' as you modestly refer to them."

His eyes met mine. "Well, Papa," he began in suddenly matter-of-fact fashion, "all my work these last two years has been increasingly dominated by a firm awareness of the fragility of the underpinnings of the good world-society we enjoy today. If certain historically-minute key events, or cusps, in only the past one hundred years had been decided differently—if another course had been chosen than the one that was—then the whole world might now be plunged in wars and worse horrors then we ever dream of. It is a chilling insight, but it bulks continually larger in my entire work, my every paper."

I felt the thrilling touch of inspiration. At that moment the wine waiter arrived with our double brandies in small goblets of cut glass. I wove the interruption into the fabric of my inspiration. "Let us drink then to what you name your chilling insight," I said. *"Prosit!"*

The bite and spreading warmth of the excellent *schnapps* quickened my inspiration further. "I believe I understand exactly what you're getting at . . ." I told my son. I set down my half-

emptied goblet and pointed at something over my son's shoulder.
He turned his head around, and after one glance back at my
pointing finger, which intentionally waggled a tiny bit from side
to side, he realized that I was not indicating the entry of the
Krähenest, but the four sizable bronze statuettes flanking it.

"For instance," I said, "if Thomas Edison and Marie Sklodowska
had not married, and especially if they had not had their super-
genius son, then Edison's knowledge of electricity and hers of
radium and other radioactives might never have been joined.
There might never have been developed the fabulous T. S. Edison
battery, which is the prime mover of all today's surface and air
traffic. Those pioneering electric trucks introduced by the *Saturday Evening Post* in Philadelphia might have remained an expensive freak. And the gas helium might never have been produced
industrially to supplement earth's meager subterranean supply."

My son's eyes brightened with the flame of pure scholarship.
"Papa," he said eagerly, "you are a genius yourself! You have
precisely hit on what is perhaps the most important of those cusp-
events I referred to. I am at this moment finishing the necessary
research for a long paper on it. Do you know, Papa, that I have
firmly established by researching Parisian records that there was
in 1894 a close personal relationship between Marie Sklodowska
and her fellow radium researcher Pierre Curie, and that she might
well have become Madame Curie—or perhaps Madame Becquerel, for he too was in that work—if the dashing and brilliant
Edison had not most opportunely arrived in Paris in December
1894 to sweep her off her feet and carry her off to the New World
to even greater achievements?

"And just think, Papa," he went on, his eyes aflame, "what might
have happened if their son's battery had not been invented—the
most difficult technical achievement, hedged by all sorts of seeming scientific impossibilities, in the entire millennium-long history
of industry. Why, Henry Ford might have manufactured automo-
biles powered by steam or by exploding natural gas or conceivably
even vaporized liquid gasoline, rather than the mass-produced
electric cars which have been such a boon to mankind everywhere

—not our smokeless cars, but cars spouting all sorts of noxious fumes to pollute the environment."

Cars powered by the danger-fraught combustion of vaporized liquid gasoline!—it almost made me shudder and certainly it was a fantastic thought, yet not altogether beyond the bounds of possibility, I had to admit.

Just then I noticed my gloomy, black-clad Jew sitting only two tables away from us, though how he had got himself into the exclusive *Krähenest* was a wonder. Strange that I had missed his entry—probably immediately after my own, while I had eyes only for my son. His presence somehow threw a dark though only momentary shadow over my bright mood. Let him get some good German food inside him and some fine German wine, I thought generously—it will fill that empty belly of his and even put a bit of a good German smile into those sunken Yiddish cheeks! I combed my little mustache with my thumbnail and swept the errant lock of hair off my forehead.

Meanwhile my son was saying, "Also, Father, if electric transport had not been developed, and if during the last decade relations between Germany and the United States had not been so good, then we might never have gotten from the wells in Texas the supply of natural helium our zeppelins desperately needed during the brief but vital period before we had put the artificial creation of helium onto an industrial footing. My researchers at Washington have revealed that there was a strong movement in the U.S. military to ban the sale of helium to any other nation, Germany in particular. Only the powerful influence of Edison, Ford, and a few other key Americans, instantly brought to bear, prevented that stupid injunction. Yet if it had gone through, Germany might have been forced to use hydrogen instead of helium to float her passenger dirigibles. That was another crucial cusp."

"A hydrogen-supported zeppelin!—ridiculous! Such an airship would be a floating bomb, ready to be touched off by the slightest spark," I protested.

"Not ridiculous, Father," my son calmly contradicted me, shaking his head. "Pardon me for trespassing in your field, but there is an inescapable imperative about certain industrial developments. If there is not a safe road of advance, then a dangerous one will invariably be taken. You must admit. Father, that the development of commercial airships was in its early stages a most perilous venture. During the 1920s there were the dreadful wrecks of the American dirigibles *Roma,* and *Shenandoah,* which broke in two, *Akron,* and *Macon,* the British *R-38,* which also broke apart in the air, and *R-101,* the French *Dixmude,* which disappeared in the Mediterranean, Mussolini's *Italia,* which crashed trying to reach the North Pole, and the Russian *Maxim Gorky,* struck down by a plane, with a total loss of no fewer than 340 crew members for the nine accidents. If that had been followed by the explosions of two or three hydrogen zeppelins, world industry might well have abandoned forever the attempt to create passenger airships and turned instead to the development of large propeller-driven, heavier-than-air craft."

Monster airplanes, in danger every moment of crashing from engine failure, competing with good old unsinkable zeppelins?—impossible, at least at first thought. I shook my head, but not with as much conviction as I might have wished. My son's suggestion was really a valid one.

Besides, he had all his facts at his fingertips and was complete master of his subject, as I also had to allow. Those nine fearful airship disasters he mentioned had indeed occurred, as I knew well, and might have tipped the scale in favor of long-distance passenger and troop-carrying airplanes, had it not been for helium, the T. S. Edison battery, and German genius.

Fortunately I was able to dump from my mind these uncomfortable speculations and immerse myself in admiration of my son's multisided scholarship. That boy was a wonder!—a real chip off the old block, and, yes, a bit more.

"And now, Dolfy," he went on, using my nickname (I did not mind), "may I turn to an entirely different topic? Or rather to a very different example of my hypothesis of historical cusps?"

I nodded mutely. My mouth was busily full with fine *Sauerbraten* and those lovely, tiny German dumplings, while my nostrils enjoyed the unique aroma of sweet-sour red cabbage. I had been so engrossed in my son's revelations that I had not consciously noted our luncheon being served. I swallowed, took a slug of the good, red Zinfandel, and said, "Please go on."

"It's about the consequences of the American Civil War, Father," he said surprisingly. "Did you know that in the decade after that bloody conflict, there was a very real danger that the whole cause of Negro freedom and rights—for which the war was fought, whatever they say—might well have been completely smashed? The fine work of Abraham Lincoln, Thaddeus Stevens, Charles Sumner, the Freedmen's Bureau, and the Union League Clubs put to naught? And even the Ku Klux Klan underground allowed free reign rather than being sternly repressed? Yes, Father, my thoroughgoing researchings have convinced me such things might easily have happened, resulting in some sort of re-enslavement of the blacks, with the whole war to be refought at an indefinite future date, or at any rate Reconstruction brought to a dead halt for many decades—with what disastrous effects on the American character, turning its deep simple faith in freedom to hypocrisy, it is impossible to exaggerate. I have published a sizable paper on this subject in the *Journal of Civil War Studies.*"

I nodded somberly. Quite a bit of this new subject matter of his was *terra incognita* to me; yet I knew enough of American history to realize he had made a cogent point. More than ever before, I was impressed by his multifaceted learning—he was indubitably a figure in the great tradition of German scholarship, a profound thinker, broad and deep. How fortunate to be his father. Not for the first time, but perhaps with the greatest sincerity yet, I thanked God and the Laws of Nature that I had early moved my family from Braunau, Austria, where I had been born in 1889, to Baden-Baden, where he had grown up in the ambience of the great new university on the edge of the Black Forest and only 150 kilometers from Count Zeppelin's dirigible factory in Württemberg, at Friedrichshafen on Lake Constance.

I raised my glass of *Kirschwasser* to him in a solemn, silent toast —we had somehow got to that stage in our meal—and downed a sip of the potent, fiery, white, cherry brandy.

He leaned toward me and said, "I might as well tell you, Dolf, that my big book, at once popular and scholarly, my *Meisterwerk,* to be titled *If Things Had Gone Wrong,* or perhaps *If Things Had Turned for the Worse,* will deal solely—though illuminated by dozens of diverse examples—with my theory of historical cusps, a highly speculative concept but firmly footed in fact." He glanced at his wristwatch, muttered, "Yes, there's still time for it. So now —" His face grew grave, his voice clear though small—"I will venture to tell you about one more cusp, the most disputable and yet most crucial of them all." He paused. "I warn you, dear Dolf, that this cusp may cause you pain."

"I doubt that," I told him indulgently. "Anyhow, go ahead."

"Very well. In November of 1918, when the British had broken the Hindenburg Line and the weary German army was defiantly dug in along the Rhine, and just before the Allies, under Marshal Foch, launched the final crushing drive which would cut a bloody swath across the heartland to Berlin—"

I understood his warning at once. Memories flamed in my mind like the sudden blinding flares of the battlefield with their deafening thunder. The company I had commanded had been among the most desperately defiant of those he mentioned, heroically nerved for a last-ditch resistance. And then Foch had delivered that last vast blow, and we had fallen back and back and back before the overwhelming numbers of our enemies with their field guns and tanks and armored cars innumerable and above all their huge aerial armadas of De Haviland and Handley-Page and other big bombers escorted by insect-buzzing fleets of Spads and other fighters shooting to bits our last Fokkers and Pfalzes and visiting on Germany a destruction greater far than our zeps had worked on England. Back, back, back, endlessly reeling and regrouping, across the devastated German countryside, a dozen times decimated yet still defiant until the end came at last amid the ruins of Berlin, and the most bold among us had to admit we were beaten and we surrendered unconditionally—

These vivid, fiery recollections came to me almost instantaneously.

I heard my son continuing, "At that cusp moment in November,

1918, Dolf, there existed a very strong possibility—I have established this beyond question—that an immediate armistice would be offered and signed, and the war ended inconclusively. President Wilson was wavering, the French were very tired, and so on.

"And if that had happened in actuality—harken closely to me now, Dolf—then the German temper entering the decade of the 1920s would have been entirely different. She would have felt she had not been really licked, and there would inevitably have been a secret recrudescence of pan-German militarism. German scientific humanism would not have won its total victory over the Germany of the—yes!—Huns.

"As for the Allies, self-tricked out of the complete victory which lay within their grasp, they would in the long run have treated Germany far less generously than they did after their lust for revenge had been sated by that last drive to Berlin. The League of Nations would not have become the strong instrument for world peace that it is today; it might well have been repudiated by America and certainly secretly detested by Germany. Old wounds would not have healed because, paradoxically, they would not have been deep enough.

"There, I've said my say. I hope it hasn't bothered you too badly, Dolf."

I let out a gusty sigh. Then my wincing frown was replaced by a brow serene. I said very deliberately, "Not one bit, my son, though you have certainly touched my own old wounds to the quick. Yet I feel in my bones that your interpretation is completely valid. Rumors of an armistice were indeed running like wildfire through our troops in that black autumn of 1918. And I know only too well that if there had been an armistice at that time, then officers like myself would have believed that the German soldier had never really been defeated, only betrayed by his leaders and by red incendiaries, and we would have begun to conspire endlessly for a resumption of the war under happier circumstances. My son, let us drink to your amazing cusps."

Our tiny glasses touched with a delicate ting, and the last drops went down of biting, faintly bitter *Kirschwasser*. I buttered a thin

slice of pumpernickel and nibbled it—always good to finish off a
meal with bread. I was suddenly filled with an immeasurable content. It was a golden moment, which I would have been happy to
have go on forever, while I listened to my son's wise words and fed
my satisfaction in him. Yes, indeed, it was a golden nugget of pause
in the terrible rush of time—the enriching conversation, the peerless food and drink, the darkly pleasant surroundings—

At that moment I chanced to look at my discordant Jew two
tables away. For some weird reason he was glaring at me with
naked hate, though he instantly dropped his gaze—

But even that strange and disquieting event did not disrupt my
mood of golden tranquillity, which I sought to prolong by saying
in summation, "My dear son, this has been the most exciting
though eerie lunch I have ever enjoyed. Your remarkable cusps
have opened to me a fabulous world in which I can nevertheless
utterly believe. A horridly fascinating world of sizzling hydrogen
zeppelins, of countless evil-smelling gasoline cars built by Ford
instead of his electrics, of re-enslaved American blackamoors, of
Madame Becquerels or Curies, a world without the T. S. Edison
battery and even T. S. himself, a world in which German scientists
are sinister pariahs instead of tolerant, humanitarian, great-souled
leaders of world thought, a world in which a mateless old Edison
tinkers forever at a powerful storage battery he cannot perfect, a
world in which Woodrow Wilson doesn't insist on Germany being
admitted at once to the League of Nations, a world of festering
hatreds reeling toward a second and worse world war. Oh, altogether an incredible world, yet one in which you have momentarily made me believe, to the extent that I do actually have the fear
that time will suddenly shift gears and we will be plunged into that
bad dream world, and our real world will become a dream—"

I suddenly chanced to see the face of my watch—

At the same time my son looked at his own left wrist—

"Dolf," he said, springing up in agitation, "I do hope that with
my stupid chatter I haven't made you miss—"

I had sprung up too—

"No, no, my son," I heard myself say in a fluttering voice, "but it's true I have little time in which to catch the *Ostwald*. *Auf Wiedersehen, mein Sohn, auf Wiedersehen!*"

And with that I was hastening, indeed almost running, or else sweeping through the air like a ghost—leaving him behind to settle our reckoning—across a room that seemed to waver with my feverish agitation, alternately darkening and brightening like an electric bulb with its fine tungsten filament about to fly to powder and wink out forever—

Inside my head a voice was saying in calm yet death-knell tones, "The lights of Europe are going out. I do not think they will be rekindled in my generation—"

Suddenly the only important thing in the world for me was to catch the *Ostwald*, get aboard her before she unmoored. That and only that would reassure me that I was in my rightful world. I would touch and feel the *Ostwald*, not just talk about her—

As I dashed between the four bronze figures, they seemed to hunch down and become deformed, while their faces became those of grotesque, aged witches—four evil kobolds leering up at me with a horrid knowledge bright in their eyes—

While behind me I glimpsed in pursuit a tall, black, white-faced figure, skeletally lean—

The strangely short corridor ahead of me had a blank end—the Departure Lounge wasn't there—

I instantly jerked open the narrow door to the stairs and darted nimbly up them as if I were a young man again and not forty-eight years old—

On the third sharp turn I risked a glance behind and down—

Hardly a flight behind me, taking great pursuing leaps, was my dreadful Jew—

I tore open the door to the hundred and second floor. There at last, only a few feet away, was the silver door I sought of the final elevator and softly glowing above it the words, *"Zum Zeppelin."* At last I would be shot aloft to the *Ostwald* and reality.

But the sign began to blink as the *Krähenest* had, while across the door was pasted askew a white cardboard sign which read "Out of Order."

I threw myself at the door and scrabbled at it, squeezing my eyes several times to make my vision come clear. When I finally fully opened them, the cardboard sign was gone.

But the silver door was gone too, and the words above it forever. I was scrabbling at seamless pale plaster.

There was a touch on my elbow. I spun around.

"Excuse me, sir, but you seem troubled," my Jew said solicitously. "Is there anything I can do?"

I shook my head, but whether in negation or rejection or to clear it, I don't know. "I'm looking for the *Ostwald,*" I gasped, only now realizing I'd winded myself on the stairs. "For the zeppelin," I explained when he looked puzzled.

I may be wrong, but it seemed to me that a look of secret glee flashed deep in his eyes, though his general sympathetic expression remained unchanged.

"Oh, the zeppelin," he said in a voice that seemed to me to have become sugary in its solicitude. "You must mean the *Hindenburg.*"

Hindenburg?—I asked myself. There was no zeppelin named *Hindenburg.* Or was there? Could it be that I was mistaken about such a simple and, one would think, immutable matter? My mind had been getting very foggy the last minute or two. Desperately I tried to assure myself that I was indeed myself and in my right world. My lips worked and I muttered to myself, *Bin Adolf Hitler, Zeppelin Fachmann. . . .*

"But the *Hindenburg* doesn't land here, in any case," my Jew was telling me, "though I think some vague intention once was voiced about topping the Empire State with a mooring mast for dirigibles. Perhaps you saw some news story and assumed—"

His face fell, or he made it seem to fall. The sugary solicitude in his voice became unendurable as he told me, "But apparently you can't have heard today's tragic news. Oh, I do hope you weren't seeking the *Hindenburg* so as to meet some beloved family member or close friend. Brace yourself, sir. Only hours ago, coming in for her landing at Lakehurst, New Jersey, the *Hindenburg* caught fire and burned up entire in a matter of seconds. Thirty or forty

at least of her passengers and crew were burned alive. Oh, steady
yourself, sir."

"But the *Hindenburg*—I mean the *Ostwald!*—couldn't burn
like that," I protested. "She's a helium zeppelin."

He shook his head. "Oh, no. I'm no scientist, but I know the
Hindenburg was filled with hydrogen—a wholly typical bit of
reckless German risk-running. At least we've never sold helium to
the Nazis, thank God."

I stared at him, wavering my face from side to side in feeble
denial.

While he stared back at me with obviously a new thought in
mind.

"Excuse me once again," he said, "but I believe I heard you start
to say something about Adolf Hitler. I suppose you know that you
bear a certain resemblance to that execrable dictator. If I were
you, sir, I'd shave my mustache."

I felt a wave of fury at this inexplicable remark with all its
baffling references, yet withal a remark delivered in the unmistak-
able tones of an insult. And then all my surroundings momentarily
reddened and flickered, and I felt a tremendous wrench in the
inmost core of my being, the sort of wrench one might experience
in transiting timelessly from one universe into another parallel to
it. Briefly I became a man still named Adolf Hitler, same as the
Nazi dictator and almost the same age, a German-American born
in Chicago, who had never visited Germany or spoke German,
whose friends teased him about his chance resemblance to the
other Hitler, and who used stubbornly to say, "No, I won't change
my name! Let that *Führer* bastard across the Atlantic change his!
Ever hear about the British Winston Churchill writing the American Winston Churchill, who wrote *The Crisis* and other novels,
and suggesting he change his name to avoid confusion, since the
Englishman had done some writing too? The American wrote
back it was a good idea, but since he was three years older, he was
senior and so the Britisher should change *his* name. That's exactly
how I feel about that son of a bitch Hitler."

The Jew still stared at me sneeringly. I started to tell him off, but then I was lost in a second weird, wrenching transition. The first had been directly from one parallel universe to another. The second was also in time—I aged fourteen or fifteen years in a single infinite instant while transiting from 1937 (where I had been born in 1889 and was forty-eight) to 1973 (where I had been born in 1910 and and was sixty-three). My name changed back to my truly own (but what is that?), and I no longer looked one bit like Adolf Hitler the Nazi dictator (or dirigible expert?), and I had a married son who was a sort of social historian in a New York City municipal university, and he had many brilliant theories, but none of historical cusps.

And the Jew—I mean the tall, thin man in black with possibly Semitic features—was gone. I looked around and around but there was no one there.

I touched my outside left breast pocket, then my hand darted tremblingly underneath. There was no zipper on the pocket inside and no precious documents, only a couple of grimy envelopes with notes I'd scribbled on them in pencil.

I don't know how I got out of the Empire State Building. Presumably by elevator. Though all my memory holds for that period is a persistent image of King Kong tumbling down from its top like a ridiculous yet poignantly pitiable giant teddy bear.

I do recollect walking in a sort of trance for what seemed hours through a Manhattan stinking with monoxide and carcinogens innumerable, half waking from time to time (usually while crossing streets that snarled, not purred), and then relapsing into trance. There were big dogs.

When I at last fully came to myself, I was walking down a twilit Hudson Street at the north end of Greenwich Village. My gaze was fixed on a distant and unremarkable pale-gray square of building top. I guessed it must be that of the World Trade Center, 1,350 feet tall.

And then it was blotted out by the grinning face of my son, the professor.

"Justin!" I said.

"Fritz!" he said. "We'd begun to worry a bit. Where did you get off to, anyhow? Not that it's a damn bit of my business. If you had an assignation with a go-go girl, you needn't tell me."

"Thanks," I said, "I do feel tired, I must admit, and somewhat cold. But no, I was just looking at some of my old stamping grounds," I told him, "and taking longer than I realized. Manhattan's changed during my years on the West Coast, but not all that much."

"It's getting chilly," he said. "Let's stop in at that place ahead with the black front. It's the White Horse. Dylan Thomas used to drink there. He's supposed to have scribbled a poem on the wall of the can, only they painted it over. But it has the authentic sawdust."

"Good," I said, "only we'll make mine coffee, not ale. Or if I can't get coffee, then cola."

I am not really a *Prosit!*-type person.

JOE HALDEMAN

End Game

Joe Haldeman was born in Oklahoma City in 1943. He grew up in Puerto Rico, New Orleans, Alaska, and Washington, D. C. He achieved a B.S. in physics and astronomy at the University of Maryland in 1967. He was drafted, sent to Viet Nam as a combat demolition engineer, wounded in action, mustered out, and has since then lived happily in Washington, Florida, and Iowa, having traveled at various times in his life in Europe, Africa, Asia, the Caribbean, and Mexico. He attended the Iowa Writers' Workshop from 1973 to 1975 on a fellowship and received the degree of Master of Fine Arts in English from the University of Iowa in 1975—but regards himself as writing full-time since 1970. He has five books published, three more sold and awaiting publication (most imminent being *Mindbridge,* due from St. Martin's Press in the summer of 1976), and four others in various states of completion. Joe and Mary Gay Haldeman were married a year before he completed his studies at the University of Maryland and report themselves "happily married for ten years; no children."

His novel, *The Forever War* (published in hardcover by St. Martin's Press and reprinted in paperback by Ballantine Books), won the Nebula Award by a wide margin and also took a Hugo at MidAmeriCon. No selection in a volume honoring Nebula Award winners can be more to the point than *The Forever War*'s "End Game."

Sometime in the Twenty-third Century they started calling it "the Forever War." Before that, it had just been the war, the only war.

And we had never met the enemy. The Taurans started the war at the end of the Twentieth Century, attacking our first starships with no provocation. We had never exchanged a word with the enemy; had never captured one alive.

I was drafted in 1997, and in 2458 still had three years to serve. I'd gone all the way from private to major in less than half a millennium. Without actually living all those years, of course; time dilation between collapsar jumps accounted for all but five of them.

Most of those five years I had been reasonably content, since the usual disadvantages of military service were offset by the fact that I was allowed to endure them in the company of the woman I loved. The three battles we had been in, we'd been in together: we'd shared a furlough on Earth, and even had the luck to be wounded at the same time, winning a year-long vacation on the hospital planet Heaven. After that, everything fell apart.

We had known for some time that neither of us would live through the war. Not only because the fighting was fierce—you had about one chance in three of surviving a battle—but also, the government couldn't afford to release us from the army: our back pay, compounded quarterly over the centuries, would cost them as much as a starship! But we did have each other, and there was always the possibility that the war might end.

But at Heaven, they separated us. On the basis of tests (and our embarrassing seniority) Marygay was made a lieutenant and I became a major. She was assigned to a Strike Force leaving from Heaven, though, and I was to go back to Stargate for combat officer training, eventually to command my own Strike Force.

I literally tried to move Heaven and Earth to get Marygay assigned to me; it didn't seem unreasonable for a commander to have a hand in the selection of his executive officer. But I found out later that the Army had good reason not to allow us together in the same company: heterosexuality was obsolete, a rare dysfunction, and we were too old to be "cured." The Army needed our experience, but the rule was one pervert per company; no exceptions.

We weren't simply lovers. Marygay and I were each other's only link to the real world, the 1990s. Everyone else came from a nightmare world that seemed to get worse as time went on. And neither was it simply separation: even if we were both to survive the battles in our future—not likely—time dilation would put us centuries out of phase with one another. There was no solution. One of us would die and the other would be alone.

My officer's training consisted of being immersed in a tank of oxygenated fluorocarbon with 239 electrodes attached to my brain and body. It was called ALSC, Accelerated Life Situation Computer, and it made my life accelerated and miserable for three weeks.

Want to know who Scipio Aemilianus was? Bright light of the Third Punic War. How to counter a knife-thrust to the abdomen? Crossed-wrists block, twist right, left side-kick to the exposed kidney.

What good all this was going to be, fighting perambulating mushrooms, was a mystery to me. But I was that machine's slave for three weeks, learning the best way to use every weapon from the sharp stick to the nova bomb, and absorbing two millennia's

worth of military observation, theory, and prejudice. It was supposed to make me a major. Kind of like making a duck by teaching
a chicken how to swim.

My separation from Marygay seemed, if possible, even more
final when I read my combat orders: Sade-138, in the Greater
Magellanic Cloud, four collapsar jumps and 150,000 light-years
away. But I had already learned to live with the fact that I'd never
see her again.

I had access to all of my new company's personnel records,
including my own. The Army's psychologist had said that I
"thought" I was tolerant toward homosexuality—which was
wounding, because I'd learned at my mother's knee that what a
person does with his plumbing is his own business and nobody
else's. Which is all very fine when you're in the majority, I found
out. When you're the one being tolerated, it can be difficult. Behind my back, most of them called me "the Old Queer," even
though no one in the company was more than nine years younger
than me. I accepted the inaccuracy along with the irony; a commander always gets names. I should have seen, though, that this
was more than the obligatory token disrespect that soldiers accord
their officers. The name symbolized an attitude of contempt and
estrangement more profound than any I had experienced during
my years as a private and noncommissioned officer.

Language, for one thing, was no small problem. English had
evolved considerably in 450 years; soldiers had to learn Twenty-
first Century English as a sort of lingua franca with which to
communicate with their officers, some of whom might be "old"
enough to be their nine-times-great-grandparents. Of course, they
only used this language when talking to their officers, or mocking
them, so they got out of practice with it.

At Stargate, maybe they should have spared some ALSC time
to teach me the language of my troops. I had an "open door"
policy, where twice weekly any soldier could come talk to me
without going up through the chain of command, everything off
the record. It never worked out well, and after a couple of months

they stopped coming altogether.

There were only three of us who were born before the Twenty-fifth Century—the only three who had been *born* at all, since they didn't make people the sloppy old-fashioned way any more. Each embryo was engineered for a specific purpose . . . and the ones that wound up being soldiers, although intelligent and physically perfect, seemed deficient in some qualities that I considered to be virtues. Attila would have loved them, though; Napoleon would have hired them on the spot.

The other two people "of woman born" were my executive officer, Captain Charlie Moore, and the senior medic, Lieutenant Diana Alsever. They were both homosexual, having been born in the Twenty-second Century, but we still had much in common, and they were the only people in the company whom I considered friends. In retrospect I can see that we insulated one another from the rest of the company, which might have been comfortable for them—but it was disastrous for me.

The rest of the officers, especially Lieutenant Hilleboe, my Field First, seemed only to tell me what they thought I wanted to hear. They didn't tell me that most of the troops thought I was inexperienced, cowardly, and had only been made their commander by virtue of seniority. All of which was more or less true—after all, I hadn't volunteered for the position—but maybe I could have done something about it if my officers had been frank with me.

Our assignment was to build a base on Sade-138's largest planet, and defend it against Tauran attack. Tauran expansion was very predictable, and we knew that they would show up there sooner or later. My company, Strike Force Gamma, would defend the place for two years, after which a garrison force would relieve us. And I would theoretically resign my commission and become a civilian again—unless there happened to be a new regulation forbidding it. Or an old one that they had neglected to tell me about.

The garrison force would automatically leave Stargate two years after we had, with no idea what would be waiting for them at Sade-138. There was no way we could get word back to them, since the trip took 340 years of "objective" time, though ship-time was only seven months, thanks to time dilation.

Seven months was long enough, trapped in the narrow corridors and tiny rooms of *Masaryk II*. It was a relief to leave the ship in orbit even though planetside meant four weeks of unrelenting hard labor under hazardous, uncomfortable conditions. Two shifts of 38.5 hours each, alternating shipboard rest and planetside work.

The planet was an almost featureless rock, an off-white billiard ball with a thin atmosphere of hydrogen and helium. The temperature at the equator varied from 25° Kelvin to 17° on a 38.5-hour cycle, daytime heat being provided by the bright blue spark of S Doradus. When it was coldest, just before dawn, hydrogen would condense out of the air in a fine mist, making everything so slippery that you had to just sit down and wait it out. At dawn a faint pastel rainbow provided the only relief from the black-and-white monotony of the landscape.

The ground was treacherous, covered with little granular chunks of frozen gas that shifted slowly, incessantly in the anemic breeze. You had to walk in a slow waddle to stay on your feet; of the four people who died during the construction of the base, three were the victims of simple falls.

From the sky down, we had three echelons of defense. First was the *Masaryk II*, with its six tachyon-drive fighters and fifty robot drones equipped with nova bombs. Commodore Antopol would take off after the Tauran ship when it flashed out of Sade-138's collapsar field. If she nailed it, we'd be home free.

If the enemy got through Antopol's swarm of fighters and drones, they would still have some difficulty attacking us. Atop our underground base was a circle of twenty-five self-aiming bevawatt lasers, with reaction times on the order of a fraction of a microsecond. And just beyond the laser's effective horizon was a broad ring with thousands of nuclear land mines that would detonate with any small distortion of the local gravitational field: a Tauran walking over one or a ship passing overhead.

If we actually had to go up and fight, which might happen if they reduced all our automatic defenses and wanted to take the base intact, each soldier was armed with a megawatt laser finger, and every squad had a tachyon rocket launcher and two repeating grenade launchers. And as a last resort, there was the stasis field.

I couldn't begin to understand the principles behind the stasis field; the gap between present-day physics and my master's degree in the same subject was as long as the time that separated Galileo and Einstein. But I knew the effects.

Nothing could move at a speed greater than 16.3 meters per second inside the field, which was a hemispherical (in space, spherical) volume about fifty meters in radius. Inside, there was no such thing as electromagnetic radiation; no electricity, no magnetism, no light. From inside your suit, you could see your surroundings in ghostly monochrome—which phenomenon was glibly explained to me as being due to "phase transference of quasi-energy leaking through from an adjacent tachyon reality," which was so much phlogiston to me.

But inside the field, all modern weapons of warfare were useless. Even a nova bomb was just an inert lump. And any creature, Terran or Tauran, caught inside without proper insulation would die in a fraction of a second.

Inside the field we had an assortment of old-fashioned weapons and one fighter, for last-ditch aerial support. I made people practice with the swords and bows and arrows and such, but they weren't enthusiastic. The consensus of opinion was that we would be doomed if the fighting degenerated to where we were forced into the stasis field. I couldn't say that I disagreed.

For five months we waited around in an atmosphere of comfortably boring routine.

The base quickly settled into a routine of training and waiting. I was almost impatient for the Taurans to show up, just to get it over with one way or the other.

The troops had adjusted to the situation much better than I had, for obvious reasons. They had specific duties to perform and ample free time for the usual soldierly anodynes to boredom. My duties were more varied but offered little satisfaction, since the problems that percolated up to me were of the "buck stops here" type: the

ones with pleasing, unambiguous solutions were taken care of in
the lower echelons.

I'd never cared much for sports or games, but found myself
turning to them more and more as a kind of safety valve. For the
first time in my life, in these tense, claustrophobic surroundings,
I couldn't escape into reading or study. So I fenced, quarterstaff
and saber, with the other officers; worked myself to exhaustion on
the exercise machines and even kept a jump rope in my office.
Most of the other officers played chess, but they could usually beat
me—whenever I won it gave me the feeling I was being humored.
And word games were difficult because my language was an archaic dialect that they had trouble manipulating. And I lacked the
time and talent to master "modern" English.

For a while I let Diana feed me mood-altering drugs, but the
cumulative effect of them was frightening—I was getting addicted
in a way that was at first too subtle to bother me—so I stopped
short. Then I tried some systematic psychoanalysis with Lieutenant Wilber. It was impossible. Although he knew all about my
problems in an academic kind of way, we didn't speak the same
cultural language; his counseling me about love and sex was like
me telling a Fourteenth Century serf how best to get along with
his priest and landlord.

And that, after all, was the root of my problem. I was sure I could
have handled the pressures and frustrations of command, of being
cooped up in a cave with these people who at times seemed
scarcely less alien than the enemy; even the near-certainty that it
could only lead to painful death in a worthless cause—if only I
could have had Marygay with me. And the feeling got more in-
tense as the months crept by.

He got very stern with me at this point and accused me of
romanticizing my position. He knew what love was, he said; he
had been in love himself. And the sexual polarity of the couple
made no difference—all right, I could accept that; that idea had
been a cliché in my parents' generation (though it had run into
some predictable resistance in my own). But love, he said, love was
a fragile blossom; love was a delicate crystal; love was an unstable

reaction with a half-life of about eight months. Crap, I said, and accused him of wearing cultural blinders; thirty centuries of prewar society taught that love was one thing that could last to the grave and even beyond *and if he had been born instead of hatched he would know that without being told!* Whereupon he would assume a wry, tolerant expression and reiterate that I was merely a victim of self-imposed sexual frustration and romantic delusion.

In retrospect, I guess we had a good time arguing with each other. Cure me, he didn't.

2.

It was exactly 400 days since the day we had begun construction. I was sitting at my desk not checking out Hilleboe's new duty roster. Charlie was stretched out in a chair reading something on the viewer. The phone buzzed and it was a voice from on high, the Commodore.

"They're here."

"What?"

"I said they're here. A Tauran ship just exited the collapsar field. Velocity .8 *c.* Deceleration thirty G's. Give or take."

Charlie was leaning over my desk. "What?"

"How long before you can pursue?" I asked.

"Soon as you get off the phone." I switched off and went over to the logistic computer, which was a twin to the one on *Masaryk II,* and had a direct data link to it. While I tried to get numbers out of the thing, Charlie fiddled with the visual display.

The display was a hologram about a meter square by half a meter thick and was programmed to show the positions of Sade-138, our planet, and a few other chunks of rock in the system. There were green and red dots to show the positions of our vessels and the Taurans'.

The computer said that the minimum time it could take the Taurans to decelerate and get back to this planet would be a little over eleven days. Of course, that would be straight maximum acceleration and deceleration all the way; Commodore Antopol could pick them off like flies on a wall. So, like us, they'd mix up their direction of flight and degree of acceleration in a random way. Based on several hundred past records of enemy behavior, the computer was able to give us a probability table:

DAYS TO CONTACT	PROBABILITY
11	.000001
15	.001514
20	.032164
25	.103287
30	.676324
35	.820584
40	.982685
45	.993576
50	.999369
MEDIAN	
28.9554	.500000

Unless, of course, Antopol and her gang of merry pirates managed to make a kill. The chances for that, I had learned in the can, were slightly less than fifty-fifty.

But whether it took 28.9554 days or two weeks, those of us on the ground had to just sit on our hands and watch. If Antopol was successful, then we wouldn't have to fight until the regular garrison troops replaced us here, and we moved on to the next collapsar.

"Haven't left yet." Charlie had the display cranked down to minimum scale; the planet was a white ball the size of a large melon and *Masaryk II* was a green dot off to the right some eight melons away; you couldn't get both on the screen at the same time.

While we were watching, a small green dot popped out of the ship's dot and drifted away from it. A ghostly number "2" drifted beside it, and a key projected on the display's lower left-hand corner identified it as 2-PURSUIT DRONE. Other numbers in the key identified the *Masaryk II*, a planetary defense fighter, and fourteen planetary defense drones. Those sixteen ships were not yet far enough away from one another to have separate dots.

"Tell Hilleboe to call a general assembly. Might as well break it to everyone at once."

The men and women didn't take it very well, and I couldn't really blame them. We had all expected the Taurans to attack much sooner—and when they persisted in not coming, the feeling grew that Strike Force Command had made a mistake, and they'd never show up at all.

I wanted them to start weapons training in earnest; they hadn't used any high-powered weapons in almost two years. So I activated their laser-fingers and passed out the grenade and rocket launchers. We couldn't practice inside the base, for fear of damaging the external sensors and defensive laser ring. So we turned off half the circle of bevawatt lasers and went out about a klick beyond the perimeter; one platoon at a time, accompanied by either me or Charlie. Rusk kept a close watch on the early-warning screens. If anything approached, she would send up a flare, and the platoon would have to get back inside the ring before the unknown came over the horizon, at which time the defensive lasers would come on automatically. Besides knocking out the unknown, they would fry the platoon in less than .02 second.

We couldn't spare anything from the base to use as a target, but that turned out to be no problem. The first tachyon rocket we fired scooped out a hole twenty meters long by ten wide by five deep; the rubble gave us a multitude of targets from twice-man-sized on down.

They were good, a lot better than they had been with the primitive weapons in the stasis field. The best laser practice turned out to be rather like skeet shooting: pair up the people and have one stand behind the other, throwing rocks at random intervals. The one who was shooting had to gauge the rock's trajectory and zap it before it hit the ground. Their eye-hand coordination was impressive (maybe the Eugenics Council had done something right). Shooting at rocks down to pebble-size, most of them could do better than nine out of ten. Old nonbioengineered me could hit maybe seven out of ten, and I'd had a good deal more practice than they'd had.

They were equally facile at estimating trajectories with the grenade launcher, which was a more versatile weapon than it had been in the past. Instead of just shooting one-microton bombs with a standard propulsive charge, it had four different charges and a choice of one-, two-, three-, or four-microton bombs. For really close-in fighting, where it was dangerous to use the lasers, the barrel of the launcher would unsnap, and you could load it with a magazine of "shotgun" rounds. Each shot would send out an expanding cloud of a thousand tiny flechettes, that were instant death out to five meters and turned to harmless vapor at six.

The tachyon rocket launcher required no skill whatsoever. All you had to do was be careful no one was standing behind you when you fired it; the backwash from the rocket was dangerous for several meters behind the launching tube. Otherwise, you just lined your target up in the crosshairs and pushed the button. You didn't have to worry about trajectory; the rocket just traveled in a straight line for all practical purposes. It reached escape velocity in less than a second.

It improved the troops' morale to get out and chew up the landscape with their new toys. But the landscape wasn't fighting back. No matter how physically impressive the weapons were, their effectiveness would depend on what the Taurans could throw back. A Greek phalanx must have looked pretty impressive, but it wouldn't do too well against a single man with a flame-thrower.

And as with any engagement, because of time dilation, there was no way to tell what sort of weaponry they would have. It depended on what the Tauran level of technology had been when their mission had begun; they could be a couple of centuries ahead of us or behind us. They might never have heard of the stasis field. Or they might be able to say a magic word and make us disappear.

I was out with the fourth platoon burning rocks, when Charlie called and asked me to come back in, urgent. I left Heimoff in charge.

"Another one?" The scale of the holograph display was such that our planet was pea-sized, about five centimeters from the X that marked the position of Sade-138. There were forty-one red and green dots scattered around the field; the key identified number forty-one as TAURAN CRUISER (2).

"That's right." Charlie was grim. "Appeared a few minutes ago. When I called. It has the same characteristics as the other one: 30 G's, .8 c."

"You called Antopol?"

"Yeah." He anticipated the next question. "It'll take almost a day for the signal to get there and back."

"It's never happened before." But of course Charlie knew that.

"Maybe this collapsar is especially important to them."

"Likely." So it was almost certain we'd be fighting on the ground. Even if Antopol managed to get the first cruiser, she wouldn't have a fifty-fifty chance on the second one. Low on drones and fighters. "I wouldn't like to be Antopol now."

"She'll just get it earlier."

"I don't know. We're in pretty good shape."

"Save it for the troops, William." He turned down the display's scale to where it showed only two objects: Sade-138 and the new red dot, slowly moving.

We spent the next two weeks watching dots blink out. And if you knew when and where to look, you could go outside and see the real thing happening, a hard bright speck of white light that faded in about a second.

In that second, a nova bomb had put out over a million times the power of a bevawatt laser. It made a miniature star half a klick in diameter and as hot as the interior of the Sun. Anything it touched it would consume. The radiation from a near miss could botch up a ship's electronics beyond repair—two fighters, one of ours and one of theirs, had evidently suffered that fate; silently drifting out of the system at a constant velocity, without power.

We had used more powerful nova bombs earlier in the war, but the degenerate matter used to fuel them was unstable in large quantities. The bombs had a tendency to explode while they were still inside the ship. Evidently the Taurans had the same problem —or they had copied the process from us in the first place—because they had also scaled down to nova bombs that used less than a hundred kilograms of degenerate matter. And they deployed them much the same way we did, the warhead separating into dozens of pieces as it approached the target, only one of which was the nova bomb.

They would probably have a few bombs left over after they finished off *Masaryk II* and her retinue of fighters and drones. So it was likely that we were just wasting time and energy in weapons practice.

The thought did slip by my conscience, that I could gather up eleven people and board the fighter we had hidden safe behind the stasis field. It was preprogrammed to take us back to Stargate.

I even went to the extreme of making a mental list of the eleven, trying to think of that many people who meant more to me than the rest. Turned out I'd be picking six at random.

I put the thought away, though. We did have a chance, maybe a damned good one, even against a fully armed cruiser. It wouldn't be easy to get a nova bomb close enough to include us inside its kill-radius.

Besides, they'd just space me for desertion. So why bother.

Spirits rose when one of Antopol's drones knocked out the first Tauran cruiser. Not counting the ships left behind for planetary defense, she still had eighteen drones and two fighters. They wheeled around to intercept the second cruiser, by then a few light-hours away, still being harassed by fifteen enemy drones.

One of the drones got her. Her ancillary craft continued the attack, but it was a rout. One fighter and three drones fled the battle at maximum acceleration, looping up over the plane of the ecliptic, and were not pursued. We watched them with morbid interest while the enemy cruiser inched back to do battle with us. The fighter was headed back for Sade-138, to escape. Nobody blamed them. In fact, we sent them a farewell solidus good-luck message; they didn't respond, naturally, being zipped up in the acceleration tanks. But it would be recorded.

It took the enemy five days to get back to the planet and be comfortably ensconced in a stationary orbit on the other side. We settled in for the inevitable first phase of the attack, which would be aerial and totally automated: their drones against our lasers. I put a force of fifty men and women inside the stasis field, in case one of the drones got through. An empty gesture, really; the enemy could just stand by and wait for them to turn off the field; fry them the second it flickered out.

Charlie had a weird idea that I almost went for.

"We could boobytrap the place."

"What do you mean?" I said. "This place is boobytrapped, out to twenty-five klicks."

"No, not the mines and such. I mean the base itself, here, underground."

"Go on."

"There are two nova bombs in that fighter." He pointed at the stasis field through a couple of hundred meters of rock. "We can roll them down here, boobytrap them, then hide everybody in the stasis field and wait."

In a way it was tempting. It would relieve me from any responsibility for decision making; leave everything up to chance. "I don't think it would work, Charlie."

He seemed hurt. "Sure it would."

"No, look. For it to work, you have to get every single Tauran inside the kill-radius before it goes off—but they wouldn't all come charging in here once they breached our defenses. Least of all if the place seemed deserted. They'd suspect something, send in an advance party. And after the advance party set off the bombs—"

"We'd be back where we started, yeah. Minus the base. Sorry."

I shrugged. "It was an idea. Keep thinking, Charlie." I turned my attention back to the display, where the lopsided space war was in progress. Logically enough, the enemy wanted to knock out that one fighter overhead before he started to work on us. About all we could do was watch the red dots crawl around the planet and try to score. So far the pilot had managed to knock out all of the drones; the enemy hadn't sent any fighters after him yet.

I'd given the pilot control over five of the lasers in our defensive ring. They couldn't do much good, though. A bevawatt laser pumps out a billion kilowatts per second at a range of a hundred meters. A thousand klicks up, though, the beam was attenuated to ten kilowatts. Might do some damage if it hit an optical sensor. At least confuse things.

"We could use another fighter. Or six."

"Use up the drones," I said. We did have a fighter, of course, and a swabbie attached to us who could pilot it. But it might turn out to be our only hope. if they got us cornered in the stasis field.

"How far away is the other guy?" Charlie asked, meaning the fighter pilot who had turned tail. I cranked down the scale and the green dot appeared at the right of the display. "About six light-hours." He had two drones left, too near to him to show as separate dots, having expended one in covering his getaway. "He's not accelerating any more, but he's doing .9 *c.*"

"Couldn't do us any good if he wanted to." Need almost a month to slow down.

At that low point, the light that stood for our own defensive fighter faded out. "Crap."

"Now the fun starts. Should I tell the troops to get ready, stand by to go topside?"

"No . . . have them suit up, in case we lose air. But I expect it'll be a little while before we have a ground attack." I turned the scale up again. Four red spots were already creeping around the globe toward us.

I got suited up and came back to Administration to watch the fireworks on the monitors.

The lasers worked perfectly. All four drones converged on us simultaneously; were targeted and destroyed. All but one of the nova bombs went off below our horizon (the visual horizon was about ten kilometers away, but the lasers were mounted high and could target something at twice that distance). The bomb that detonated on our horizon had melted out a semicircular chunk that glowed brilliantly white for several minutes. An hour later, it was still glowing dull orange, and the ground temperature outside had risen to 50° Absolute, melting most of our snow, exposing an irregular dark gray surface.

The next attack was also over in a fraction of a second, but this time there had been eight drones, and four of them got within ten klicks. Radiation from the glowing craters raised the temperature to nearly 300°. That was above the melting point of water, and I was starting to get worried. The fighting suits were good to over 1000°, but the automatic lasers depended on low-temperature superconductors for their speed.

I asked the computer what the lasers' temperature limit was, and it printed out TR 398–734–009–265, "Some Aspects Concerning the Adaptability of Cryogenic Ordnance to Use in Relatively High-Temperature Environments," which had lots of handy advice about how we could insulate the weapons if we had access to a fully equipped armorer's shop. It did note that the response time of automatic-aiming devices increased as the temperature increased, and that above some "critical temperature," the weapons would not aim at all. But there was no way to predict any individual weapon's behavior, other than to note that the highest critical temperature recorded was 790° and the lowest was 420°.

Charlie was watching the display. His voice was flat over the suit's radio: "Sixteen this time."

"Surprised?" One of the few things we knew about Tauran psychology was a certain compulsiveness about numbers, especially primes and powers of two.

"Let's just hope they don't have thirty-two left." I queried the computer on this; all it could say was that the cruiser had thus far launched a total of forty-four drones, and some cruisers had been known to carry as many as 128.

We had more than a half-hour before the drones would strike. I could evacuate everybody to the stasis field, and they would be temporarily safe if one of the nova bombs got through. Safe, but trapped. How long would it take the crater to cool down, if three or four—let alone sixteen—of the bombs made it through? You couldn't live forever in a fighting suit, even though it recycled everything with remorseless efficiency. One week was enough to make you thoroughly miserable. Two weeks, suicidal. Nobody had ever gone three weeks, under field conditions.

Besides, as a defensive position, the stasis field could be a death-trap. The enemy has all the options, since the dome is opaque; the only way you can find out what they're up to is to stick your head out. They didn't have to wade in with primitive weapons unless they were impatient. They could just keep the dome saturated with laser fire and wait for you to turn off the generator. Meanwhile harassing you by throwing spears, rocks, arrows into the dome—you could return fire, but it was pretty futile.

Of course, if one man stayed inside the base, the others could wait out the next half-hour in the stasis field. If he didn't come get them, they'd know the outside was hot. I chinned the combination that would give me a frequency available to everybody Echelon 5 and above.

"This is Major Mandella." That still sounded like a bad joke.

I outlined the situation to them and asked them to tell their troops that everyone in the company was free to move into the stasis field. I would stay behind and come retrieve them if things went well—not out of nobility, of course; I preferred taking the chance of being vaporized in a nanosecond, rather than almost certain slow death under the gray dome.

I chinned Charlie's frequency. "You can go, too. I'll take care of things here."

"No, thanks," he said slowly. "I'd just as soon . . . hey, look at this."

The cruiser had launched another red dot, a couple of minutes behind the others. The display's key identified it as being another drone. "That's curious."

"Superstitious bastards," he said without feeling.

It turned out that only eleven people chose to join the fifty who had been ordered into the dome. That shouldn't have surprised me, but it did.

As the drones approached, Charlie and I stared at the monitors, carefully not looking at the holograph display, tacitly agreeing that it would be better not to know when they were one minute away, thirty seconds . . . and then, like the other times, it was over before we knew it had started. The screens glared white and there was a yowl of static, and we were still alive.

But this time there were fifteen new holes on the horizon—or closer!—and the temperature was rising so fast that the last digit in the readout was an amorphous blur. The number peaked in the high 800s and began to slide down.

We had never seen any of the drones, not during that tiny fraction of a second it took the lasers to aim and fire. But then the seventeenth one flashed over the horizon, zig-zagging crazily, and stopped directly overhead. For an instant it seemed to hover, and then it began to fall. Half the lasers had detected it, and they were firing steadily, but none of them could aim; they were all stuck in their last firing position.

It glittered as it dropped, the mirror polish of its sleek hull reflecting the white glow from the craters and the eerie flickering of the constant, impotent laser fire. I heard Charlie take one deep breath and the drone fell so close you could see spidery Tauran numerals etched on the hull, and a transparent porthole near the tip—then its engine flared and it was suddenly gone.

"What the hell?" Charlie said, quietly.

The porthole. "Maybe reconnaissance."

"I guess. So we can't touch them, and they know it."

"Unless the lasers recover." Didn't seem likely. "We better get everybody under the dome. Us; too."

He said a word whose vowel had changed over the centuries, but whose meaning was clear. "No hurry. Let's see what they do."

We waited for several hours. The temperature outside stabilized at 690°—just under the melting point of zinc, I remembered to no purpose—and I tried the manual controls for the lasers, but they were still frozen.

"Here they come," Charlie said. "Eight again."

I started for the display. "Guess we'll—"

"Wait! They aren't drones." The key identified all eight with the legend TROOP CARRIER.

"Guess they want to take the base," he said. "Intact."

That, and maybe try out new weapons and techniques. "It's not much of a risk for them. They can always retreat and drop a nova bomb in our laps."

I called Brill and had her go get everybody who was in the stasis field; set them up with the remainder of her platoon as a defensive line circling around the northeast and northwest quadrants.

"I wonder," Charlie said. "Maybe we shouldn't put everyone topside at once. Until we know how many Taurans there are."

That was a point. Keep a reserve, let the enemy underestimate our strength. "It's an idea . . . there might be just 64 of them in eight carriers." Or 128 or 256. I wished our spy satellites had a finer sense of discrimination. But you can only cram so much into a machine the size of a grape.

I decided to let Brill's seventy people be our first line of defense, and ordered them into a ring in the ditches we had made outside the base's perimeter. Everybody else would stay downstairs until needed.

If it turned out that the Taurans, either through numbers or new technology, could field an unstoppable force, I'd order everyone into the stasis field. There was a tunnel from the living quarters to the dome, so the people underground could go straight there in safety. The ones in the ditches would have to fall back under fire. If any of them were still alive when I gave the order.

I called in Hilleboe and had her and Charlie keep watch over the lasers. If they came unstuck, I'd call Brill and her people back. Turn on the automatic aiming system again, then just sit back and watch the show. But even stuck, the lasers could be useful. Charlie marked the monitors to show where the rays would go; he and Hilleboe could fire them manually whenever something moved into a weapon's line-of-sight.

We had about twenty minutes. Brill was walking around the

perimeter with her men and women, ordering them into the ditches a squad at a time, setting up overlapping fields of fire. I broke in and asked her to set up the heavy weapons so that they could be used to channel the enemy's advance into the path of the lasers.

There wasn't much else to do but wait. I asked Charlie to measure the enemy's progress and try to give us an accurate countdown, then sat at my desk and pulled out a pad, to diagram Brill's arrangement and see whether I could improve on it.

The first line that I drew ripped through four sheets of paper. It had been some time since I'd done any delicate work in a suit. I remembered how, in training, they'd made us practice controlling the strength-amplification circuits by passing eggs from person to person, messy business. I wondered if they still had eggs on Earth.

The diagram completed, I couldn't see any way to add to it. All those reams of theory crammed in my brain; there was plenty of tactical advice about envelopment and encirclement, but from the wrong point of view. If you were the one who was being encircled, you didn't have many options. Just sit tight and fight. Respond quickly to enemy concentrations of force, but stay flexible so the enemy can't employ a diversionary force to divert strength from some predictable section of your perimeter. *Make full use of air and space support,* always good advice. Keep your head down and your chin up and pray for the cavalry. Hold your position and don't contemplate Dien Bien Phu, the Alamo, the Battle of Hastings.

"Eight more carriers out," Charlie said. "Five minutes. Until the first eight get here."

So they were going to attack in two waves. At least two. What would I do, in the Tauran commander's position? That wasn't too far-fetched; the Taurans lacked imagination in tactics and tended to copy human patterns.

The first wave could be a throwaway, a kamikaze attack to soften us up and evaluate our defenses. Then the second would come in more methodically and finish the job. Or vice versa; the first group would have twenty minutes to get entrenched, then the second could skip over their heads and hit us hard at one spot —breach the perimeter and overrun the base.

Or maybe they sent out two forces simply because two was a magic number. Or they could only launch eight troop carriers at a time (that would be bad, implying that the carriers were large; in different situations they had used carriers holding as few as 4 troops or as many as 128).

"Three minutes." I stared at the cluster of monitors that showed various sectors of the mine field. If we were lucky, they'd land out there, out of caution. Or maybe pass over it low enough to detonate mines.

I was feeling vaguely guilty. I was safe in my hole, doodling, ready to start calling out orders. How did those seventy sacrificial lambs feel about their absentee commander?

Then I remembered how I had felt about Captain Stott, that first mission, when he'd elected to stay safely in orbit while we fought on the ground. The rush of remembered hate was so strong I had to bite back nausea.

"Hilleboe, can you handle the lasers by yourself?"

"I don't see why not, sir."

I tossed down the pen and stood up. "Charlie, you take over the unit coordination; you can do it as well as I could. I'm going topside."

"I wouldn't advise that, sir."

"Hell no, William. Don't be an idiot."

"I'm not taking orders, I'm giv—"

"You wouldn't last ten seconds up there," Charlie said.

"I'll take the same chance as everybody else."

"Don't you hear what I'm saying? *They'll* kill you!"

"The troops? Nonsense. I know they don't like me especially, but—"

"You haven't listened in on the squad frequencies?" No, they didn't speak my brand of English when they talked among themselves. "They think you put them out on the line for punishment, for cowardice. After you'd told them anyone was free to go into the dome."

"Didn't you, sir?" Hilleboe said.

"To punish them? No, of course not." Not consciously. "They were just up there when I needed . . . hasn't Lieutenant Brill said anything to them?"

"Not that I've heard," Charlie said. "Maybe she's been too busy to tune in."

Or she agreed with them. "I'd better get—"

"There!" Hilleboe shouted. The first enemy ship was visible in one of the mine field monitors; the others appeared in the next second. They came in from random directions and weren't evenly distributed around the base. Five in the northeast quadrant and only one in the southwest. I relayed the information to Brill.

But we had predicted their logic pretty well; all of them were coming down in the ring of mines. One came close enough to one of the tachyon devices to set it off. The blast caught the rear end of the oddly streamlined craft, causing it to make a complete flip and crash nose-first. Side ports opened up and Taurans came crawling out. Twelve of them; probably four left inside. If all the others had sixteen as well, there were only slightly more of them than of us.

In the first wave.

The other seven had landed without incident, and yes, there were sixteen each. Brill shuffled a couple of squads to conform to the enemy's troop concentration, and we waited.

They moved fast across the mine field, striding in unison like bow-legged, top-heavy robots, not even breaking stride when one of them was blown to bits by a mine, which happened eleven times.

When they came over the horizon, the reason for their apparently random distribution was obvious: they had analyzed beforehand which approaches would give them the most natural cover, from the rubble that the drones had kicked up. They would be able to get within a couple of kilometers of the base before we got any clear line of sight on them. And their suits had augmentation circuits similar to ours, so they could cover a kilometer in less than a minute.

Brill had her troops open fire immediately, probably more for morale than out of any hope of actually hitting the enemy. They probably were getting a few, though it was hard to tell. At least the tachyon rockets did an impressive job of turning boulders into gravel.

The Taurans returned fire with some weapon similar to the tachyon rocket, maybe exactly the same. They rarely found a mark, though; our people were at and below ground level, and if the rocket didn't hit something it would keep on going forever, amen. They did score a hit on one of the bevawatt lasers, though, and the concussion that filtered down to us was strong enough to make me wish we had burrowed a little deeper than twenty meters.

The bevawatts weren't doing us any good. The Taurans must have figured out the lines of sight ahead of time, and gave them wide berth. That turned out to be fortunate, because it caused Charlie to let his attention wander from the laser monitors for a moment.

"What the hell?"

"What's that, Charlie?" I didn't take my eyes off the monitors. Waiting for something to happen.

"The ship, the cruiser—it's gone." I looked at the holograph display. He was right, the only red lights were those that stood for the troop carriers.

"Where did it go?" I asked inanely.

"Let's play it back." He programmed the display to go back a couple of minutes and cranked out the scale to where both planet and collapsar showed on the cube. The cruiser showed up, and with it, three green dots. Our "coward," attacking the cruiser with only two drones.

But he had a little help from the laws of physics.

Instead of going into collapsar insertion, he had skimmed *around* the collapsar field in a slingshot orbit. He had come out going .9 *c;* the drones were going .99 *c,* headed straight for the enemy cruiser. Our planet was about a thousand light-seconds from the collapsar, so the Tauran ship had only ten seconds to detect and stop both drones. And at that speed, it didn't matter whether you'd been hit by a nova bomb or a spitball.

The first drone disintegrated the cruiser and the other one, .01 second behind, glided on down to impact on the planet. The fighter missed the planet by a couple of hundred kilometers and hurtled on into space, decelerating with the maximum twenty-five G's. He'd be back in a couple of months.

But the Taurans weren't going to wait. They were getting close enough to our lines for both sides to start using lasers, but they were also within easy grenade range. A good-sized rock could shield them from laser fire, but the grenades and rockets were slaughtering them.

At first, Brill's troops had the overwhelming advantage: fighting from ditches, they could only be harmed by an occasional lucky shot or an extremely well-aimed grenade (which the Taurans threw by hand, with a range of several hundred meters). Brill had lost four, but it looked as if the Tauran force was down to less than half its original size.

Eventually, the landscape had been torn up enough so that the bulk of the Tauran force was also able to fight from holes in the ground. The fighting slowed down to individual laser duels, punctuated occasionally by heavier weapons. But it wasn't smart to use up a tachyon rocket against a single Tauran, not with another force of unknown size only a few minutes away.

Something had been bothering me about that holographic replay. Now, with the battle's lull, I knew what it was.

When that second drone crashed at near-light-speed, how much damage had it done to the planet? I stepped over to the computer and punched it up; found out how much energy had been released in the collision, and then compared it with geological information in the computer's memory.

Twenty times as much energy as the most powerful earthquake ever recorded. On a planet three-quarters the size of Earth.

On the general frequency: "Everybody—topside! Right now!" I palmed the button that would cycle and open the airlock and tunnel that led from Administration to the surface.

"What the hell, Will—"

"Earthquake!" How long? "Move!"

Hilleboe and Charlie were right behind me.

"Safer in the ditches?" Charlie said.

"I don't know," I said. "Never been in an earthquake." Maybe the walls of the ditch would close up and crush you.

I was surprised at how dark it was on the surface. S Doradus had almost set; the monitors had compensated for the low light level.

An enemy laser raked across the clearing to our left, making a quick shower of sparks when it flicked by a bevawatt mounting. We hadn't been seen yet. We all decided yes, it would be safer in the ditches, and made it to the nearest one in three strides.

There were four men and women in the ditch, one of them badly wounded or dead. We scrambled down the ledge and I turned up my image amplifier to log two, to inspect our ditch-mates. We were lucky; one was a grenadier and they also had a rocket launcher. I could just make out the names on their helmets. We were in Brill's ditch, but she hadn't noticed us yet. She was at the opposite end, cautiously peering over the edge, directing two squads in a flanking movement. When they were safely in position, she ducked back down. "Is that you, Major?"

"That's right," I said cautiously. I wondered whether any of the people in the ditch were among the ones after my scalp.

"What's this about an earthquake?"

She had been told about the cruiser being destroyed, but not about the other drone. I explained in as few words as possible.

"Nobody's come out of the airlock," she said. "Not yet. I guess they all went into the stasis field."

"Yeah, they were just as close to one as the other." Maybe some of them were still down below, hadn't taken my warning seriously. I chinned the general frequency to check, and then all hell broke loose.

The group dropped away and then flexed back up; slammed us so hard that we were airborne, tumbling out of the ditch. We flew several meters, going high enough to see the pattern of bright orange and yellow ovals, the craters where nova bombs had been stopped. I landed on my feet but the ground was shifting and slithering so much that it was impossible to stay upright.

With a basso grinding I could feel through my suit, the cleared area above our base crumbled and fell in. Part of the stasis field's underside was exposed when the ground subsided; it settled to its new level with aloof grace.

I hoped everybody had had time and sense enough to get under the dome.

A figure came staggering out of the ditch nearest to me and I realized with a start that it wasn't human. At this range, my laser burned a hole straight through his helmet; he took two steps and fell over backward. Another helmet peered over the edge of the ditch. I sheared the top of it off before he could raise his weapon.

I couldn't get my bearings. The only thing that hadn't changed was the stasis dome, and it looked the same from any angle. The bevawatt lasers were all buried, but one of them had switched on, a brilliant flickering searchlight that illuminated a swirling cloud of vaporized rock.

Obviously, though, I was in enemy territory. I started across the trembling ground toward the dome.

I couldn't raise any platoon leaders. All of them but Brill were probably inside the dome. I did get Hilleboe and Charlie; told Hilleboe to go inside the dome and roust everybody out. If the next wave also had 128, we were going to need everybody.

The tremors died down and I found my way into a "friendly" ditch—the cooks' ditch, in fact, since the only people there were Orban and Rudkoski.

I got a beep from Hilleboe and chinned her on. "Sir . . . there were only ten people there. The rest didn't make it."

"They stayed behind?" Seemed like they'd had plenty of time.

"I don't know, sir."

"Never mind. Get me a count, how many people we have, all totaled." I tried the platoon leaders' frequency again and it was still silent.

The three of us watched for enemy laser fire, for a couple of minutes, but there was none. Probably waiting for reinforcements.

Hilleboe called back. "I only get fifty-three, sir. Some others may be unconscious."

"All right. Have them sit tight until—" Then the second wave showed up, the troop carriers roaring over the horizon with their jets pointed our way, decelerating. *"Get some rockets on those bastards!"* Hilleboe yelled to everyone in particular. But nobody had managed to stay attached to a rocket launcher while he was being tossed around. No grenade launchers, either, and the range was too far for the hand lasers to do any damage.

These carriers were four or five times the size of the ones in the first wave. One of them grounded about a kilometer in front of us, barely stopping long enough to disgorge its troops. Of which there were over fifty, probably sixty-four times eight made 512. No way we could hold them back.

"Everybody listen, this is Major Mandella." I tried to keep my voice even and quiet. "We're going to retreat back into the dome, quickly but in an orderly way. I know we're scattered all over hell. If you belong to the second or fourth platoon, stay put for a minute and give covering fire while the first and third platoons, and support, fall back.

"First and third and support, fall back to about half your present distance from the dome, then take cover and defend the second and fourth as they come back. They'll go to the edge of the dome and cover you while you come back the rest of the way." I shouldn't have said "retreat"; that word wasn't in the book. Retrograde action.

There was a lot more retrograde than action. Eight or nine people were firing, and all the rest were in full flight. Rudkoski and Orban had vanished. I took a few carefully aimed shots, to no great effect, then ran down to the other end of the ditch, climbed out and headed for the dome.

The Taurans started firing rockets, but most of them seemed to be going too high. I saw two of us get blown away before I got to my half-way point; found a nice big rock and hid behind it. I peeked out and decided that only two or three of the Taurans were close enough to be even remotely possible laser targets, and the better part of valor would be in not drawing unnecessary attention to myself. I ran the rest of the way to the edge of the field and stopped to return fire. After a couple of shots, I realized that I was just making myself a target; as far as I could see there was only one other person who was still running toward the dome.

A rocket zipped by, so close I could have touched it. I flexed my knees and kicked, and entered the dome in a rather undignified posture.

3.

Inside, I could see the rocket that had missed me drifting lazily through the gloom, rising slightly as it passed through to the other side of the dome. It would vaporize the instant it came out the other side, since all of the kinetic energy it had lost in abruptly slowing down to 16.3 meters per second would come back in the form of heat.

Nine people were lying dead, face-down just inside of the field's edge. It wasn't unexpected, though it wasn't the sort of thing you were supposed to tell the troops.

Their fighting suits were intact—otherwise they wouldn't have made it this far—but sometime during the past few minutes rough-and-tumble, they had damaged the coating of special insulation that protected them from the stasis field. So as soon as they entered the field, all electrical activity in their bodies ceased, which killed them instantly. Also, since no molecule in their bodies could move faster than 16.3 miles per second, they instantly froze solid, their body temperatures stabilized at a cool $0.426°$ Absolute.

I decided not to turn any of them over to find out their names, not yet. We had to get some sort of defensive position worked out, before the Taurans came through the dome. If they decided to slug it out rather than wait.

With elaborate gestures, I managed to get everybody collected in the center of the field, under the fighter's tail, where the weapons were racked.

There were plenty of weapons, since we had been prepared to

outfit three times this number of people. After giving each person a shield and short-sword, I traced a question in the snow: GOOD ARCHERS? RAISE HANDS. I got five volunteers, then picked out three more so that all the bows would be in use. Twenty arrows per bow. They were the most effective long-range weapon we had; the arrows were almost invisible in their slow flight, heavily weighted and tipped with a deadly sliver of diamond-hard crystal.

I arranged the archers in a circle around the fighter (its landing fins would give them partial protection from missiles coming in from behind) and between each pair of archers put four other people: two spear-throwers, one quarterstaff, and a person armed with battleax and a dozen chakram throwing knives. This arrangement would theoretically take care of the enemy at any range from the edge of the field to hand-to-hand combat.

Actually, at some 600-to-42 odds, they could probably walk in with a rock in each hand, no shields or special weapons, and still beat the crap out of us.

Assuming they knew what the stasis field was. Their technology seemed up to date in all other respects.

For several hours nothing happened. We got about as bored as anyone could, waiting to die. No one to talk to, nothing to see but the unchanging gray dome, gray snow, gray space-ship, and a few identically gray soldiers. Nothing to hear, taste, or smell but yourself.

Those of us who still had any interest in the battle were keeping watch on the bottom edge of the dome, waiting for the first Taurans to come through. So it took us a second to realize what was going on when the attack did start. It came from above, a cloud of catapulted darts swarming in through the dome some thirty meters above the ground, headed straight for the center of the hemisphere.

The shields were big enough that you could hide most of your body behind them by crouching slightly; the people who saw the darts coming could protect themselves easily. The ones who had their backs to the action, or were just asleep at the switch, had to rely on dumb luck for survival; there was no way to shout a warning, and it only took three seconds for a missile to get from the edge of the dome to its center.

We were lucky, losing only five. One of them was an archer, Shubik. I took over her bow and we waited, expecting a ground attack immediately.

It didn't come. After a half-hour, I went around the circle and explained with gestures that the first thing you were supposed to do, if anything happened, was to touch the person on your right. He'd do the same, and so on down the line.

That might have saved my life. The second dart attack, a couple of hours later, came from behind me. I felt the nudge, slapped the person on my right, turned around and saw the cloud descending. I got the shield over my head and they hit a split-second later.

I set down my bow to pluck three darts from the shield and the ground attack started.

It was a weird, impressive sight. Some 300 of them stepped into the field simultaneously, almost shoulder-to-shoulder around the perimeter of the dome. They advanced in step, each one holding a round shield barely large enough to hide his massive chest. They were throwing darts similar to the ones we had been barraged with.

I set the shield up in front of me—it had little extensions on the bottom to keep it upright—and with the first arrow I shot, I knew we had a chance. It struck one of them in the center of his shield, went straight through, and penetrated his suit.

It was a one-sided massacre. The darts weren't very effective without the element of surprise—but when one came sailing over my head from behind, it did give me a crawly feeling between the shoulderblades.

With twenty arrows I got twenty Taurans. They closed ranks every time one dropped; you didn't even have to aim. After running out of arrows, I tried throwing their darts back at them. But their light shields were quite adequate against the small missiles.

We'd killed more than half of them with arrows and spears, long before they got into range of the hand-to-hand weapons. I drew my sword and waited. They still outnumbered us by better than three to one.

When they got within ten meters, the people with the chakram throwing knives had their own field day. Although the spinning disc was easy enough to see, and it took more than a half-second to get from thrower to target, most of the Taurans reacted the same ineffective way, raising up the shield to ward it off. The razor-sharp, tempered heavy blade cut through the light shield like a buzz-saw through cardboard.

The first hand-to-hand contact was with the quarterstaffs, which were metal rods two meters long, that tapered at the ends to a double-edged, serrated knife blade. The Taurans had a cold-blooded—or valiant, if your mind works that way—method for dealing with them. They would simply grab the blade and die. While the human was trying to extricate his weapon from the frozen death-grip, a Tauran swordsman, with a scimitar over a meter long, would step in and kill him.

Besides the swords, they had a bolo-like thing that was a length of elastic cord that ended with about ten centimeters of something like barbed wire, and a small weight to propel it. It was a danger-ous weapon for all concerned; if they missed their target it would come snapping back unpredictably. But they hit their target pretty often, going under the shields and wrapping the thorny wire around ankles.

I stood back-to-back with Private Erikson and with our swords we managed to stay alive for the next few minutes. When the Taurans were down to a couple of dozen survivors, they just turned around and started marching out. We threw some darts after them, getting three, but we didn't want to chase after them. They might turn around and start hacking again.

There were only twenty-eight of us left standing. Nearly ten times that number of dead Taurans littered the ground, but there was no satisfaction in it.

They could do the whole thing over, with a fresh 300. And this time it would work.

We moved from body to body, pulling out arrows and spears,

then took up places around the fighter again. Nobody bothered to retrieve the quarterstaffs. I counted noses: Charlie and Diana were still alive (Hilleboe had been one of the quarterstaff victims) as well as two supporting officers, Wilber and Szydlowska. Rudkoski was still alive but Orban had taken a dart.

After a day of waiting, it looked as if the enemy had decided on a war of attrition, rather than repeating the ground attack. Darts came in constantly, not in swarms anymore, but in twos and threes and tens. And from all different angles. You couldn't stay alert forever; they'd get somebody every three or four hours.

We took turns sleeping, two at a time, on top of the stasis field generator. Sitting directly under the bulk of the fighter, it was the safest place in the dome.

Every now and then, a Tauran would appear at the edge of the field, evidently to see whether any of us were left. Sometimes we'd shoot an arrow at him, for practice.

The darts stopped falling after a couple of days. I supposed it was possible that they'd simply run out of them. Or maybe they'd decided to stop when we were down to twenty survivors.

There was a more likely possibility. I took one of the quarterstaffs down to the edge of the field and poked it through, a centimeter or so. When I drew it back, the point was melted off. When I showed it to Charlie, he just rocked back and forth (the only way you can nod in a suit); this sort of thing had happened before, one of the first times the stasis field hadn't worked. They simply saturated it with laser fire and waited for us to go stir-crazy and turn off the generator. They were probably sitting in their ships playing the Tauran equivalent of pinochle.

I tried to think. It was hard to keep your mind on something for any length of time in that hostile environment, sense-deprived, looking over your shoulder every few seconds. Something Charlie had said. Only yesterday, I couldn't track it down. It wouldn't have worked then; that was all I could remember. Then finally it came to me.

I called everyone over and wrote in the snow:
GET NOVA BOMBS FROM SHIP.

CARRY TO EDGE OF FIELD.

MOVE FIELD.

Szydlowska knew where the proper tools would be, aboard ship. Luckily, we had left all of the entrances open before turning on the stasis field: they were electronic and would have been frozen shut. We got an assortment of wrenches from the engine room and climbed up to the cockpit. He knew how to remove the access plate that exposed a crawl space into the bomb-bay. I followed him in through the meter-wide tube.

Normally, I supposed, it would have been pitch-black. But the stasis field illuminated the bomb-bay with the same dim, shadowless light that prevailed outside. The bomb-bay was too small for both of us, so I stayed at the end of the crawl space and watched.

The bomb-bay doors had a "manual override" so they were easy; Szydlowska just turned a hand-crank and we were in business. Freeing the two nova bombs from their cradles was another thing. Finally, he went back down to the engine room and brought back a crowbar. He pried one loose and I got the other, and we rolled them out the bomb-bay.

Sergeant Anghelov was already working on them by the time we climbed back down. All you had to do to arm the bomb was to unscrew the fuse on the nose of it and poke something around in the fuse socket to wreck the delay mechanism and safety restraints.

We carried them quickly to the edge, six people per bomb, and set them down next to each other. Then we waved to the four people who were standing by at the field generator's handles. They picked it up and walked ten paces in the opposite direction. The bombs disappeared as the edge of the field slid over them.

There was no doubt that the bombs had gone off. For a couple of seconds it was hot as the interior of a star outside, and even the stasis field took notice of the fact: about a third of the dome glowed a dull pink for a moment, then was gray again. There was a slight acceleration, like you would feel in a slow elevator. That meant we were drifting down to the bottom of the crater. Would there be a solid bottom? Or would we sink down through molten rock to be trapped like a fly in amber—didn't pay to even think about that. Perhaps if it happened, we could blast our way out with the fighter's bevawatt laser.

Twelve of us, anyhow.

HOW LONG? Charlie scraped in the snow at my feet.

That was a damned good question. About all I knew was the amount of energy two nova bombs released. I didn't know how big a fireball they would make, which would determine the temperature at detonation and the size of the crater. I didn't know the heat capacity of the surrounding rock, or its boiling point. I wrote ONE WEEK, SHRUG? HAVE TO THINK.

The ship's computer could have told me in a thousandth of a second, but it wasn't talking. I started writing equations in the snow, trying to get a maximum and minimum figure for the length of time it would take for the outside to cool down to 500°. Anghelov, whose physics was much more up-to-date, did his own calculations on the other side of the ship.

My answer said anywhere from six hours to six days (although for six hours, the surrounding rock would have to conduct heat like pure copper), and Anghelov got five hours to four and a half days. I voted for six and nobody else got a vote.

We slept a lot. Charlie and Diana played chess by scraping symbols in the snow; I was never able to hold the shifting positions of the pieces in my mind. I checked my figures several times and kept coming up with six days. I checked Anghelov's computations, too, and they seemed all right, but I stuck to my guns. It wouldn't hurt us to stay in the suits an extra day and a half. We argued good-naturedly in terse shorthand.

There had been nineteen of us left the day we tossed the bombs outside. There were still nineteen six days later, when I paused with my hand over the generator's cutoff switch. What was waiting for us out there? Surely we had killed all the Taurans within several klicks of the explosion. But there might have been a reserve force farther away, now waiting patiently on the crater's lip. At least you could push a quarterstaff through the field and have it come back whole.

I dispersed the people evenly around the area, so they might not get us with a single shot. Then, ready to turn it back on immediately if anything went wrong. I pushed.

4.

My radio was still tuned to the general frequency; after more than a week of silence my ears were suddenly assaulted with loud, happy babbling.

We stood in the center of a crater almost a kilometer wide and deep. Its sides were a shiny black crust shot through with red cracks, hot but no longer dangerous. The hemisphere of earth that we rested on had sunk a good forty meters into the floor of the crater, while it had still been molten, so now we stood on a kind of pedestal.

Not a Tauran in sight.

We rushed to the ship, sealed it and filled it with cold air and popped our suits. I didn't press seniority for the one shower; just sat back in an acceleration couch and took deep breaths of air that didn't smell like recycled Mandella.

The ship was designed for a maximum crew of twelve, so we stayed outside in shifts of seven to keep from straining the life-support systems. I sent a repeating message to the other fighter, which was still over six weeks away, that we were in good shape and waiting to be picked up. I was reasonably certain he would have seven free berths, since the normal crew for a combat mission was only three.

It was good to walk around and talk again. I officially suspended all things military for the duration of our stay on the planet. Some of the people were survivors of Brill's mutinous bunch, but they didn't show any hostility toward me.

We played a kind of nostalgia game, comparing the various eras we'd experienced on Earth, wondering what it would be like in the 700-years-future we were going back to. Nobody mentioned the fact that we would at best go back to a few months' furlough, and then be assigned to another Strike Force, another turn of the wheel.

Wheels. One day Charlie asked me from what country my name originated; it sounded weird to him. I told him it originated from the lack of a dictionary and that if it were spelled right, it would look even weirder.

I got to kill a good half-hour explaining all the peripheral details to that. Basically, though, my parents were "hippies" (a kind of subculture in late Twentieth Century America, that rejected materialism and embraced a broad spectrum of odd ideas) who lived with a group of other hippies in a small agricultural community. When my mother got pregnant, they wouldn't be so conventional as to get married: this entailed the woman taking the man's name, and implied that she was his property. But they got all intoxicated and sentimental and decided they would both change their names to be the same. They rode into the nearest town, arguing all the way as to what name would be the best symbol for the love-bond between them—I narrowly missed having a much shorter name —and they settled on Mandala.

A mandala is a wheel-like design the hippies had borrowed from a foreign religion, that symbolized the cosmos, the cosmic mind, God, or whatever needed a symbol. Neither my mother nor my father really knew how to spell the word, and the magistrate in town just wrote it down the way it sounded to him. And they named me William in honor of a wealthy uncle, who unfortunately died penniless.

The six weeks passed rather pleasantly: talking, reading, resting. The other ship landed next to ours and did have nine free berths. We shuffled crews so that each ship had someone who could get it out of trouble if the preprogrammed jump sequence malfunctioned. I assigned myself to the other ship, hoping it would have some new books. It didn't.

We zipped up in the tanks and took off simultaneously.

We wound up spending a lot of time in the tanks, just to keep from looking at the same faces all day long in the crowded ship. The added periods of acceleration got us back to Stargate in ten months, subjective. Of course it was still 340 years (minus seven months) to the hypothetical objective observer.

There were hundreds of cruisers in orbit around Stargate. Bad news: with that kind of backlog we probably wouldn't get any furlough at all.

I supposed I was more likely to get a court martial than a furlough, anyhow. Losing eighty-eight percent of my company, many of them because they didn't have enough confidence in me to obey that direct earthquake order. And we were back where we'd started on Sade-138; no Taurans there but no base, either.

We got landing instructions and went straight down, no shuttle. There was another surprise waiting at the spaceport. More dozens of cruisers were standing around on the ground—they'd never done that before for fear that Stargate would be hit—and two captured Tauran cruisers as well. We'd never managed to get one intact.

Seven centuries could have brought us a decisive advantage, of course. Maybe we were winning.

We went through an airlock under a "returnees" sign. After the air cycled and we'd popped our suits, a beautiful young woman came in with a cartload of tunics and told us, in perfectly accented English, to get dressed and go to the lecture hall at the end of the corridor to our left.

The tunic felt odd, light yet warm. It was the first thing I'd worn besides a fighting suit or bare skin in almost a year.

The lecture hall was about a hundred times too big for the twenty-two of us. The same girl was there, and asked us to move down to the front. That was unsettling; I could have sworn she had gone down the corridor the other way—I *knew* she had; I'd been captivated by the sight of her clothed behind.

Hell, maybe they had matter transmitters. Or teleportation. Wanted to save herself a few steps.

We sat for a minute and a man, clothed in the same kind of unadorned tunic we and the girl were wearing, walked across the stage with a stack of thick notebooks under each arm.

The same girl followed him on, also carrying notebooks.

I looked behind me and she was still standing in the aisle. To make things even more odd, the man was virtually a twin to both of the women.

The man riffled through one of the notebooks and cleared his throat. "These books are for your convenience." he said, also with perfect accent, "and you don't have to read them if you don't want to. You don't have to do anything you don't want to do, because . . . you're free men and women. The war is over."

Disbelieving silence.

"As you will read in this book, the war ended 221 years ago. Accordingly, this is the year 220. Old style, of course, it is 3138 A.D.

"You are the last group of soldiers to return. When you leave here, I will leave as well. And destroy Stargate. It exists only as a rendezvous point for returnees, and as a monument to human stupidity. And shame. As you will read. Destroying it will be a cleansing."

He stopped speaking and the woman started without a pause. "I am sorry for what you've been through and wish I could say that it was for good cause, but as you will read, it was not.

"Even the wealth you have accumulated, back salary and compound interest, is worthless, as I no longer use money or credit. Nor is there such a thing as an economy, in which to use these . . . things."

"As you must have guessed by now," the man took over, "I am, we are, clones of a single individual. Some 250 years ago, my name was Kahn. Now it is Man.

"I had a direct ancestor in your company, a Corporal Larry Kahn. It saddens me that he didn't come back."

"I am over ten billion individuals but only one consciousness," she said. "After you read, I will try to clarify this. I know that it will be difficult to understand.

"No other humans are quickened, since I am the perfect pattern. Individuals who die are replaced. There are planets, however, on which humans are born in the normal, mammalian way. If my society is too alien for you, you may go to one of these planets. If you wish to take part in procreation, we will not discourage it. Many veterans ask us to change their polarity to heterosexual so that they can more easily fit into these other societies. This I can do very easily."

Don't worry about that, Man, just make out my ticket.

"You will be my guest here at Stargate for ten days, after which you will be taken wherever you want to go," he said. "Please read this book in the meantime. Feel free to ask any questions, or request any service." They both stood and walked off the stage.

Charlie was sitting next to me. "Incredible," he said. "They let . . . they encourage . . . men and women to do *that* again? Together?"

The female aisle Man was sitting behind us, and she answered before I could frame a reasonably sympathetic, hypocritical reply. "It isn't a judgment on your society," she said, probably not seeing that he took it a little more personally than that. "I only feel that it's necessary as a eugenic safety device. I have no evidence that there is anything wrong with cloning only one ideal individual, but if it turns out to have been a mistake, there will be a large genetic pool with which to start again."

She patted him on the shoulder. "Of course, you don't have to go to these breeder planets. You can stay on one of my planets. I make no distinction between heterosexual play and homosexual."

She went up on the stage to give a long spiel about where we were going to stay and eat and so forth while we were on Stargate. "Never been seduced by a computer before," Charlie muttered.

The 1,143-year-long war had been begun on false pretenses and only continued because the two races were unable to communicate.

Once they could talk, the first question was "Why did you start this thing?" and the answer was "Me?"

The Taurans hadn't known war for millennia, and toward the beginning of the Twenty-first Century it looked as if mankind was ready to outgrow the institution as well. But the old soldiers were still around, and many of them were in positions of power. They virtually ran the United Nations Exploratory and Colonization Group, that was taking advantage of the newly discovered collapsar jump to explore interstellar space.

Many of the early ships met with accidents and disappeared. The ex-military men were suspicious. They armed the colonizing vessels and the first time they met a Tauran ship, they blasted it.

They dusted off their medals and the rest was going to be history.

You couldn't blame it all on the military, though. The evidence they presented for the Taurans' having been responsible for the earlier casualties was laughably thin. The few people who pointed this out were ignored.

The fact was, Earth's economy needed a war, and this one was ideal. It gave a nice hole to throw buckets of money into, but would unify humanity rather than divide it.

The Taurans relearned war, after a fashion. They never got really good at it, and would eventually have lost.

The Taurans, the book explained, couldn't communicate with humans because they had no concept of the individual; they had been natural clones for millions of years. Eventually, Earth's cruisers were manned by Man, Kahn-clones, and they were for the first time able to get through to each other.

The book stated this as a bald fact. I asked a Man to explain what it meant, what was special about clone-to-clone communication, and he said that I *a priori* couldn't understand it. There were no words for it, and my brain wouldn't be able to accommodate the concepts even if there were words.

All right. It sounded a little fishy, but I was willing to accept it. I'd accept that up was down if it meant the war was over.

I'd just finished dressing after my first good night's sleep in years, when someone tapped lightly on my door. I opened it and it was a female Man, standing there with an odd expression on her face. Almost a leer; was she trying to look seductive?

"Major Mandella," she said, "may I come in?" I motioned her to a chair but she went straight to the bed and sat daintily on the rumpled covers.

"I have a proposition for you, Major." I wondered whether she knew the word's archaic second meaning. "Come sit beside me, please."

Lacking Charlie's reservations about being seduced by a computer, I sat. "What do you propose?" I touched her warm thigh and found it disappointingly easy to control myself. Can reflexes get out of practice?

"I need permission to clone you, and a few grams of flesh. In return, I offer you immortality."

Not the proposition I'd expected. "Why me? I thought you were already the perfect pattern."

"For my own purposes, and within my powers to judge, I am. But I need you for a function . . . contrary to my own nature. And contrary to my Tauran brother's nature."

"A nasty job." Spend all eternity cleaning out the sewers; immortality of a sort.

"You might not find it so." She shifted restlessly and I removed my hand. "Thank you. You have read the first part of the book?"

"Scanned it."

"Then you know that both Man and Tauran are gentle beings. We do not fight among ourselves or with each other, because physical aggressiveness has been bred out of our sensibilities. Engineered out."

"A laudable accomplishment." I saw where this was leading and the answer was going to be no.

"But it was just this lack of aggressiveness that allowed Earth, in your time, to successfully wage war against a culture uncountable millennia older. I am afraid it could happen again."

"This time to Man."

"Man and Tauran; philosophically there is little difference."

"What you want, then, is for me to provide you with an army. A band of barbarians to guard your frontiers."

"That's an unpleasant way of—"

"It's not a pleasant idea." My idea of hell. "No. I can't do it."

"Your only chance to live forever."

"Absolutely not." I stared at the floor. "Your aggressiveness was bred out of you. Mine was knocked out of me."

She stood up and smoothed the tunic over her perfect hips. "I cannot use guile. I will not withhold this body from you, if you desire it."

I considered that but didn't say anything.

"Besides immortality, all I can offer you is the abstract satisfaction of service. Protecting humanity against unknown perils."

I'd put in my thousand-odd years of service, and hadn't got any great satisfaction. "No. Even if I thought of you as humanity, the answer would still be no."

She nodded and went to the door.

"Don't worry," I said. "You can get one of the others."

She opened the door and addressed the corridor outside. "No, the others have already declined. You were the least likely, and the last one I approached."

Man was pretty considerate, especially so in light of our refusal to cooperate. Just for us twenty-two throwbacks, he went to the trouble of rejuvenating a little restaurant/tavern and staffing it at all hours (I never saw a Man eat or drink—guess they'd discovered a way around it). I was sitting in there one evening, drinking beer and reading their book, when Charlie came in and sat down.

Without preamble, he said, "I'm going to give it a try."

"Give what a try?"

"Women. Hetero." He shuddered. "No offense . . . it's not really very appealing." He patted my hand, looking distracted. "But the alternative . . . have you tried it?"

"Well . . . no, I haven't." Female Man was a visual treat, but only in the same sense as a painting or a piece of sculpture. I just couldn't see them as human beings.

"Don't." He didn't elaborate. "Besides, they say—he says, she says, it says—that they can change me back just as easily. If I don't like it."

"You'll like it, Charlie."

"Sure, that's what *they* say." He ordered a stiff drink. "Just seems unnatural. Anyway, since, uh, I'm going to make the switch, do you mind if . . . why don't we plan on going to the same planet?"

"Sure, Charlie, that'd be great." I meant it. "You know where you're going?"

"Hell, I don't care. Just away from here."

"I wonder if Heaven's still as nice—"

"No." Charlie jerked a thumb at the bartender. "*He* lives there."

"I don't know. I guess there's a list."

A Man came into the tavern, pushing a car piled high with folders. "Major Mandella? Captain Moore?"

"That's us," Charlie said.

"These are your military records. I hope you find them of interest. They were transferred to paper when your Strike Force was the only one outstanding, because it would have been impractical to keep the normal data retrieval networks running to preserve so few data."

They always anticipated your questions, even when you didn't have any.

My folder was easily five times as thick as Charlie's. Probably thicker than any other, since I seemed to be the only trooper who'd made it through the whole duration. Poor Marygay. "Wonder what kind of report old Stott filed about me." I flipped to the front of the folder.

Stapled to the front page was a small square of paper. All the other pages were pristine white, but this one was tan with age and crumbling around the edges.

The handwriting was familiar, too familiar even after so long. The date was over 250 years old.

I winced and was blinded by sudden tears. I'd had no reason to suspect that she might be alive. But I hadn't really known she was dead, not until I saw that date.

"William? What's—"

"Leave me be, Charlie. Just for a minute." I wiped my eyes and closed the folder. I shouldn't even read the damned note. Going to a new life, I should leave old ghosts behind.

But even a message from the grave was contact of a sort. I opened the folder again.

11 Oct 2878

William—

All this is in your personnel file. But knowing you, you might just chuck it. So I made sure you'd get this note.

Obviously, I lived. Maybe you will, too. Join me.

I know from the records that you're out at Sade-138 and won't be back for a couple of centuries. No problem.

I'm going to a planet they call Middle Finger, the fifth planet out from Mizar. It's two collapsar jumps, ten months subjective. Middle Finger is a kind of Coventry for heterosexuals. They call it a "eugenic control baseline."

No matter. It took all of my money, and all the money of five other old-timers, but we bought a cruiser from UNEF. And we're using it as a time machine.

So I'm on a relativistic shuttle, waiting for you. All it does is go out five light-years and come back to Middle Finger, very fast. Every ten years I age about a month. So if you're on schedule and still alive. I'll only be twenty-eight when you get here. Hurry!

I never found anybody else and I don't want anybody else. I don't care whether you're ninety years old or thirty. If I can't be your lover, I'll be your nurse.

—Marygay

"Say, bartender."

"Yes, Major?"

"Do you know of a place called Middle Finger? Is it still there?"

"Of course it is. Where would it be?" Reasonable question. "A very nice place. Garden planet. Some people don't think it's exciting enough."

"What's this all about?" Charlie said.

I handed the bartender my empty glass. "I just found out where we're going."

5. Epilog

From *The New Voice*,
Paxton, Middle Finger 24-6
14/2/3143

OLD-TIMER HAS FIRST BOY

Marygay Potter-Mandella (24 Post Road, Paxton) gave birth Friday last to a fine baby boy, 3.1 kilos.

Marygay lays claim to being the second-"oldest" resident of Middle Finger, having been born in 1977. She fought through most of the

Forever War and then waited for her mate on the time shuttle, 261 years. Her mate, William Mandella-Potter, is two years older.

The baby, not yet named, was delivered at home with the help of a friend of the family, Dr. Diana Alsever-Moore.

PETER NICHOLLS

1975: The Year in Science Fiction, or Let's Hear It for the Decline and Fall of the Science Fiction Empire!

Peter Nicholls, now resident in London, was born in Melbourne, Australia, in 1939. He lectured in English Literature for eight years after graduation, while also scripting television documentaries and reviewing science fiction for the newspapers in his spare time. He went to the U.S.A. on a Harkness Fellowship in 1968 to study film direction for two years. He has served as administrator of the Science Fiction Foundation at North East London Polytechnic since 1971—a job he acquired after seeing it advertised in *The London Times.* He has served as editor of the journal *Foundation: The Review of Science Fiction* and of *Science Fiction at Large,* a series of diverse statements about sf.

Nicholls is also the author of the forthcoming *Infinity, Eternity and the Pulp Magazines,* a critical survey of science fiction. He has set himself to evaluate a smaller slice of space and time—one year—in the following original essay.

Perhaps the view isn't very good from this, the British side of the Atlantic, but I'm not so sure it's easy to talk about "science fiction" itself any more, let alone "the year in science fiction."

Let's face it, "science fiction" is a term that was invented by publishers to sell magazines and books, and these days, they're not always consistent about the way they use it—less than they ever were. Some publishers sell science fiction without labeling it as such, and conversely, many of them do put the label science fiction on fantasy or even occult books. Bookshops can be pretty confusing for the innocent reader, who may find *Brak the Barbarian* on the same shelf as *The Dispossessed*, alongside *Lord of the Rings, Concrete Island, The Bermuda Triangle, Conjure Wife, Ringworld,* and *Dhalgren*. The ingenuity of scholars is severely tested by this sort of thing, and underneath all the learned talk about *genre* and cognition, our definitions all come out as one form or another of a weak instruction to the bookseller, "Hey, buddy, you've got that book on the wrong shelf." The bookseller, who has put the book on that particular shelf because experience tells him it will sell better there, ignores the whine in our voice, and leaves the book where it is.

But this has always been true, and I'm talking specifically about the situation now. A lot of you will have read Gibbon's *Decline and*

Fall of the Roman Empire, either in the original eighteenth-century English, or in the abridged Asimov version (often known as the "Foundation" trilogy). Now, as I remember that book (I won't say which version), large empires, like the Roman one, tend to get decadent, and then split up into a lot of semi-independent, often belligerent mini-empires. While all this is going on, back home in Rome or Byzantium or the World Convention, the propaganda machine rolls ponderously into action, and a lot of Press Releases are sent out to the Provinces, explaining that the Empire has never been in better shape; that a special bureaucracy has been set up to dissect it, docket it, and put the Imperial Facts on to a Data Bank programmed for Instant Information Retrieval; that Imperial Engineering is in fine fettle, and a new viaduct, the eighth wonder of the world, has just been built in southern France and this year's Hugo has just been given to the most literate candidate yet.

I belong to just such a bureaucracy, and in my view (which has been formed in a Great Britain from which Scotland, Wales, and Northern Ireland are threatening to secede, so I might be biased) the Science Fiction Empire is in the full flood of decadence. Now I see some of you turning pale and pouring yourselves a stiff drink, but you needn't worry. Decadence is not such an awful thing. Lots of people have a good time while decadence is happening, and it's often a stimulus for artists to be creative, and anyway, if empires didn't crumble, then we'd all be subject to bosses who live too far away to understand our problems, and neither England nor America would be free.

Getting back to plain English: the propaganda machines (I edit one myself) were active in 1975, which was the year of the coffee table science fiction book: James Gunn's *Alternate Worlds,* Aldiss's *Science Fiction Art,* Frewin's *One Hundred Years of Science Fiction Illustration,* and a whole slew of other histories, picture books, academic studies, and who's whos. No less than three academic journals about science fiction (my own journal *Foundation, Science-Fiction Studies,* and *Extrapolation*) and a number of fanzines such as *Algol, Maya, Locus,* and *Science Fiction Review* are thriving and increasing their circulation. The fanzines should certainly be included, if only because in many cases their circulation is considerably larger than that of their academic counterparts. Is it only a cynical person who would suppose that with such a chorus of voices crying out that all is well, something must be wrong?

The proliferation of science fiction conventions is another aspect of the propaganda machine's success. They even had a *world* convention in my quiet hometown, Melbourne, Australia, in 1975. England has three or four conventions a year, where it used to have one. Poznan, in Poland, behind an iron curtain which has obviously rusted badly, is hosting the Europe Convention for 1976.

Nostalgia for an imagined golden age is always a sign of decadence, and sure enough, a steady stream of anthologies has been recently reminding us of the thirties and forties, back when the Empire was at its most brash and confident. Nineteen seventy-five saw four brand-new series of collectors' hardcover reprint editions —by no means cheap, either. Whoever scooped up the reprint rights on Doc Smith's novels must be gleefully chuckling, too. When I started to read science fiction around 1950, Robert Howard and Edgar Rice Burroughs were almost impossible to obtain. I was eleven at the time, and bitterly resented the deprivation. Now their books (and comics based on their books) are so thickly piled up that traffic is impeded in some areas.

What about new work? Can we see signs here that the Empire is tottering, about to succumb to the hairy barbarians and slant-eyed Mongol hordes? Leaving aside the fact that much new science fiction is actually *about* hairy barbarians or slant-eyed Mongol hordes (e.g., Piers Anthony's new novel, *Steppe*), there are other, more sophisticated registers. The first, already implied, is Fragmentation. Here we need to distinguish between the periphery and the center. Out around the periphery, in the border provinces, there is plenty of vigor, and no two provinces are alike. An occasional Roman legate may even do secret deals with the enemy across the border, outside the provinces altogether. I don't want to spread disaffection and lower morale, but *in this very volume you hold in your hand,* containing the Nebula Award winners for the best science fiction of 1975, there are some stories which back in the decaying slums of the center they'd call "fantasy." (I won't tell anyone, if you don't.) Now the really upsetting thing is this: Individual acts of treason can be expected, though deplored, but these treasons have been ratified by the science fiction writers themselves! We are faced not with one or two Benedict Arnolds, but 1,500 of them.

There has been plenty of drama. More than one glamorous centurion has run amuck in 1975, and instead of sneaking across the border in the dead of night, they have made their escape in the full glare of day, shouting anti-Imperial slogans, and having the sheer gall to look proud of themselves. Both Robert Silverberg and Barry Malzberg announced in '75 that they'd never write science fiction again. Jim Ballard and Michael Moorcook, both of whom defected years ago, have already built comfortable city-states for themselves, somewhere on the far side of the wall. It makes you wonder if the wall is really there, or is it just the product of mass hypnosis, like the chalk line which, beginning at the rooster's beak and drawn across the floor, is rumored to keep the unfortunate bird glued to the spot in stupefaction? I tried it once, and the fowl merely cackled derisively. Harlan Ellison's experience seems to be similar. He has skipped backward and forward across the Imperial Wall so often that the weary guards don't even bother asking for the password any more.

The fragmentation is on the fringes of the Science Fiction Empire. Back in the center, things seem unified—at least on the surface—and cheered on by gung-ho patriotic shouts. There may be a few shanty towns built out of hammered-flat kerosene tins in the provinces, but behind the gaudy advertising hoardings in the Imperial Center, are decaying tenements. I believe that these slums are even more squalid in America than over here in England, because the cynicism of some of the publishers (not all) is more extreme.

Publishers of science fiction know well that there is a rapid turnover of readership. Mr. Average Fan starts buying sf paper-

backs at seventeen, and by age twenty-one he is losing interest.
This means that there need not be a premium on originality. You
may know, and I may know, that sf writer Otis Truehack has never
had an original thought in his life, and that his most recent opus
contains nothing but reworked items of Pohl and Kornbluth,
Heinlein, van Vogt, and Eric Frank Russell. But the seventeen-
year-old Average Fan doesn't know this. In his innocence he as-
sumes that all these mind-blowing concepts are Otis Truehack's
very own, and he considers the man a genius.

In the glittering Capital of science fiction, the Center, we find
a constantly bubbling stock-pot of new writing which is not really
new at all. The same old concepts, once gleaming but now dulled
by repetition and time, are given a brisk stir with the writer's
spoon, fractionally rearrange themselves, and Eureka! A new sf
novel is born. That's where the real decadence is.

We are faced with the paradox that a field of literature famous
for its originality is subject, partly for economic reasons (give the
customers what we *know* they want), to a rigid conservatism.
Once the center of an empire becomes frozen into stiff, hieratic
rituals, even at its most commonplace levels, then we know that
the decline and fall has set in. This is as true of science fiction as
it was of ancient Egypt or Byzantium. You can see why a writer
like Robert Silverberg could miserably mistake the Center for the
whole Science Fiction Empire, and get out. My analogy isn't exact,
but to continue it for a moment, the Center is where most of the
publishers live, and no matter where in the Empire the writer
makes his home, he takes his instructions and his wages from the
Center.

I'm simplifying what is really a very complicated question. No
one *forces* the writer to work within set conventions which can
come to seem as confining as prison bars. It isn't desirable on the
other hand, it isn't even *possible*, for a writer to be wholly original
all of the time. A writer needs tact. His job is to communicate, not
to baffle, and to communicate with the reader he must first make
him sufficiently at home in his company that the reader is willing
to join him on the trip. The really good science fiction story is

always a tactful balance between fulfilling the reader's comfortable expectations, and surprising him, making him think a new thought, or perhaps putting two old thoughts together so that he gets a new meaning from them.

I don't mean to suggest that all traditional sf is bad. On the contrary, much good work is being done. Even in the much despised sf series, where a brawny-thewed hero has a new adventure in each successive paperback, not all the news is bad. The young English writer Brian Stableford, for instance, writes traditional series sf—space opera—but his books all contain a leavening of good, imaginative sociology and some really ingenious exobiology. To take another example, Bob Shaw's books are very much, at first sight, in the time-honored *Astounding-Analog* tradition, but they remain fresh and stimulating. Good traditions don't die easily, and some of the traditional themes have such intrinsic strength that they live on as vigorously as ever when nursed by skilled hands, though only too often they wither beneath the frenzied manipulations of the hack.

I don't think many of us will remember 1975 as a vintage year for sf novels, although there was plenty of action. But there was no sense of the sf novel advancing in an irresistible wave, whether old or new. There *were* pointers to new directions, perhaps too many of them. The sf novel in 1975 rode off furiously in every direction. This is what I mean by the fragmentation at the outskirts of the Empire. I don't believe that it was possible for any science fiction reader in 1975 to come away from the ten or twenty best novels of the year with any sense of science fiction having a coherent identity. He is more likely to have been confused, but not, I think, depressed. I can't repeat too strongly that fragmentation can point to a new beginning, as well as signaling an end.

Nineteen seventy-five saw (in either the U.S.A. or the U.K., though not necessarily both) the publication of the following novels, among many others (beyond giving the Nebula Winner pride of place, they are in no special order):

Joe Haldeman's *The Forever War,* with its witty, bitter upending of the old sf theme most famously enunciated by Robert Heinlein in *Starship Troopers;* Ian Watson's *The Embedding,* a book which excitingly models concepts about how we model concepts (what happens if you raise children by computers?); the new novelist Chris Boyce's *Catchworld* with its scary and metaphysical thoughts about the machine-human interface; John Crowley's *The Deep* (fantasy, mystery, or science fiction?); Joanna Russ's *The Female Man* (its anger at men, for their condescension, cruelty, and smugness, stung a lot of readers, and made it possibly the most controversial sf book of the year); Robert Silverberg's *The Stochastic Man,* not one of his major works, but full of cool, ironic, sociological extrapolation, plus a lively if not profound contribution to the old free-will-versus-determinism debate; Jerry Pournelle and Larry Niven's *The Mote in God's Eye,* one of the most ambitious man-meets-alien stories yet, which contains certain assumptions about society which have caused some readers to cheer, and others to cry out, or yawn, with horror; Samuel Delany's *Dhalgren,* the *longest* sf novel of the year and, as far as I know, the longest ever published, about a ruined future city with ambiguous inhabitants (are they healthy or decayed?); Arthur Clarke's *Imperial Earth* (as a long-time Clarke fan, I was saddened by what seemed a lack of the old zest and spirit in this one); J. G. Ballard's *High Rise,* with its sociological and metaphysical chaos in its totally self-enclosed and microcosmic Apartment Block (it's rather like one of those "social breakdown into primitive tribalism after the holocaust" stories, without a causative holocaust—written with barbed precision, and even a sense that such a breakdown might not be the worst of fates); Keith Roberts's tortured, visionary futures in *The Chalk Giants;* Michael Moorcock's sophisticates dancing their elegant minuets at the end of Time, unable to relate to the unfortunate time travelers who periodically arrive, and perversely place morals before style, in *The Hollow Lands;* John Brunner's *Shockwave Rider,* a frightening but by no means hopeless near-future scenario; Michael Coney's *Hello Summer, Goodbye* (published as *Rax* in the U.S.A.), his best yet, a wistful, touching story, extracting much feeling from a basically hard sf theme; Jack

Vance's *Showboat World* (vintage Vance, baroque, colorful, witty, and badly constructed—all his old strengths and weaknesses); and Alfred Bester's *Extro* (titled *The Computer Connection* in the U.S.A.), with all the fiendish ingenuity he used to show two decades ago, but without that vindictive, obsessive hero which used to mark out a Bester story as the closest thing to the Jacobean Revenge Drama in science fiction.

How can a reader make any meaningful conclusions about such a diverse list? It is really quite distinguished, I find, after putting it all down in black and white, and I'm having second thoughts. Perhaps 1975 *was* a vintage year after all. Any generalities which follow must be cautious and tentative indeed. I do get the impression, from the above sampling of novels, and also from many short stories of the year (*especially* the short stories) that advances in style are, at the moment, outdistancing advances in concept. But even if 1975 wasn't a year for conceptual breakthrough in sf (with the notable exception of Ian Watson's *Embedding,* in which the thought triumphantly survives both the occasionally awkward style and melodramatic plotting), there is much solid thinking in these novels and, generally, a workmanlike marriage of form and content—Ballard, especially, writes as beautifully as ever. In one or two cases, though, there is an imbalance, such that the style seems unnecessarily elaborate and self-indulgent, overornate for the comparatively light freight of meaning it is required to carry. At one time the more familiar fault in science fiction's narrative style, as well as its dialogue, was the reverse of overelaboration— a crude, slangy punchiness derived from the pulps—but this seems to be disappearing from sf, at least in these higher echelons, though traces are still visible in the Niven-Pournelle book.

The reader may be more struck by the variety of these novels than by anything else: the old forms, the hard sf extrapolation and the baroque space opera, are still with us, but the metaphysical thriller is obviously gaining ground, and so is the "what is the nature of intelligence" story, the latter especially in the U.K., but see also Roger Zelazny's gripping "Home is the Hangman" in this volume. The alternative-life-style story is stronger than before, as in the Delany, Russ, and Ballard novels—in three very different ways.

Turning to short stories, we find that a new generation of writers has definitely arrived. Frank Herbert and Ursula Le Guin, Tom Disch and R. A. Lafferty, all the bright names of the late sixties—it seems like only yesterday—are practically Senior Citizens, grave members of The Establishment by now, and I suppose they've got mixed feelings about it! The following are some of the names of the seventies: T. J. Bass, Michael Bishop, Ed Bryant, Jack Dann, Gardner Dozois, Gordon Eklund, Felix Gottschalk, M. John Harrison, Joe Haldeman, George Martin, Vonda McIntyre, Doris Piserchia, P. J. Plauger, Christopher Priest, Tom Reamy, Joanna Russ, Pamela Sargent, Craig Strete, James Tiptree, Jr., Ian Watson, and Gene Wolfe. The list is very partial; obviously it could be extended three or four times.

Not everyone will like the work of *all* the above writers—I don't myself—but I think anyone familiar with the work of some or all of them will admit that there is a move, as in the sf novel, toward a greater sophistication and confidence in style, and a greater vulnerability of manner (toughness is not very "in" at the moment, and the unkind older reader, reared on the *Astounding* of the forties, might be tempted to murmur "bleeding hearts" of some of them, not entirely without justice). Let's not nitpick though; there are some fine writers in that list, and I will be very surprised if two or three of them do not grow into being the sf "classics" of the next decade. The same list reveals that an already established shift from hard sf (chemistry, physics, astronomy, technology) to soft sf (psychology, biology, anthropology, sociology, and even—in the case of Ian Watson and Samuel Delany—linguistics) is continuing more strongly than ever. Even black holes are being assimilated into psychological rather than physical landscapes (spacescapes?).

A last generalization. Increasingly it seems to me that the strength of American sf is the short story; the strength of British sf is the novel. I am perfectly aware of a great many distinguished exceptions on both sides of the ocean, but I feel it to be so nevertheless. I have no idea why it should be. I do get the impression

(I have said that the view from this side of the Atlantic is sometimes foggy, and I can't be sure) that commercial pressures on the young sf writer to "conform" to a predetermined pattern are stronger in the U.S.A. than in the U.K., but clearly there are plenty of American writers, including a number of those named above, who are strong enough to resist, if this dubious proposition is actually so.

In the very act of writing this piece, I feel a surge of confidence about science fiction. The Empire *is* crumbling, but it has been unwieldy for a long time, and the dissolution might be all to the good. Real Soon Now the label "science fiction" may be seen as archaic as the Roman Empire, or at least—if it is retained—seen as a token courtesy-label, much as "British Commonwealth" is a token nostalgia-term for a bunch of nations that pretty well mind their own business and sing the National Anthem, if at all, with a marked absence of enthusiasm. If science fiction splits into a chain of autonomous provinces, friendly but self-contained, a kind of Common Market of Speculative Fiction, then the decline and fall of the Science Fiction Empire might come to seem a happy event, providing at the very least some memorable orgies along the way.

Someone reading over my shoulder has just pointed out that it's possible to take what I have been saying as meaning that there's no longer much good sf around. Not true. There's more good sf than ever, and more bad as well. The simple fact is, that there's more sf. According to the ever-reliable magazine *Locus* (I don't know what sort of definition they used), there were 890 sf titles published in the U.S.A. alone in 1975, an increase of 23 percent over the previous year. Only half of these were reprints. But sf is less monolithic than it was, and the publishers themselves are showing signs of recognizing this in their terminology. Individual sf writers are as vigorous as ever, but the links that bind them together as part of a ghetto or exclusive club or Empire, are weakening.

Readers are asked to note that, by a supreme effort of will, I nowhere used the term "mainstream" in the above essay to designate the area outside the Imperial Wall. I beg you all to follow my example.

ROGER ZELAZNY

Home is the Hangman

Roger Zelazny was born May 13, 1937 in Euclid, Ohio. He won his B.A. at Western Reserve University in 1959 and his M.A. at Columbia University in 1962. He served in the Ohio National Guard from 1960 to 1963 and was a member of the Army Reserves from 1963 to 1966. He was employed by the Social Security Administration as a claims representative for three years (beginning in 1962) in Cleveland and thereafter as a claims policy specialist (until 1969) in Baltimore. He married Judith Alene Callahan in 1966, and they have one son, Devin Joseph, now five years old. Their current residence is Santa Fe, New Mexico.

He began writing professionally in 1962, full-time in 1969. He has had approximately seventy short stories and articles published, almost entirely within the genre, and has fulfilled many speaking engagements. In addition since winning one Hugo (for . . . *And Call Me Conrad*) and *two* Nebulas (for the novella, "He Who Shapes," and the novelette, "The Doors of His Face, the Lamps of His Mouth") in 1966, he has published more than sixteen books. Three separate awards for three separate titles made a dazzling beginning to a decade which now comes full term with a Nebula, again awarded by his peers, again for a novella. One might also mention the *Prix Apollo* (the 1972 French literary prize awarded for *Isle of the Dead*) and make reference in passing to the fact that various of the above mentioned sixteen books have appeared in French, Spanish, Italian, German, Dutch, Swedish, Greek, Hebrew, and Japanese. It can be noted also that he was guest of honor at the 1974 World Science Fiction Convention, in Washington, D.C.

It is clear that Roger Zelazny's is a hard act to follow.

Big fat flakes down the night, silent night, windless night. And I never count them as storms unless there is wind. Not a sigh or a whimper, though. Just a cold, steady whiteness, drifting down outside the window, and a silence confirmed by gunfire, driven deeper now it had ceased. In the main room of the lodge the only sounds were the occasional hiss and sputter of the logs turning to ashes on the grate.

I sat in a chair turned sidewise from the table to face the door. A tool kit rested on the floor to my left. The helmet stood on the table, a lopsided basket of metal, quartz, porcelain, and glass. If I heard the click of a microswitch followed by a humming sound from within it, then a faint light would come on beneath the meshing near to its forward edge and begin to blink rapidly. If these things occurred, there was a very strong possibility that I was going to die.

I had removed a black ball from my pocket when Larry and Bert had gone outside, armed, respectively, with a flame thrower and what looked like an elephant gun. Bert had also taken two grenades with him.

I unrolled the black ball, opening it out into a seamless glove, a dollop of something resembling moist putty stuck to its palm. Then I drew the glove on over my left hand and sat with it upraised, elbow resting on the arm of the chair. A small laser flash pistol in which I had very little faith lay beside my right hand on the tabletop, next to the helmet.

If I were to slap a metal surface with my left hand, the substance would adhere there, coming free of the glove. Two seconds later it would explode, and the force of the explosion would be directed in against the surface. Newton would claim his own by way of right-angled redistributions of the reaction, hopefully tearing lateral hell out of the contact surface. A smother-charge, it was called, and its possession came under concealed weapons and possession of burglary tools statutes in most places. The molecularly gimmicked goo, I decided, was great stuff. It was just the delivery system that left more to be desired.

Beside the helmet, next to the gun, in front of my hand, stood a small walkie-talkie. This was for purposes of warning Bert and Larry if I should hear the click of a microswitch followed by a humming sound, should see a light come on and begin to blink rapidly. Then they would know that Tom and Clay, with whom we had lost contact when the shooting began, had failed to destroy the enemy and doubtless lay lifeless at their stations now, a little over a kilometer to the south. Then they would know that they, too, were probably about to die.

I called out to them when I heard the click. I picked up the helmet and rose to my feet as its light began to blink.

But it was already too late.

The fourth place listed on the Christmas card I had sent Don Walsh the previous year was Peabody's Book Shop and Beer Stube in Baltimore, Maryland. Accordingly, on the last night in October I sat in its rearmost room, at the final table before the alcove with the door leading to the alley. Across that dim chamber, a woman dressed in black played the ancient upright piano, up-tempoing everything she touched. Off to my right, a fire wheezed and spewed fumes on a narrow hearth beneath a crowded mantelpiece overseen by an ancient and antlered profile. I sipped a beer and listened to the sounds.

I half-hoped that this would be one of the occasions when Don
failed to show up. I had sufficient funds to hold me through spring
and I did not really feel like working. I had summered farther
north, was anchored now in the Chesapeake, and was anxious to
continue Caribbeanwards. A growing chill and some nasty winds
told me I had tarried overlong in these latitudes. Still, the understanding was that I remain in the chosen bar until midnight. Two
hours to go.

I ate a sandwich and ordered another beer. About halfway into
it, I spotted Don approaching the entranceway, topcoat over his
arm, head turning. I manufactured a matching quantity of surprise
when he appeared beside my table with a, "Ron! Is that really
you?"

I rose and clasped his hand.

"Alan! Small world, or something like that. Sit down! Sit down!"

He settled onto the chair across from me, draped his coat over
the one to his left.

"What are you doing in this town?" he asked.

"Just a visit," I answered. "Said hello to a few friends." I patted
the scars, the stains of the venerable surface before me. "And this
is my last stop. I'll be leaving in a few hours."

He chuckled.

"Why is it that you knock on wood?"

I grinned.

"I was expressing affection for one of Henry Mencken's favorite
speakeasies."

"This place dates back that far?"

I nodded.

"It figures," he said. "You've got this thing for the past—or
against the present. I'm never sure which."

"Maybe a little of both," I said. "I wish Mencken would stop in.
I'd like his opinion on the present. What are you doing with it?"

"What?"

"The present. Here. Now."

"Oh." He spotted the waitress and ordered a beer. "Business
trip," he said then. "To hire a consultant."

"Oh. And how *is* business?"

"Complicated," he said, "complicated."

We lit cigarettes and after a while his beer arrived. We smoked and drank and listened to the music.

I've sung this song and I'll sing it again: the world is like an up-tempoed piece of music. Of the many changes which came to pass during my lifetime, it seems that the majority have occurred during the past few years. It also struck me that way several years ago, and I'd a hunch I might be feeling the same way a few years hence—that is, if Don's business did not complicate me off this mortal coil or condenser before then.

Don operates the second largest detective agency in the world, and he sometimes finds me useful because I do not exist. I do not exist now because I existed once at the time and the place where we attempted to begin scoring the wild ditty of our times. I refer to the World Data Bank project and the fact that I had had a significant part in that effort to construct a working model of the real world, accounting for everyone and everything in it. How well we succeeded and whether possession of the world's likeness does indeed provide its custodians with a greater measure of control over its functions are questions my former colleagues still debate as the music grows more shrill and you can't see the maps for the pins. I made my decision back then and saw to it that I did not receive citizenship in that second world, a place which may now have become more important than the first. Exiled to reality, my own sojourns across the line are necessarily those of an alien guilty of illegal entry. I visit periodically because I go where I must to make my living. That is where Don comes in. The people I can become are often very useful when he has peculiar problems. Unfortunately, at that moment, it seemed that he did, just when the whole gang of me felt like turning down the volume and loafing.

We finished our drinks, got the bill, settled it.

"This way," I said, indicating the rear door, and he swung into his coat and followed me out.

"Talk here?" he asked, as we walked down the alley.

"Rather not," I said. "Public transportation, then private conversation."

He nodded and came along.

About three-quarters of an hour later we were in the saloon of the *Proteus* and I was making coffee. We were rocked gently by the Bay's chill waters, under a moonless sky. I'd only a pair of the smaller lights burning. Comfortable. On the water, aboard the *Proteus*, the crowding, the activities, the tempo, of life in the cities, on the land, are muted, slowed—fictionalized—by the metaphysical distancing a few meters of water can provide. We alter the landscape with great facility, but the ocean has always seemed unchanged, and I suppose by extension we are infected with some feelings of timelessness whenever we set out upon her. Maybe that's one of the reasons I spend so much time there.

"First time you've had me aboard," he said. "Comfortable. Very."

"Thanks. Cream? Sugar?"

"Yes. Both."

We settled back with our steaming mugs and I said, "What have you got?"

"One case involving two problems," he said. "One of them sort of falls within my area of competence. The other does not. I was told that it is an absolutely unique situation and would require the services of a very special specialist."

"I'm not a specialist at anything but keeping alive."

His eyes came up suddenly and caught my own.

"I had always assumed that you knew an awful lot about computers," he said.

I looked away. That was hitting below the belt. I had never held myself out to him as an authority in that area, and there had always been a tacit understanding between us that my methods of manipulating circumstance and identity were not open to discussion. On the other hand, it was obvious to him that my knowledge of the system was both extensive and intensive. Still, I didn't like talking about it. So I moved to defend.

"Computer people are a dime a dozen," I said. "It was probably different in your time, but these days they start teaching computer science to little kids their first year in school. So, sure I know a lot about it. This generation, everybody does."

"You know that is not what I meant," he said. "Haven't you known me long enough to trust me a little more than that? The question springs solely from the case at hand. That's all."

I nodded. Reactions by their very nature are not always appropriate, and I had invested a lot of emotional capital in a heavy duty set. So, "OK, I know more about them than the school kids," I said.

"Thanks. That can be our point of departure." He took a sip of coffee. "My own background is in law and accounting, followed by the military, military intelligence, and civil service, in that order. Then I got into this business. What technical stuff I know I've picked up along the way, a scrap here, a crash course there. I know a lot about what things can do, not so much about how they work. I did not understand the details on this one, so I want you to start at the top and explain things to me, for as far as you can go. I need the background review, and if you are able to furnish it I will also know that you are the man for the job. You can begin by telling me how the early space exploration robots worked—like, say, the ones they used on Venus."

"That's not computers," I said. "and for that matter, they weren't really robots. They were telefactoring devices."

"Tell me what makes the difference."

"A robot is a machine which carries out certain operations in accordance with a program of instructions. A telefactor is a slave machine operated by remote control. The telefactor functions in a feedback situation with its operator. Depending on how sophisticated you want to get, the links can be audio-visual, kinesthetic, tactile, even olfactory. The more you want to go in this direction, the more anthropomorphic you get in the thing's design. In the case of Venus, if I recall correctly, the human operator in orbit wore an exoskeleton which controlled the movements of the body, legs, arms, and hands of the device on the surface below, receiving motion and force feedback through a system of airjet transducers. He had on a helmet controlling the slave device's television camera—set, obviously enough, in its turret—which filled his field of vision with the scene below. He also wore earphones connected with its audio pickup. I read the book he wrote later. He said that for long stretches of time, he would forget the cabin, forget that he was at the boss end of a control loop and actually feel as if he were stalking through that hellish landscape. I remember being very impressed by it, just being a kid, and I wanted a supertiny one all my own, so that I could wade around in puddles picking fights with microorganisms."

"Why?"

"Because there weren't any dragons on Venus. Anyhow, that is a telefactoring device, a thing quite distinct from a robot."

"I'm still with you," he said. "Now tell me the difference between the early telefactoring devices and the later ones."

I swallowed some coffee.

"It was a bit trickier with respect to the outer planets and their satellites," I said. "There, we did not have orbiting operators at first. Economics, and some unresolved technical problems. Mainly economics. At any rate, the devices were landed on the target worlds, but the operators stayed home. Because of this, there was of course a time lag in the transmissions along the control loop. It took a while to receive the on-site input, and then there was another time-lapse before the response movements reached the telefactor. We attempted to compensate for this in two ways. The first was by the employment of a simple wait-move, wait-move sequence. The second was more sophisticated and is actually the point where computers come into the picture in terms of participating in the control loop. It involved the setting up of models of known environmental factors, which were then enriched during the initial wait-move sequences. On this basis, the computer was then used to anticipate short-range developments. Finally, it could take over the loop and run it by a combination of 'predictor controls' and wait-move reviews. It still had to holler for human help though, when unexpected things came up. So, with the outer planets, it was neither totally automatic nor totally manual—nor totally satisfactory—at first."

"OK," he said, lighting a cigarette. "And the next step?"

"The next wasn't really a technical step forward in telefactoring. It was an economic shift. The purse strings were loosened and we could afford to send men out. We landed them where we could land them, and in many of the places where we could not we sent down the telefactors and orbited the men again. Like in the old days. The time lag problem was removed because the operator was on top of things once more. If anything, you can look at it as a reversion to earlier methods. It is what we still often do, though, and it works."

He shook his head.

"You left something out," he said, "between the computers and the bigger budget."

I shrugged.

"A number of things were tried during that period," I said, "but none of them proved as effective as what we already had going in the human-computer partnership with the telefactors."

"There was one project," he said, "which attempted to get around the time lag troubles by sending the computer along with the telefactor as part of the package. Only the computer wasn't exactly a computer and the telefactor wasn't exactly a telefactor. Do you know which one I am referring to?"

I lit a cigarette of my own while I thought about it, then, "I think you are talking about the Hangman," I said.

"That's right," he said, "and this is where I get lost. Can you tell me how it works?"

"Ultimately, it was a failure," I said.

"But it worked at first."

"Apparently. But only on the easy stuff, on Io. It conked out later and had to be written off as a failure, albeit a noble one. The venture was overly ambitious from the very beginning. What seems to have happened was that the people in charge had the opportunity to combine vanguard projects—stuff that was still under investigation and stuff that was extremely new. In theory it all seemed to dovetail so beautifully that they yielded to the temptation and incorporated too much. It started out well, but it fell apart later."

"But what all was involved in the thing?"

"Lord! What wasn't? The computer that wasn't exactly a computer . . . OK, we'll start there. Last century, three engineers at the University of Wisconsin—Nordman, Parmentier, and Scott—developed a device known as a superconductive tunnel junction neuristor. Two tiny strips of metal with a thin insulating layer between. Supercool it and it passed electrical impulses without resistance. Surround it with magnetized material and pack a mass of them together—billions—and what have you got?"

He shook his head.

"Well, for one thing you've got an impossible situation to schematize when considering all the paths and interconnections that may be formed. There is an obvious similarity to the structure of the brain. So, they theorized, you don't even attempt to hook up such a device. You pulse in data and let it establish its own preferential pathways, by means of the magnetic material's becoming increasingly magnetized each time the current passes through it, thus cutting the resistance. So the material establishes its own routes in a fashion analogous to the functioning of the brain when it is learning something. In the case of the Hangman, they used a setup very similar to this and they were able to pack over ten billion neuristor-type cells into a very small area—around a cubic foot. They aimed for that magic figure because that is approximately the number of nerve cells in the human brain. That is what I meant when I said that it wasn't really a computer. They were actually working in the area of artificial intelligence, no matter what they called it."

"If the thing had its own brain—computer or quasi-human—then it was a robot rather than a telefactor, right?"

"Yes and no and maybe," I said. "It was operated as a telefactor device here on Earth—on the ocean floor, in the desert, in mountainous country—as part of its programming. I suppose you could also call that its apprenticeship or kindergarten. Perhaps that is even more appropriate. It was being shown how to explore in difficult environments and to report back. Once it mastered this, then theoretically they could hang it out there in the sky without a control loop and let it report its own findings."

"At that point would it be considered a robot?"

"A robot is a machine which carries out certain operations in accordance with a program of instructions. The Hangman made its own decisions, you see. And I suspect that by trying to produce something that close to the human brain in structure and function the seemingly inevitable randomness of its model got included in. It wasn't just a machine following a program. It was too complex. That was probably what broke it down."

Don chuckled.

"Inevitable free will?"

"No. As I said, they had thrown too many things into one bag. Everybody and his brother with a pet project that might be fitted in seemed a supersalesman that season. For example, the psychophysics boys had a gimmick they wanted to try on it, and it got used. Ostensibly, it was a communications device. Actually, they were concerned as to whether the thing was truly sentient."

"Was it?"

"Apparently so, in a limited fashion. What they had come up with, to be made part of the initial telefactor loop, was a device which set up a weak induction field in the brain of the operator. The machine received and amplified the patterns of electrical activity being conducted in the Hangman's—might as well call it 'brain'—then passed them through a complex modulator and pulsed them into the induction field in the operator's head. I am out of my area now and into that of Weber and Fechner, but a neuron has a threshold at which it will fire, and below which it will not. There are some forty thousand neurons packed together in a square millimeter of the cerebral cortex, in such a fashion that each one has several hundred synaptic connections with others about it. At any given moment, some of them may be way below the firing threshold while others are in a condition Sir John Eccles once referred to as 'critically poised'—ready to fire. If just one is pushed over the threshold, it can affect the discharge of hundreds of thousands of others within twenty milliseconds. The pulsating field was to provide such a push in a sufficiently selective fashion to give the operator an idea as to what was going on in the Hangman's brain. And vice versa. The Hangman was to have its own built-in version of the same thing. It was also thought that this might serve to humanize it somewhat, so that it would better appreciate the significance of its work—to instill something like loyalty, you might say."

"Do you think this could have contributed to its later break-down?"

"Possibly. How can you say in a one-of-a-kind situation like this? If you want a guess, I'd say yes. But it's just a guess."

"Uh-huh," he said, "and what were its physical capabilities?"

"Anthropomorphic design," I said, "both because it was originally telefactored and because of the psychological reasoning I just mentioned. It could pilot its own small vessel. No need for a life-support system, of course. Both it and the vessel were powered by fusion units, so that fuel was no real problem. Self-repairing. Capable of performing a great variety of sophisticated tests and measurements, of making observations, completing reports, learning new material, broadcasting its findings back here. Capable of surviving just about anywhere. In fact, it required less energy on the outer planets—less work for the refrigeration units, to maintain that supercooled brain in its midsection."

"How strong was it?"

"I don't recall all the specs. Maybe a dozen times as strong as a man, in things like lifting and pushing."

"It explored Io for us and started in on Europa."

"Yes."

"Then it began behaving erratically, just when we thought it had really learned its job."

"That sounds right," I said.

"It refused a direct order to explore Callisto, then headed out toward Uranus."

"Yes. It's been years since I read the reports. . . ."

"The malfunction worsened after that. Long periods of silence interspersed with garbled transmissions. Now that I know more about its make-up, it almost sounds like a man going off the deep end."

"It seems similar."

"But it managed to pull itself together again for a brief while. It landed on Titania, began sending back what seemed like appropriate observation reports. This only lasted a short time, though. It went irrational once more, indicated that it was heading for a landing on Uranus itself, and that was it. We didn't hear from it after that. Now that I know about that mind-reading gadget I understand why a psychiatrist on this end could be so positive it would never function again."

"I never heard about that part."

"I did."

I shrugged.

"This was all around twenty years ago," I said, "and, as I mentioned, it has been a long while since I've read anything about it."

"The Hangman's ship crashed or landed, as the case may be, in the Gulf of Mexico," he said, "two days ago."

I just stared at him.

"It was empty," he said, "when they finally got out and down to it."

"I don't understand."

"Yesterday morning," he went on, "restaurateur Manny Burns was found beaten to death in the office of his establishment, the *Maison Saint-Michel,* in New Orleans."

"I still fail to see . . ."

"Manny Burns was one of the four original operators who programmed—pardon me, 'taught'—the Hangman."

The silence lengthened, dragged its belly on the deck.

"Coincidence . . . ?" I finally said.

"My client doesn't think so."

"Who is your client?"

"One of the three remaining members of the training group. He is convinced that the Hangman has returned to Earth to kill its former operators."

"Has he made his fears known to his old employers?"

"No."

"Why not?"

"Because it would require telling them the reason for his fears."

"That being . . . ?"

"He wouldn't tell me either."

"How does he expect you to do a proper job?"

"He told me what he considered a proper job. He wants two things done, neither of which requires a full case history. He wanted to be furnished with good bodyguards, and he wanted the Hangman found and disposed of. I have already taken care of the first part."

"And you want me to do the second?"

"That's right. You have confirmed my opinion that you are the man for the job."

"I see," I said. "Do you realize that if the thing is truly sentient this will be something very like murder? If it is not, of course, then it will only amount to the destruction of expensive government property."

"Which way do you look at it?"

"I look at it as a job," I said.

"You'll take it?"

"I need more facts before I can decide. Like . . . Who is your client? Who are the other operators? Where do they live? What do they do? What—"

He raised his hand.

"First," he said, "the Honorable Jesse Brockden, senior senator from Wisconsin, is our client. Confidentiality, of course, is written all over it."

I nodded.

"I remember his being involved with the space program before he went into politics. I wasn't aware of the specifics, though. He could get government protection so easily—"

"To obtain it, he would apparently have to tell them something he doesn't want to talk about. Perhaps it would hurt his career. I simply do not know. He doesn't want them. He wants us."

I nodded again.

"What about the others? Do they want us, too?"

"Quite the opposite. They don't subscribe to Brockden's notions at all. They seem to think he is something of a paranoid."

"How well do they know one another these days?"

"They live in different parts of the country, haven't seen each other in years. Been in occasional touch, though."

"Kind of flimsy basis for that diagnosis, then."

"One of them *is* a psychiatrist."

"Oh. Which one?"

"Leila Thackery is her name. Lives in St. Louis. Works at the State Hospital there."

"None of them have gone to any authority, then—Federal or local?"

"That's right. Brockden contacted them when he heard about the Hangman. He was in Washington at the time. Got word on its return right away and managed to get the story killed. He tried to reach them all, learned about Burns in the process, contacted me, then tried to persuade the others to accept protection by my people. They weren't buying. When I talked to her, Dr. Thackery pointed out—quite correctly—that Brockden is a very sick man—"

"What's he got?"

"Cancer. In his spine. Nothing they can do about it once it hits there and digs in. He even told me he figures he has maybe six months to get through what he considers a very important piece of legislation—the new criminal rehabilitation act. I will admit that he did sound kind of paranoid when he talked about it. But hell! Who wouldn't? Dr. Thackery sees that as the whole thing, though, and she doesn't see the Burns killing as being connected with the Hangman. Thinks it was just a traditional robbery gone sour, thief surprised and panicky, maybe hopped-up, et cetera."

"Then she is not afraid of the Hangman?"

"She said that she is in a better position to know its mind than anyone else, and she is not especially concerned."

"What about the other operator?"

"He said that Dr. Thackery may know its mind better than anyone else, but he knows its brain, and he isn't worried either."

"What did he mean by that?"

"David Fentris is a consulting engineer—electronics, cybernetics. He actually had something to do with the Hangman's design."

I got to my feet and went after the coffee pot. Not that I'd an overwhelming desire for another cup at just that moment. But I had known, had once worked with a David Fentris. And he had at one time been connected with the space program.

About fifteen years my senior, Dave had been with the Data Bank project when I had known him. Where a number of us had begun having second thoughts as the thing progressed, Dave had never been anything less than wildly enthusiastic. A wiry five-eight, white-cropped, gray eyes back of hornrims and heavy glass, cycling between preoccupation and near-frantic darting, he had had a way of verbalizing half-completed thoughts as he went along, so that you might begin to think him a representative of that tribe which had come into positions of small authority by means of nepotism or politics. If you would listen a few more minutes though, you would begin revising your opinion as he started to pull his musings together into a rigorous framework. By the time he had finished you generally wondered why you hadn't seen it all along and what a guy like that was doing in a position of such small authority. Later, it might strike you, though, that he seemed sad whenever he wasn't enthusiastic about something, and while the gung-ho spirit is great for short-range projects, larger ventures generally require something more of equanimity. I wasn't at all surprised that he had wound up as a consultant. The big question now, of course, was would he remember me? True, my appearance was altered, my personality hopefully more mature, my habits shifted around. But would that be enough, should I have to encounter him as part of this job? That mind behind those hornrims could do a lot of strange things with just a little data.

"Where does he live?" I asked.

"Memphis, and what's the matter?"

"Just trying to get my geography straight," I said. "Is Senator Brockden still in Washington?"

"No. He's returned to Wisconsin and is currently holed up in a lodge in the northern part of the state. Four of my people are with him."

"I see."

I refreshed our coffee supply and reseated myself. I didn't like
this one at all and I resolved not to take it. I didn't like just giving
Don a flat no, though. His assignments had become a very important part of my life, and this one was not mere legwork. It was
obviously important to him, and he wanted me on it. I decided to
look for holes in the thing, to find some way of reducing it to the
simple bodyguard job already in progress.

"It does seem peculiar," I said, "that Brockden is the only one
afraid of the device."

"Yes."

". . . And that he gives no reasons."

"True."

". . . Plus his condition, and what the doctor said about its effect
on his mind."

"I have no doubt that he is neurotic," Don said. "Look at this."

He reached for his coat, withdrew a sheaf of papers from within
it. He shuffled through them and extracted a single sheet, which
he passed to me. It was a piece of Congressional letterhead station-
ery, with the message scrawled in longhand: "Don," it said, "I've
got to see you. Frankenstein's monster has just come back from
where we hung him and he's looking for me. The whole damn
universe is trying to grind me up. Call me between eight and ten.
—Jess." I nodded, started to pass it back, paused, then handed it
over. Double damn it deeper than hell! I took a drink of coffee. I
thought that I had long ago given up hope in such things, but I had
noticed something which immediately troubled me. In the margin
where they list such matters, I had seen that Jesse Brockden was
on the committee for review of the Data Bank program. I recalled
that that committee was supposed to be working on a series of
reform recommendations. Offhand, I could not remember Brockden's position on any of the issues involved, but—oh hell! The
thing was simply too big to alter significantly now. . . . But it *was*
the only real Frankenstein monster I cared about, and there was
always the possibility. . . . On the other hand—hell, again. What
if I let him die when I might have saved him, and he had been the
one who . . . ?

I took another drink of coffee. I lit another cigarette. There might be a way of working it so that Dave didn't even come into the picture. I could talk to Leila Thackery first, check further into the Burns killing, keep posted on new developments, find out more about the vessel in the Gulf. . . . I might be able to accomplish something, even if it was only the negation of Brockden's theory, without Dave's and my paths ever crossing.

"Have you got the specs on the Hangman?" I asked.

"Right here."

He passed them over.

"The police report on the Burns killing?"

"Here it is."

"The whereabouts of everyone involved, and some background on them?"

"Here."

"The place or places where I can reach you during the next few days—around the clock? This one may require some coordination."

He smiled and reached for his pen.

"Glad to have you aboard," he said.

I reached over and tapped the barometer. I shook my head.

The ringing of the phone awakened me. Reflex bore me across the room, where I took it on audio.

"Yes?"

"Mr. Donne? It is eight o'clock."

"Thanks."

I collapsed into the chair. I am what might be called a slow starter. I tend to recapitulate phylogeny every morning. Basic desires inched their ways through my gray matter to close a connection. Slowly, I extended a cold-blooded member and clicked my talons against a couple numbers. I croaked my desire for food and lots of coffee to the voice that responded. Half an hour later I would only have growled. Then I staggered off to the place of flowing waters to renew my contact with basics.

In addition to my normal adrenaline and blood-sugar bearishness, I had not slept much the night before. I had closed up shop after Don had left, stuffed my pockets with essentials, departed the *Proteus,* gotten myself over to the airport and onto a flight which took me to St. Louis in the dead, small hours of the dark. I was unable to sleep during the flight, thinking about the case, deciding on the tack I was going to take with Leila Thackery. On arrival, I had checked into the airport motel, left a message to be awakened at an unreasonable hour, and collapsed.

As I ate, I regarded the factsheet Don had given me: Leila Thackery was currently single, having divorced her second husband a little over two years ago, was forty-six years old, and lived in an apartment near to the hospital where she worked. Attached to the sheet was a photo which might have been ten years old. In it, she was brunette, light-eyed, barely on the right side of that border between ample and overweight, with fancy glasses straddling an upturned nose. She had published a number of books and articles with titles full of alienations, roles, transactions, social contexts, and more alienations.

I hadn't had the time to go my usual route, becoming an entire new individual with a verifiable history. Just a name and a story, that's all. It did not seem necessary this time, though. For once, something approximating honesty actually seemed a reasonable approach.

I took a public vehicle over to her apartment building. I did not phone ahead, because it is easier to say no to a voice than to a person. According to the record, today was one of the days when she saw out-patients in her home. Her idea, apparently: break down the alienating institution image, remove resentments by turning the sessions into something more like social occasions, et cetera. I did not want all that much of her time, I had decided that Don could make it worth her while if it came to that, and I was sure my fellows' visits were scheduled to leave her with some small breathing space—*inter alia,* so to speak.

I had just located her name and apartment number amid the buttons in the entrance foyer when an old woman passed behind me and unlocked the door to the lobby. She glanced at me and held it open, so I went on in without ringing. The matter of presence, again.

I took the elevator to Leila's floor, the second. I located her door and knocked on it. I was almost ready to knock again when it opened, part-way.

"Yes?" she asked, and I revised my estimate as to the age of the photo. She looked just about the same.

"Dr. Thackery," I said, "my name is Donne. You could help me quite a bit with a problem I've got."

"What sort of problem?"

"It involves a device known as the Hangman."

She sighed and showed me a quick grimace. Her fingers tightened on the door.

"I've come a long way but I'll be easy to get rid of. I've only a few things I'd like to ask you about it."

"Are you with the Government?"

"No."

"Do you work for Brockden?"

"No. I'm something different."

"All right," she said. "Right now I've got a group session going. It will probably last around another half-hour. If you don't mind waiting down in the lobby, I'll let you know as soon as it is over. We can talk then."

"Good enough," I said. "Thanks."

She nodded, closed the door. I located the stairway and walked back down.

A cigarette later, I decided that the devil finds work for idle hands and thanked him for his suggestion. I strolled back toward the foyer. Through the glass, I read the names of a few residents of the fifth floor. I elevated up and knocked on one of the doors. Before it was opened I had my notebook and pad in plain sight.

"Yes?"—short, fiftyish, curious.

"My name is Stephen Foster, Mrs. Gluntz. I am doing a survey for the North American Consumers League. I would like to pay you for a couple minutes of your time, to answer some questions about products you use."

"Why—Pay me?"

"Yes, ma'am. Ten dollars. Around a dozen questions. It will just take a minute or two."

"All right." She opened the door wider. "Won't you come in?"

"No, thank you. This thing is so brief I'd just be in and out. The first question involves detergents—"

Ten minutes later I was back in the lobby adding the thirty bucks for the three interviews to the list of expenses I was keeping. When a situation is full of unpredictables and I am playing makeshift games, I like to provide for as many contingencies as I can.

Another quarter of an hour or so slipped by before the elevator opened and discharged three guys, young, young, and middle-aged, casually dressed, chuckling over something. The big one on the nearest end strolled over and nodded.

"You the fellow waiting to see Dr. Thackery?"

"That's right."

"She said to tell you to come on up now."

"Thanks."

I rode up again, returned to her door. She opened to my knock, nodded me in, saw me seated in a comfortable chair at the far end of her living room.

"Would you care for a cup of coffee?" she asked. "It's fresh. I made more than I needed."

"That would be fine. Thanks."

Moments later, she brought in a couple of cups, delivered one to me and seated herself on the sofa to my left. I ignored the cream and sugar on the tray and took a sip.

"You've gotten me interested," she said. "Tell me about it."

"O.K. I have been told that the telefactor device known as the Hangman, now possibly possessed of an artificial intelligence, has returned to Earth—"

"Hypothetical," she said, "unless you know something I don't. I have been told that the Hangman's vehicle reentered and crashed in the Gulf. There is no evidence that the vehicle was occupied."

"It seems a reasonable conclusion, though."

"It seems just as reasonable to me that the Hangman sent the vehicle off toward an eventual rendezvous point many years ago and that it only recently reached that point, at which time the reentry program took over and brought it down."

"Why should it return the vehicle and strand itself out there?"

"Before I answer that," she said, "I would like to know the reason for your concern. News media?"

"No," I said. "I am a science writer—straight tech, popular and anything in between. But I am not after a piece for publication. I was retained to do a report on the psychological make-up of the thing."

"For whom?"

"A private investigation outfit. They want to know what might influence its thinking, how it might be likely to behave—if it has indeed come back. I've been doing a lot of homework, and I gathered there is a likelihood that its nuclear personality was a composite of the minds of its four operators. So, personal contacts seemed in order, to collect your opinions as to what it might be like. I came to you first for obvious reasons."

She nodded.

"A Mr. Walsh spoke with me the other day. He is working for Senator Brockden."

"Oh? I never got into an employer's business beyond what he's asked me to do. Senator Brockden is on my list though, along with a David Fentris."

"You were told about Manny Burns?"

"Yes. Unfortunate."

"That is apparently what set Jesse off. He is—how shall I put it? He is clinging to life right now, trying to accomplish a great many things in the time he has remaining. Every moment is precious to him. He feels the old man in the white nightgown breathing down his neck. Then the ship returns and one of us is killed. From what we know of the Hangman, the last we heard of it, it had become irrational. Jesse saw a connection, and in his condition the fear is understandable. There is nothing wrong with humoring him if it allows him to get his work done."

"But you don't see a threat in it?"

"No. I was the last person to monitor the Hangman before communications ceased, and I could see then what had happened.

The first things that it had learned were the organization of perceptions and motor activities. Multitudes of other patterns had been transferred from the minds of its operators, but they were too sophisticated to mean much initially. Think of a child who has learned the Gettysburg Address. It is there in his head, that is all. One day, however, it may be important to him. Conceivably, it may even inspire him to action. It takes some growing up first, of course. Now think of such a child with a great number of conflicting patterns—attitudes, tendencies, memories—none of which are especially bothersome for so long as he remains a child. Add a bit of maturity, though—and bear in mind that the patterns originated with four different individuals, all of them more powerful than the words of even the finest of speeches, bearing as they do their own built-in feelings. Try to imagine the conflicts, the contradictions involved in being four people at once—"

"Why wasn't this imagined in advance?" I asked.

"Ah!" she said, smiling. "The full sensitivity of the neuristor brain was not appreciated at first. It was assumed that the operators were adding data in a linear fashion and that this would continue until a critical mass was achieved, corresponding to the construction of a model or picture of the world which would then serve as a point of departure for growth of the Hangman's own mind. And it did seem to check out this way. What actually occurred, however, was a phenomenon amounting to imprinting. Secondary characteristics of the operators' minds, outside the didactic situations, were imposed. These did not immediately become functional and hence were not detected. They remained latent until the mind had developed sufficiently to understand them. And then it was too late. It suddenly acquired four additional personalities and was unable to coordinate them. When it tried to compartmentalize them it went schizoid; when it tried to integrate them it went catatonic. It was cycling back and forth between these alternatives at the end. Then it just went silent. I felt it had undergone the equivalent of an epileptic seizure. Wild currents through that magnetic material would, in effect, have erased its mind, resulting in its equivalent of death or idiocy."

"I follow you," I said. "Now, just for the sake of playing games, I see the alternatives as a successful integration of all this material or the achievement of a viable schizophrenia. What do you think its behavior would be like if either of these were possible?"

"All right," she agreed. "As I just said, though, I think there were physical limitations to its retaining multiple personality structures for a very long period of time. If it did, however, it would have continued with its own plus replicas of the four operators', at least for a while. The situation would differ radically from that of a human schizoid of this sort in that the additional personalities were valid images of genuine identities rather than self-generated complexes which had become autonomous. They might continue to evolve, they might degenerate, they might conflict to the point of destruction or gross modification of any, or all of them. In other words, no prediction is possible as to the nature of whatever might remain."

"Might I venture one?"

"Go ahead."

"After considerable anxiety, it masters them. It asserts itself. It beats down this quartet of demons which has been tearing it apart, acquiring in the process an all-consuming hatred for the actual individuals responsible for this turmoil. To free itself totally, to revenge itself, to work its ultimate catharsis, it resolves to seek them out and destroy them."

She smiled.

"You have just dispensed with the 'viable schizophrenia' you conjured up, and you have now switched over to its pulling through and becoming fully autonomous. That is a different situation, no matter what strings you put on it."

"OK, I accept the charge. But what about my conclusion?"

"You are saying that if it did pull through, it would hate us. That strikes me as an unfair attempt to invoke the spirit of Sigmund Freud: Oedipus and Electra in one being, out to destroy all its parents—the authors of every one of its tensions, anxieties, hang-ups, burned into the impressionable psyche at a young and defenseless age. Even Freud didn't have a name for that one. What should we call it?"

"A Hermacis complex?" I suggested.

"Hermacis?"

"Hermaphroditus having been united in one body with the nymph Salmacis, I've just done the same with their names. That being would then have had four parents against whom to react."

"Cute," she said, smiling. "If the liberal arts do nothing else they provide engaging metaphors for the thinking they displace. This one is unwarranted and overly anthropomorphic, though. You wanted my opinion. All right. If the Hangman pulled through at all it could only have been by virtue of that neuristor brain's differences from the human brain. From my own professional experience, a human could not pass through a situation like that and attain stability. If the Hangman did, it would have to have resolved all the contradictions and conflicts, to have mastered and understood the situation so thoroughly that I do not believe whatever remained could involve that sort of hatred. The fear, the uncertainty, the things that feed hate would have been analyzed, digested, turned to something more useful. There would probably be distaste, and possibly an act of independence, of self-assertion. That was why I suggested its return of the ship."

"It is your opinion, then, that if the Hangman exists as a thinking individual today, this is the only possible attitude it would possess toward its former operators? It would want nothing more to do with you?"

"That is correct. Sorry about your Hermacis complex. But in this case we must look to the brain, not the psyche. And we see two things: schizophrenia would have destroyed it, and a successful resolution of its problem would preclude vengeance. Either way, there is nothing to worry about."

How could I put it tactfully? I decided that I could not.

"All of this is fine," I said, "for as far as it goes. But getting away from both the purely psychological and the purely physical, could there be a particular reason for its seeking your deaths—that is, a plain old-fashioned motive for a killing, based on events rather than having to do with the way its thinking equipment goes together?"

Her expression was impossible to read, but considering her line of work I had expected nothing less.

"What events?" she said.

"I have no idea. That's why I asked."

She shook her head.

"I'm afraid that I don't either."

"Then that about does it," I said. "I can't think of anything else to ask you."

She nodded.

"And I can't think of anything else to tell you."

I finished my coffee, returned the cup to the tray.

"Thanks, then," I said, "for your time, for the coffee. You have been very helpful."

I rose. She did the same.

"What are you going to do now?" she asked.

"I haven't quite decided," I said. "I want to do the best report I can. Have you any suggestions on that?"

"I suggest that there isn't any more to learn, that I have given you the only possible constructions the facts warrant."

"You don't feel David Fentris could provide any additional insights?"

She snorted, then sighed.

"No," she said, "I do not think he could tell you anything useful."

"What do you mean? From the way you say it . . ."

"I know. I didn't mean to. Some people find comfort in religion. Others . . . you know. Others take it up late in life with a vengeance and a half. They don't use it quite the way it was intended. It comes to color all their thinking."

"Fanaticism?" I said.

"Not exactly. A misplaced zeal. A masochistic sort of thing. Hell! I shouldn't be diagnosing at a distance—or influencing your opinion. Forget what I said. Form your own opinion when you meet him."

She raised her head, appraising my reaction.

"Well," I said, "I am not at all certain that I am going to see him. But you have made me curious. How can religion influence engineering?"

"I spoke with him after Jesse gave us the news on the vessel's return," she said. "I got the impression at the time that he feels we were tampering in the province of the Almighty by attempting the creation of an artificial intelligence. That our creation should go mad was only appropriate, being the work of imperfect man. He seemed to feel that it would be fitting if it had come back for retribution, as a sign of judgment upon us."

"Oh," I said.

She smiled then. I returned it.

"Yes," she said, "but maybe I just got him in a bad mood. Maybe you should go see for yourself."

Something told me to shake my head—a bit of a difference between this view of him, my recollections, and Don's comment that Dave had said he knew its brain and was not especially concerned. Somewhere among these lay something I felt I should know, felt I should learn without seeming to pursue. So, "I think I have enough right now," I said. "It was the psychological side of things I was supposed to cover, not the mechanical—or the theological. You have been extremely helpful. Thanks again."

She carried her smile all the way to the door.

"If it is not too much trouble," she said, as I stepped into the hall, "I would like to learn how this whole thing finally turns out—or any interesting developments, for that matter."

"My connection with the case ends with this report," I said, "and I am going to write it now. Still, I may get some feedback."

"You have my number . . . ?"

"Probably, but . . ."

I already had it, but I jotted it again, right after Mrs. Gluntz's answers to my inquiries on detergents.

Moving in a rigorous line, I made beautiful connections for a change. I headed directly for the airport, found a flight aimed at Memphis, bought passage and was the last to board. Ten score seconds, perhaps, made all the difference. Not even a tick or two to spare for checking out of the motel. No matter. The good head doctor had convinced me that, like it or not, David Fentris was next, damn it. I had too strong a feeling that Leila Thackery had not told me the entire story. I had to take a chance, to see these changes in the man for myself, to try to figure out how they related to the Hangman. For a number of reasons, I'd a feeling they might.

I disembarked into a cool, partly overcast afternoon, found transportation almost immediately and set out for Dave's office address. A before-the-storm feeling came over me as I entered and crossed the town. A dark wall of clouds continued to build in the west. Later, standing before the building where Dave did business, the first few drops of rain were already spattering against its dirty brick front. It would take a lot more than that to freshen it, though, or any of the others in the area. I would have thought he'd have come a little farther than this by now. I shrugged off some moisture and went inside.

The directory gave me directions, the elevator elevated me, my feet found the way to his door. I knocked on it.

After a time, I knocked again and waited again. Again, nothing. So I tried it, found it open and went on in.

It was a small, vacant waiting room, green-carpeted. The reception desk was dusty. I crossed and peered around the plastic partition behind it.

The man had his back to me. I drummed my knuckles against the partitioning. He heard it and turned.

"Yes?"

Our eyes met, his still framed by hornrims and just as active; glasses thicker, hair thinner, cheeks a trifle hollower. His question mark quivered in the air, and nothing in his gaze moved to replace it with recognition. He had been bending over a sheaf of schematics; a lopsided basket of metal, quartz, porcelain, and glass rested on a nearby table.

"My name is Donne, John Donne," I said. "I am looking for David Fentris."

"I am David Fentris."

"Good to meet you," I said, crossing to where he stood. "I am assisting in an investigation concerning a project with which you were once associated—"

He smiled and nodded, accepted my hand and shook it.

"—The Hangman, of course," he said. "Glad to know you, Mr. Donne."

"Yes, the Hangman," I said. "I am doing a report. . . ."

". . . And you want my opinion as to how dangerous it is. Sit down." He gestured toward a chair at the end of his work bench. "Care for a cup of tea?"

"No thanks."

"I'm having one."

"Well, in that case . . ."

He crossed to another bench.

"No cream. Sorry."

"That's all right.—How did you know it involved the Hangman?"

He grinned as he brought my cup.

"Because it's come back," he said, "and it's the only thing I've been connected with that warrants that much concern."

"Do you mind talking about it?"

"Up to a point, no."

"What's the point?"

"If we get near it, I'll let you know."

"Fair enough. How dangerous *is* it?"

"I would say that it is harmless," he replied, "except to three persons."

"Formerly four?"

"Precisely."

"How come?"

"We were doing something we had no business doing."

"That being . . . ?"

"For one thing, attempting to create an artificial intelligence."

"Why had you no business doing that?"

"A man with a name like yours shouldn't have to ask."

I chuckled.

"If I were a preacher," I said, "I would have to point out that there is no biblical injunction against it—unless you've been worshiping it on the sly."

He shook his head.

"Nothing that simple, that obvious, that explicit. Times have changed since the Good Book was written, and you can't hold with a purely Fundamentalist approach in complex times. What I was getting at was something a little more abstract. A form of pride, not unlike the classical *hubris*—the setting up of oneself on a level with the Creator."

"Did you feel that—pride?"

"Yes."

"Are you sure it wasn't just enthusiasm for an ambitious project that was working well?"

"Oh, there was plenty of that. A manifestation of the same thing."

"I do seem to recall something about man being made in the Creator's image, and something else about trying to live up to that. It would seem to follow that exercising one's capacities along similar lines would be a step in the right direction—an act of conformance with the Divine Ideal, if you'd like."

"But I don't like. Man cannot really create. He can only rearrange what is already present. Only God can create."

"Then you have nothing to worry about."

He frowned, then, "No," he said. "Being aware of this and still trying is where the presumption comes in."

"Were you really thinking that way when you did it? Or did all this occur to you after the fact?"

"I am no longer certain."

"Then it would seem to me that a merciful God would be inclined to give you the benefit of the doubt."

He gave me a wry smile.

"Not bad, John Donne. But I feel that judgment may already have been entered and that we may have lost four to nothing."

"Then you see the Hangman as an avenging angel?"

"Sometimes. Sort of. I see it as being returned to exact a penalty."

"Just for the record," I said, "if the Hangman had had full access to the necessary equipment and was able to construct another unit such as itself, would you consider it guilty of the same thing that is bothering you?"

He shook his head.

"Don't get all cute and Jesuitical with me, Donne. I'm not that far away from fundamentals. Besides, I'm willing to admit I might be wrong and that there may be other forces driving it to the same end."

"Such as?"

"I told you I'd let you know when we reached a certain point. That's it."

"OK," I said. "But that sort of blank-walls me, you know. The people I am working for would like to protect you people. They want to stop the Hangman. I was hoping you would tell me a little more—if not, for your own sake, then for the others'. They might not share your philosophical sentiments, and you have just admitted you may be wrong. Despair, by the way, is also considered a sin by a great number of theologians."

He sighed and stroked his nose, as I had often seen him do in times long past.

"What do you do, anyhow?" he asked me.

"Me, personally? I'm a science writer. I'm putting together a report on the device for the agency that wants to do the protecting. The better my report, the better their chances."

He was silent for a time, then, "I read a lot in the area, but I don't recognize your name," he said.

"Most of my work has involved petrochemistry and marine biology," I said.

"Oh. You were a peculiar choice then, weren't you?"

"Not really. I was available, and the boss knows my work, knows I'm good."

He glanced across the room, to where a stack of cartons partly obscured what I then realized to be a remote access terminal. OK. If he decided to check out my credentials now, John Donne would fall apart.It seemed a hell of a time to get curious, though, *after* sharing his sense of sin with me. He must have thought so too, because he did not look that way again.

"Let me put it this way," he finally said, and something of the old David Fentris at his best took control of his voice. "For one reason or the other, I believe that it wants to destroy its former operators. If it is the judgment of the Almighty, that's all there is to it. It will succeed. If not, however, I don't want any outside protection. I've done my own repenting and it is up to me to handle the rest of the situation myself, too. I will stop the Hangman personally, right here, before anyone else is hurt."

"How?" I asked him.

He nodded toward the glittering helmet.

"With that," he said.

"How?" I repeated.

"Its telefactor circuits are still intact. They have to be. They are an integral part of it. It could not disconnect them without shutting itself down. If it comes within a quartermile of here, that unit will be activated. It will emit a loud humming sound and a light will begin to blink behind that meshing beneath the forward ridge. I will then don the helmet and take control of the Hangman. I will bring it here and disconnect its brain."

"How would you do the disconnect?"

He reached for the schematics he had been looking at when I had come in.

"Here," he said. "The thoracic plate has to be unlugged. There are four subunits that have to be uncoupled. Here, here, here, and here."

He looked up.

"You would have to do them in sequence though, or it could get mighty hot," I said. "First this one, then these two. Then the other."

When I looked up again, the gray eyes were fixed on my own.

"I thought you were in petrochemistry and marine biology," he said.

"I am not really 'in' anything," I said. "I am a tech writer, with bits and pieces from all over—and I did have a look at these before, when I accepted the job."

"I see."

"Why don't you bring the space agency in on this?" I said, working to shift ground. "The original telefactoring equipment had all that power and range—"

"It was dismantled a long time ago," he said. "I thought you were with the Government."

I shook my head.

"Sorry. I didn't mean to mislead you. I am on contract with a private investigation outfit."

"Uh-huh. Then that means Jesse. Not that it matters. You can tell him that one way or the other everything is being taken care of."

"What if you are wrong on the supernatural," I said, "but correct on the other? Supposing it is coming under the circumstances you feel it proper to resist? But supposing you are not next on its list? Supposing it gets to one of the others next instead of you? If you are so sensitive about guilt and sin, don't you think that you would be responsible for that death—if you could prevent it by telling me just a little bit more? If it is confidentiality you are worried about—"

"No," he said. "You cannot trick me into applying my principles to a hypothetical situation which will only work out the way that you want it to. Not when I am certain that it will not arise. Whatever moves the Hangman, it will come to me next. If I cannot stop it, then it cannot be stopped until it has completed its job."

"How do you know that you are next?"

"Take a look at a map," he said. "It landed in the Gulf. Manny was right there in New Orleans. Naturally, he was first. The Hangman can move underwater like a controlled torpedo, which makes the Mississippi its logical route for inconspicuous travel. Proceeding up it then, here I am in Memphis. Then Leila, up in St. Louis, is obviously next after me. It can worry about getting to Washington after that."

I thought about Senator Brockden in Wisconsin and decided it would not even have that problem. All of them were fairly accessible, when you thought of the situation in terms of river travel.

"But how is it to know where you all are?" I asked.

"Good question," he said. "Within a limited range, it was once sensitive to our brain waves, having an intimate knowledge of them and the ability to pick them up. I do not know what that range would be today. I might have been able to construct an amplifier to extend this area of perception. But to be more mundane about it, I believe that it simply consulted the Data Bank's national directory. There are booths all over, even on the waterfront. It could have hit one late at night and gimmicked it. It certainly had sufficient identifying information—and engineering skill."

"Then it seems to me the best bet for all of you would be to move away from the river till this business is settled. That thing won't be able to stalk about the countryside very long without being noticed."

"It would find a way. It is extremely resourceful. At night, in an overcoat, a hat, it could pass. It requires nothing that a man would need. It could dig a hole and bury itself, stay underground during daylight. It could run without resting all night long. There is no place it could not reach in a surprisingly short while. No. I must wait here for it."

"Let me put it as bluntly as I can," I said. "If you are right that it is a divine avenger, I would say that it smacks of blasphemy to try to tackle it. On the other hand, if it is not, then I think you are guilty of jeopardizing the others by withholding information that would allow us to provide them with a lot more protection than you are capable of giving them all by yourself."

He laughed.

"I'll just have to learn to live with that guilt too, as they do with theirs," he said. "After I've done my best, they deserve anything they get."

"It was my understanding," I said, "that even God doesn't judge people until after they're dead—if you want another piece of presumption to add to your collection."

He stopped laughing and studied my face.

"There is something familiar about the way you talk, the way you think," he said. "Have we ever met before?"

"I doubt it. I would have remembered."

He shook his head.

"You've got a way of bothering a man's thinking that rings a faint bell," he went on. "You trouble me, sir."

"That was my intention."

"Are you staying here in town?"

"No."

"Give me a number where I can reach you, will you? If I have any new thoughts on this thing I'll call you."

"I wish you would have them now if you are going to have them."

"No," he said, "I've got some thinking to do. Where can I get hold of you later?"

I gave him the name of the motel I was still checked into in St. Louis, I could call back periodically for messages.

"All right," he said, and he moved toward the partition by the reception area and stood beside it.

I rose and followed him, passing into that area and pausing at the door to the hall.

"One thing . . ." I said.

"Yes?"

"If it does show up and you do stop it, will you call me and tell me that?"

"Yes, I will."

"Thanks then—and good luck."

Impulsively, I extended my hand. He gripped it and smiled faintly.

"Thank you, Mr. Donne."

Next. Next, next, next . . .

I couldn't budge Dave, and Leila Thackery had given me everything she was going to. No real sense in calling Don yet—not until I had more to say. I thought it over on my way back to the airport. The pre-dinner hours always seem best for talking to people in any sort of official capacity, just as the night seems best for dirty work. Heavily psychological, but true nevertheless. I hated to waste the

rest of the day if there was anyone else worth talking to before I
called Don. Going through the folder, I decided that there was.

Manny Burns had a brother, Phil. I wondered how worthwhile
it might be to talk with him. I could make it to New Orleans at a
sufficiently respectable hour, learn whatever he was willing to tell
me, check back with Don for new developments and then decide
whether there was anything I should be about with respect to the
vessel itself. The sky was gray and leaky above me. I was anxious
to flee its spaces. So I decided to do it. I could think of no better
stone to upturn at the moment.

At the airport, I was ticketed quickly, in time for another close
connection. Hurrying to reach my flight, my eyes brushed over a
half-familiar face on the passing escalator. The reflex reserved for
such occasions seemed to catch us both, because he looked back
too, with the same eyebrow twitch of startle and scrutiny. Then
he was gone. I could not place him, though. The half-familiar face
becomes a familiar phenomenon in a crowded, highly mobile society. I sometimes think that this is all that will eventually remain
of any of us: patterns of features, some a trifle more persistent than
others, impressed on the flow of bodies. A small town boy in a big
city. Thomas Wolfe must long ago have felt the same thing when
he had coined the word *manswarm.* It might have been someone
I had once met briefly, or simply someone or someone like someone I had passed on sufficient other occasions such as this.

As I flew the unfriendly skies out of Memphis, I mulled over
musings past on artificial intelligence, or AI as they have tagged
it in the think box biz. When talking about computers, the AI
notion had always seemed hotter than I deemed necessary, partly
because of semantics. The word "intelligence" has all sorts of tag-
along associations of the nonphysical sort. I suppose it goes back
to the fact that early discussions and conjectures concerning it
made it sound as if the potential for intelligence was always
present in the array of gadgets, and the correct procedures, the
right programs, simply had to be found to call it forth. When you
looked at it that way, as many did, it gave rise to an uncomfortable
déjà vu—namely, vitalism. The philosophical battles of the Nine-

teenth Century were hardly so far behind that they had been forgotten, and the doctrine which maintained that life is caused and sustained by a vital principle apart from physical and chemical forces and that life is self-sustaining and self-evolving, had put up quite a fight before Darwin and his successors had produced triumph after triumph for the mechanistic view. Then vitalism sort of crept back into things again when the AI discussions arose in the middle of the past century. It would seem that Dave had fallen victim to it, and that he had come to believe he had helped provide an unsanctified vessel and filled it with something intended only for those things which had made the scene in the first chapter of Genesis.

With computers it was not quite as bad as with the Hangman though, because you could always argue that no matter how elaborate the program it was basically an extension of the programmer's will and the operations of causal machines merely represented functions of intelligence, rather than intelligence in its own right backed by a will of its own. And there was always Gödel for a theoretical *cordon sanitaire*, with his demonstration of the true but mechanically unprovable proposition. But the Hangman was quite different. It had been designed along the lines of a brain and at least partly educated in a human fashion; and to further muddy the issue with respect to anything like vitalism, it had been in direct contact with human minds from which it might have acquired almost anything—including the spark that set it on the road to whatever selfhood it may have found. What did that make it? Its own creature? A fractured mirror reflecting a fractured humanity? Both? Or neither? I certainly could not say, but I wondered how much of its "self" had been truly its own. It had obviously acquired a great number of functions, but was it capable of having real feelings? Could it, for example, feel something like love? If not, then it was still only a collection of complex abilities, and not a thing with all the tag-along associations of the nonphysical sort which made the word "intelligence" such a prickly item in AI discussions; and if it were capable of, say, something like love, and if I were Dave, I would not feel guilty about having helped to bring it into being. I would feel proud, though not in the fashion he was concerned about, and I would also feel humble. Offhand though, I do not know how intelligent I would feel, because I am still not sure what the hell intelligence is.

The day's-end sky was clear when we landed. I was into town before the sun had finished setting, and on Philip Burns's doorstep just a little while later.

My ring was answered by a girl, maybe seven or eight years old. She fixed me with large brown eyes and did not say a word.

"I would like to speak with Mr. Burns," I said.

She turned and retreated around a corner.

A heavyset man, slacked and undershirted, bald about halfway back and very pink, padded into the hall moments later and peered at me. He bore a folded newssheet in his left hand.

"What do you want?" he asked.

"It's about your brother," I said.

"Yeah?"

"Well, I wonder if I could come in? It's kind of complicated."

He opened the door. But instead of letting me in, he came out.

"Tell me about it out here," he said.

"OK, I'll be quick. I just wanted to find out whether he ever spoke with you about a piece of equipment he once worked with called the Hangman."

"Are you a cop?"

"No."

"Then what's your interest?"

"I am working for a private investigation agency trying to track down some equipment once associated with the project. It has apparently turned up in this area and it could be rather dangerous."

"Let's see some identification."

"I don't carry any."

"What's your name?"

"John Donne."

"And you think my brother had some stolen equipment when he died? Let me tell you something—"

"No. Not stolen," I said, "and I don't think he had it."

"What then?"

"It was—well, robotic in nature. Because of some special training Manny once received, he might have had a way of detecting
it. He might even have attracted it. I just want to find out whether
he had said anything about it. We are trying to locate it."

"My brother was a respectable businessman, and I don't like
accusations. Especially right after his funeral, I don't. I think I'm
going to call the cops and let them ask *you* a few questions."

"Just a minute," I said. "Supposing I told you we had some
reason to believe it might have been this piece of equipment that
killed your brother?"

His pink turned to bright red and his jaw muscles formed sudden ridges. I was not prepared for the stream of profanities that
followed. For a moment, I thought he was going to take a swing
at me.

"Wait a second," I said when he paused for breath. "What did
I say?"

"You're either making fun of the dead or you're stupider than
you look!"

"Say I'm stupid. Then tell me why."

He tore at the paper he carried, folded it back, found an item,
thrust it at me.

"Because they've got the guy who did it! That's why," he said.

I read it. Simple, concise, to the point. Today's latest. A suspect
had confessed. New evidence had corroborated it. The man was
in custody. A surprised robber who had lost his head and hit too
hard, hit too many times. I read it over again. I nodded as I passed
it back.

"Look, I'm sorry," I said, "I really didn't know about this."

"Get out of here," he said. "Go on."

"Sure."

"Wait a minute."

"What?"

"That's his little girl who answered the door."

"I'm very sorry."

"So am I. But I know her Daddy didn't take your damned equipment."

I nodded and turned away.

I heard the door slam behind me.

After dinner, I checked into a small hotel, called for a drink and stepped into the shower. Things were suddenly a lot less urgent than they had been earlier. Senator Brockden would doubtless be pleased to learn that his initial estimation of events had been incorrect. Leila Thackery would give me an I-told-you-so smile when I called her to pass along the news—a thing I now felt obliged to do. Don might or might not want me to keep looking for the device now that the threat had been lessened. It would depend on the Senator's feelings on the matter, I supposed. If urgency no longer counted for as much, Don might want to switch back to one of his own, fiscally less burdensome operatives. Toweling down, I caught myself whistling. I felt almost off the hook.

Later, drink beside me, I paused before punching out the number he had given me and hit the sequence for my motel in St. Louis instead. Merely a matter of efficiency, in case there was a message worth adding to my report.

A woman's face appeared on the screen and a smile appeared on her face. I wondered whether she would always smile whenever she heard a bell ring, or if the reflex was eventually extinguished in advanced retirement. It must be rough, being afraid to chew gum, yawn or pick your nose.

"Airport Accommodations," she said. "May I help you?"

"This is Donne. I'm checked into Room 106," I said. "I'm away right now and I wondered whether there had been any messages for me."

"Just a moment," she said, checking something off to her left. Then, "Yes," she continued, consulting a piece of paper she now held. "You have one on tape. But it is a little peculiar. It is for someone else in care of you."

"Oh? Who is that?"

She told me and I exercised self-control.

"I see," I said. "I'll bring him around later and play it for him. Thank you."

She smiled again and made a good-bye noise and I did the same and broke the connection.

So Dave had seen through me after all. . . . Who else could have that number *and* my real name?

I might have given her some line or other and had her transmit the thing. Only I was not certain but that she might be a silent party to the transmission, should life be more than usually boring for her at that moment. I had to get up there myself, as soon as possible, and personally see that the thing was erased.

I took a big swallow of my drink, then fetched the folder on Dave. I checked out his number—there were two, actually—and spent fifteen minutes trying to get hold of him. No luck.

O.K. Good-bye New Orleans, good-bye peace of mind. This time I called the airport and made a reservation. Then I chugged the drink, put myself in order, gathered up my few possessions and went to check out again. Hello Central. . . .

During my earlier flights that day I had spent time thinking about Teilhard de Chardin's ideas on the continuation of evolution within the realm of artifacts, matching them against Gödel on mechanical undecidability, playing epistemological games with the Hangman as a counter, wondering, speculating, even hoping, hoping that truth lay with the nobler part, that the Hangman, sentient, had made it back, sane, that the Burns killing had actually been something of the sort that now seemed to be the case, that the washed-out experiment had really been a success of a different sort, a triumph, a new link or fob for the chain of being. . . . And Leila had not been wholly discouraging with respect to the neuristor-type brain's capacity for this. . . . Now, though, now I had troubles of my own, and even the most heartening of philosophical vistas is no match for, say, a toothache, if it happens to be your own. Accordingly, the Hangman was shunted aside and the stuff of my thoughts involved, mainly, myself. There was, of course, the possibility that the Hangman had indeed showed up

and Dave had stopped it and then called to report it as he had
promised. However, he had used my name.

There was not too much planning that I could do until I received the substance of the communication. It did not seem
that as professedly religious a man as Dave would suddenly be
contemplating the blackmail business. On the other hand, he
was a creature of sudden enthusiasms and had already undergone one unanticipated conversion. It was difficult to say. . . .
His technical background plus his knowledge of the Data Bank
program did put him in an unusually powerful position should
he decide to mess me up. I did not like to think of some of the
things I have done to protect my nonperson status; I especially
did not like to think of them in connection with Dave, whom I
not only still respected but still liked. Since self-interest dominated while actual planning was precluded, my thoughts tooled
their way into a more general groove.

It was Karl Mannheim, a long while ago, who made the observation that radical, revolutionary, and progressive thinkers tend to
employ mechanical metaphors for the state, whereas those of conservative inclination make vegetable analogies. He said it well
over a generation before the cybernetics movement and the ecology movement beat their respective paths through the wilderness
of general awareness. If anything, it seemed to me that these two
developments served to elaborate the distinction between a pair
of viewpoints which, while no longer necessarily tied in with the
political positions Mannheim assigned them, do seem to represent
a continuing phenomenon in my own time. There are those who
see social/economic/ecological problems as malfunctions which
can be corrected by simple repair, replacement or streamlining—
a kind of linear outlook where even innovations are considered to
be merely additive. Then there are those who sometimes hesitate
to move at all, because their awareness follows events in the directions of secondary and tertiary effects as they multiply and cross-
fertilize throughout the entire system. I digress to extremes. The
cyberneticists have their multiple feedback loops, though it is
never quite clear how they know what kind of, which, and how

many to install, and the ecological gestaltists do draw lines representing points of diminishing returns, though it is sometimes equally difficult to see how they assign their values and priorities. Of course they need each other, the vegetable people and the Tinker toy people. They serve to check one another, if nothing else. And while occasionally the balance dips, the tinkerers have, in general, held the edge for the past couple centuries. However, today's can be just as politically conservative as the vegetable people Mannheim was talking about, and they are the ones I fear most at the moment. They are the ones who saw the Data Bank program, in its present extreme form, as a simple remedy for a great variety of ills and a provider of many goods. Not all of the ills have been remedied, however, and a new brood has been spawned by the program itself. While we need both kinds, I wish that there had been more people interested in tending the garden of state rather than overhauling the engine of state when the program was inaugurated. Then I would not be a refugee from a form of existence I find repugnant, and I would not be concerned whether a former associate had discovered my identity.

Then, as I watched the lights below, I wondered. . . . Was I a tinkerer because I would like to further alter the prevailing order, into something more comfortable on my anarchic nature? Or was I a vegetable dreaming I was a tinkerer? I could not make up my mind. The garden of life never seems to confine itself to the plots philosophers have laid out for its convenience. Maybe a few more tractors would do the trick.

I pressed the button. The tape began to roll. The screen remained blank. I heard Dave's voice ask for John Donne in Room 106 and I heard him told that there was no answer. Then I heard him say that he wanted to record a message, for someone else, in care of Donne, that Donne would understand. He sounded out of breath. The girl asked him whether he wanted visual, too. He told her to turn it on. There was a pause. Then she told him go ahead. Still no picture. No words either. His breathing and a slight scraping noise. Ten seconds. Fifteen. . . .

". . . Got me," he finally said, and he mentioned that name again.

". . . Had to let you know I'd figured you out, though. . . . It wasn't any particular mannerism—any single thing you said. . . . Just your general style—thinking, talking—the electronics—everything—after I got more and more bothered by the familiarity—after I checked you on petrochem—and marine bio—Wish I knew what you've really been up to all these years. . . . Never know now. But I wanted you—to know—you hadn't put one—over on me." There followed another quarter-minute of heavy breathing, climaxed by a racking cough. Then a choked, "Said too much—too fast—too soon. . . . All used up. . . ."

The picture came on then. He was slouched before the screen, head resting on his arms, blood all over him. His glasses were gone and he was squinting and blinking. The right side of his head looked pulpy and there was a gash on his left cheek and one on his forehead.

". . . Sneaked up on me—while I was checking you out," he managed then. "Had to tell you what I learned. . . . Still don't know —which of us is right. . . . Pray for me!"

His arms collapsed and the right one slid forward. His head rolled to the right and the picture went away. When I replayed it I saw it was his knuckle that had hit the cutoff.

Then I erased it. It had been recorded only a little over an hour after I had left him. If he had not also placed a call for help, if no one had gotten to him quickly after that, his chances did not look good. Even if they had, though. . . .

I used a public booth to call the number Don had given me, got hold of him after some delay, told him Dave was in bad shape if not worst, that a team of Memphis medics was definitely in order, if one had not been there already, and that I hoped to call him back and tell him more shortly, good-bye.

Then I tried Leila Thackery's number. I let it go for a long while, but there was no answer. I wondered how long it would take a controlled torpedo moving up the Mississippi to get from Memphis to St. Louis. I did not feel it was time to start leafing through that section of the Hangman's specs. Instead, I went looking for transportation.

At her apartment, I tried ringing her from the entrance foyer. Again, no answer. So I rang Mrs. Gluntz. She had seemed the most guileless of the three I had interviewed for my fake consumer survey.

"Yes?"

"It's me again, Mrs. Gluntz: Stephen Foster. I've just a couple follow-up questions on that survey I was doing today, if you could spare me a few moments."

"Why, yes," she said. "All right. Come up."

The door hummed itself loose and I entered. I duly proceeded to the fifth floor, composing my questions on the way. I had planned this maneuver as I had waited earlier solely to provide a simple route for breaking and entering, should some unforeseen need arise. Most of the time my ploys such as this go unused, but sometimes they simplify matters a lot.

Five minutes and half-a-dozen questions later, I was back down on the second floor, probing at the lock on Leila's door with a couple of little pieces of metal it is sometimes awkward to be caught carrying.

Half a minute later I hit it right and snapped it back. I pulled on some tissue-thin gloves I keep rolled in the corner of one pocket, opened the door and stepped inside.

I closed it behind me immediately. She was lying on the floor, her neck at a bad angle. One table lamp still burned, though it was lying on its side. Several small items had been knocked from the table, a magazine rack pushed over, a cushion partly displaced from the sofa. The cable to her phone unit had been torn from the wall.

A humming noise filled the air, and I sought its source.

I saw where the little blinking light was reflected on the wall, on-off, on-off. . . .

I moved quickly.

It was a lopsided basket of metal, quartz, porcelain, and glass, which had rolled to a position on the far side of the chair in which I had been seated earlier that day. The same rig I had seen in Dave's workshop not all that long ago, though it now seemed so. A device to detect the Hangman, and hopefully to control it.

I picked it up and fitted it over my head.

Once, with the aid of a telepath, I had touched minds with a dolphin as he composed dreamsongs somewhere in the Caribbean, an experience so moving that its mere memory had often been a comfort. This sensation was hardly equivalent.

Analogies & impressions: a face seen through a wet pane of glass; a whisper in a noisy terminal; scalp massage with an electric vibrator; Edvard Munch's *The Scream;* the voice of Yma Sumac, rising and rising and rising; the disappearance of snow; a deserted street, illuminated as through a sniperscope I'd once used, rapid movement past darkened storefronts that line it, an immense feeling of physical capability, compounded of proprioceptive awareness of enormous strength, a peculiar array of sensory channels, a central, undying sun that fed me a constant flow of energy, a memory vision of dark waters, passing, flashing, echo-location within them, the need to return to that place, reorient, move north; Munch & Sumac, Munch & Sumac, Munch & Sumac—Nothing.

Silence.

The humming had ceased, the light gone out. The entire experience had lasted only a few moments. There had not been time enough to try for any sort of control, though an afterimpression akin to a biofeedback cue hinted at the direction to go, the way to think, to achieve it. I felt that it might be possible for me to work the thing, given a better chance.

I removed the helmet and approached Leila. I knelt beside her and performed a few simple tests, already knowing their outcome. In addition to the broken neck, she had received some bad bashes about the head and shoulders. There was nothing that anyone could do for her now.

I did a quick run-through then, checking over the rest of her apartment. There were no apparent signs of breaking and entering, though if I could pick one lock, a guy with built-in tools could easily go me one better.

I located some wrapping paper and string in the kitchen and turned the helmet into a parcel. It was time to call Don again, to tell him that the vessel had indeed been occupied and that river traffic was probably bad in the north-bound lane.

Don had told me to get the helmet up to Wisconsin, where I would be met at the airport by a man named Larry who would fly me to the lodge in a private craft. I did that, and this was done. I also learned, with no real surprise, that David Fentris was dead.

The temperature was down, and it began to snow on the way up. I was not really dressed for the weather. Larry told me I could borrow some warmer clothing once we reached the lodge, though I probably would not be going outside that much. Don had told them that I was supposed to stay as close to the Senator as possible and that any patrols were to be handled by the four guards themselves. Larry was curious as to what exactly had happened so far and whether I had actually seen the Hangman. I did not think it my place to fill him in on anything Don may not have cared to, so I might have been a little curt. We didn't talk much after that.

Bert met us when we landed. Tom and Clay were outside the building, watching the trail, watching the woods. All of them were middle-aged, very fit-looking, very serious, and heavily armed. Larry took me inside then and introduced me to the old gentleman himself.

Senator Brockden was seated in a heavy chair in the far corner of the room. Judging from the layout, it appeared that the chair might recently have occupied a position beside the window in the opposite wall where a lonely watercolor of yellow flowers looked down on nothing. The Senator's feet rested on a hassock, a red plaid blanket lay across his legs. He had on a dark green shirt, his hair was very white and he wore rimless reading glasses which he removed when we entered.

He tilted his head back, squinted and gnawed his lower lip slowly as he studied me. He remained expressionless as we advanced. A big-boned man, he had probably been beefy much of his life. Now he had the slack look of recent weight loss and an unhealthy skin tone. His eyes were a pale gray within it all. He did not rise.

"So you're the man," he said, offering me his hand. "I'm glad to meet you. How do you want to be called?"

"John will do," I said.

He made a small sign to Larry and Larry departed.

"It's cold out there. Go get yourself a drink, John. It's on the shelf." He gestured off to his left. ". . . and bring me one while you're at it. Two fingers of bourbon in a water glass. That's all."

I nodded and went and poured a couple.

"Sit down." He motioned at a nearby chair as I delivered his. "But first let me see that gadget you've brought."

I undid the parcel and handed him the helmet. He sipped his drink and put it aside. He took the helmet in both hands and studied it, brows furrowed, turning it completely around. He raised it and put it on his head.

"Not a bad fit," he said, and then he smiled for the first time, becoming for a moment the face I had known from newscasts past. Grinning or angry—it was almost always one or the other. I had never seen his collapsed look in any of the media.

He removed the helmet and set it on the floor.

"Pretty piece of work," he said. "Nothing quite that fancy in the old days. But then David Fentris built it. Yes, he told us about it. . . ." He raised his drink and took a sip. "You are the only one who has actually gotten to use it, apparently. What do you think? Will it do the job?"

"I was only in contact for a couple seconds," I said, "so I've only got a feeling to go on, not much better than a hunch. But yes, I'd a feeling that if I'd had more time I might have been able to work its circuits."

"Tell me why it didn't save Dave."

"In the message he left me he indicated that he had been distracted at his computer access station. Its noise probably drowned out the humming."

"Why wasn't this message preserved?"

"I erased it for reasons not connected with the case."

"What reasons?"

"My own."

His face went from sallow to ruddy.

"A man can get in a lot of trouble for suppressing evidence, obstructing justice," he said.

"Then we have something in common, don't we, sir?"

His eyes caught mine with a look I had only encountered before from those who did not wish me well. He held the glare for a full four heartbeats, then sighed and seemed to relax.

"Don said there were a number of points you couldn't be pressed on," the Senator finally said.

"That's right."

"He didn't betray any confidences, but he had to tell me something about you, you know."

"I'd imagine."

"He seems to think highly of you. Still, I tried to learn more about you on my own."

"And . . . ?"

"I couldn't—and my usual sources are good at that kind of thing."

"So . . . ?"

"So, I've done some thinking, some wondering. . . . The fact that my sources could not come up with anything is interesting in itself. Possibly even revealing. I am in a better position than most to be aware of the fact that there was not perfect compliance with the registration statute some years ago. It didn't take long for a great number of the individuals involved—I should probably say 'most'—to demonstrate their existence in one fashion or another and be duly entered, though. And there were three broad categories: those who were ignorant, those who disapproved, and those who would be hampered in an illicit life style. I am not attempting to categorize you or to pass judgment. But I am aware that there are a number of nonpersons passing through society without casting shadows and it has occurred to me that you may be such a one."

I tasted my drink.

"And if I am?" I asked.

He gave me his second, nastier smile and said nothing.

I rose and crossed the room to where I judged his chair had once stood. I looked at the watercolor.

"I don't think you could stand an inquiry," he said.

I did not reply.

"Aren't you going to say something?"

"What do you want me to say?"

"You might ask me what I am going to do about it."

"What are you going to do about it?"

"Nothing," he said. "So come back here and sit down."

I nodded and returned.

He studied my face.

"Was it possible you were close to violence just then?"

"With four guards outside?"

"With four guards outside."

"No," I said.

"You're a good liar."

"I am here to help you, sir. No questions asked. That was the deal, as I understood it. If there has been any change, I would like to know about it now."

He drummed with his fingertips on the plaid.

"I've no desire to cause you any difficulty," he said. "Fact of the matter is, I need a man just like you, and I was pretty sure someone like Don might turn him up. Your unusual maneuverability and your reported knowledge of computers, along with your touchiness in certain areas, made you worth waiting for. I've a great number of things I would like to ask you."

"Go ahead," I said.

"Not yet. Later, if we have time. All that would be bonus material, for a report I am working on. Far more important, to me personally, there are things that I want to tell you."

I frowned.

"Over the years," he said. "I have learned that the best man for purposes of keeping his mouth shut concerning your business is someone for whom you are doing the same."

"You have a compulsion to confess something?" I said.

"I don't know whether 'compulsion' is the right word. Maybe so, maybe not. Either way, though, someone among those working to defend me should have the whole story. Something somewhere in it may be of help—and you are the ideal choice to hear it."

"I buy that," I said, "and you are as safe with me as I am with you."

"Have you any suspicions as to why this business bothers me so?"

"Yes," I said.

"Let's hear them."

"You used the Hangman to perform some act or acts—illegal, immoral, whatever. This is obviously not a matter of record. Only you and the Hangman now know what it involved. You feel it was sufficiently ignominious that when that device came to appreciate the full weight of the event it suffered a breakdown which may well have led to a final determination to punish you for using it as you did."

He stared down into his glass.

"You've got it," he said.

"You were all party to it?"

"Yes, but I was the operator when it happened. You see . . . we—I—killed a man. It was—actually, it all started as a celebration. We had received word that afternoon that the project had cleared. Everything had checked out in order and the final approval had come down the line. It was go, for that Friday. Leila, Dave, Manny, and myself—we had dinner together. We were in high spirits. After dinner, we continued celebrating and somehow the party got adjourned back to the installation. As the evening wore on, more and more absurdities seemed less and less preposterous, as is sometimes the case. We decided—I forget which of us suggested it—that the Hangman should really have a share in the festivities. After all, it was, in a very real sense, his party. Before too much longer, it sounded only fair and we were discussing how we could go about it. You see, we were in Texas and the Hangman was at the Space Center in California. Getting together with him was out of the question. On the other hand, the teleoperator station was right up the hall from us. What we finally decided to do was to activate him and take turns working as operator. There was already a rudimentary consciousness there, and we felt it fitting that we each get in touch to share the good news. So that is what we did."

He sighed, took another sip, glanced at me.

"Dave was the first operator," he continued. "He activated the Hangman. Then—well, as I said, we were all in high spirits. We had not originally intended to remove the Hangman from the lab where he was situated, but Dave decided to take him outside briefly—to show him the sky and to tell him he was going there, after all. Then he suddenly got enthusiastic about outwitting the guards and the alarm system. It was a game. We all went along with it. In fact, we were clamoring for a turn at the thing ourselves. But Dave stuck with it, and he wouldn't turn over control until he had actually gotten the Hangman off the premises, out into an uninhabited area next to the Center. By the time Leila persuaded him to give her a go at the controls, it was kind of anticlimactic. That game had already been played. So she thought up a new one. She took the Hangman into the next town. It was late, and the sensory equipment was superb. It was a challenge—passing through the town without being detected. By then, everyone had suggestions as to what to do next, progressively more outrageous suggestions. Then Manny took control, and he wouldn't say what he was doing—wouldn't let us monitor him. Said it would be more fun to surprise the next operator. Now, he was higher than the rest of us put together, I think, and he stayed on so damn long that we started to get nervous. A certain amount of tension is partly sobering, and I guess we all began to think what a stupid thing it was we were doing. It wasn't just that it would wreck our careers—which it would—but it could blow the entire project if we got caught playing games with such expensive hardware. At least, I was thinking that way, and I was also thinking that Manny was no doubt operating under the very human wish to go the others one better. I started to sweat. I suddenly just wanted to get the Hangman back where he belonged, turn him off—you could still do that, before the final circuits went in—shut down the station and start forgetting it had ever happened. I began leaning on Manny to wind up his diversion and turn the controls over to me. Finally, he agreed."

He finished his drink and held out the glass.

"Would you freshen this a bit?"

"Surely."

I went and got him some more, added a touch to my own, returned to my chair, and waited.

"So I took over," he said. "I took over, and where do you think that idiot had left me? I was inside a building, and it didn't take but an eyeblink to realize it was a bank. The Hangman carries a lot of tools, and Manny had apparently been able to guide him through the doors without setting anything off. I was standing right in front of the main vault. Obviously, he thought that should be my challenge. I fought down a desire to turn and make my own exit in the nearest wall and start running. I went back to the doors and looked outside. I didn't see anyone. I started to let myself out. The light hit me as I emerged. It was a hand flash. The guard had been standing out of sight. He'd a gun in his other hand. I panicked. I hit him. Reflex. If I am going to hit someone I hit him as hard as I can. Only I hit him with the strength of the Hangman. He must have died instantly. I started to run and I didn't stop till I was back in the little park area near the Center. Then I stopped and the others had to take me out of the harness."

"They monitored all this?"

"Yes, someone cut the visual in on a side viewscreen again a few seconds after I took over. Dave, I think."

"Did they try to stop you at any time while you were running away?"

"No. I wasn't aware of anything but what I was doing at the time. But afterward they said they were too shocked to do anything but watch, until I gave out."

"I see."

"Dave took over then, ran his initial route in reverse, got the Hangman back into the lab, cleaned him up, turned him off. We shut down the operator station. We were suddenly very sober."

He sighed and leaned back and was silent for a long while.

Then, "You are the only person I've ever told this to," he said.

I tasted my own drink.

"We went over to Leila's place then," he continued, "and the rest is pretty much predictable. Nothing we could do would bring the guy back, we decided, but if we told what had happened it would wreck an expensive, important program. It wasn't as if we were criminals in need of rehabilitation. It was a once-in-a-lifetime lark that happened to end tragically. What would you have done?"

"I don't know," I said. "Maybe the same thing. I'd have been scared, too."

He nodded.

"Exactly. And that's the story."

"Not all of it, is it?"

"What do you mean?"

"What about the Hangman? You said there was already a detectable consciousness there. Then you were aware of it, as it was aware of you. It must have had some reaction to the whole business. What was it like?"

"Damn you," he said flatly.

"I'm sorry."

"Are you a family man?" he asked.

"No," I said. "I'm not."

"Did you ever take a small child to a zoo?"

"Yes."

"Then maybe you know the experience. When my son was around four I took him to the Washington Zoo one afternoon. We must have walked past every cage in the place. He made appreciative comments every now and then, asked a few questions, giggled at the monkeys, thought the bears were very nice, probably because they made him think of oversized toys. But do you know what the finest thing of all was? The thing that made him jump up and down and point and say, 'Look, Daddy! Look!'?"

I shook my head.

"A squirrel looking down from the limb of a tree," he said, and he chuckled briefly. "Ignorance of what's important and what isn't. Inappropriate responses. Innocence. The Hangman was a child, and up until the time I took over, the only thing he had gotten from us was the idea that it was a game. He was playing with us, that's all. Then something horrible happened. . . . I hope you never know what it feels like to do something totally rotten to a child, while he is holding your hand and laughing. . . . He felt all my reactions, and all of Dave's as he guided him back."

We sat there for a long while then.

"So we—traumatized it," he said, "or whatever other fancy terminology you might want to give it. That is what happened that night. It took a while for it to take effect, but there is no doubt in my mind that that is the cause of its finally breaking down."

I nodded.

"I see," I said. "And you believe it wants to kill you for this?"

"Wouldn't you?" he said. "If you had started out as a thing and we had turned you into a person and then used you as a thing again, wouldn't you?"

"Leila left a lot out of her diagnosis," I said.

"No, she just omitted it in talking to you. It was all there. But she read it wrong. She wasn't afraid. It *was* just a game it had played—with the others. Its memories of that part might not be as bad. I was the one that really marked it. As I see it, Leila was betting that I was the only one it was after. Obviously, she read it wrong."

"Then what I do not understand," I said, "is why the Burns killing did not bother her more. There was no way of telling immediately that it had been a panicky hoodlum rather than the Hangman."

"The only thing that I can see is that, being a very proud woman —which she was—she was willing to hold with her diagnosis in the face of the apparent evidence."

"I don't like it," I said, "but you know her and I don't, and as it turned out her estimate of that part was correct. Something else bothers me just as much, though: the helmet. It looks as though the Hangman killed Dave, then took the trouble to bear the helmet in his watertight compartment all the way to St. Louis, solely for purposes of dropping it at the scene of his next killing. That makes no sense whatsoever."

"It does, actually," he said. "I was going to get to that shortly, but I might as well cover it now. You see, the Hangman possessed no vocal mechanism. We communicated by means of the equipment. Don says you know something about electronics. . . ."

"Yes."

"Well, shortly, I want you to start checking over that helmet, to see whether it has been tampered with—"

"That is going to be difficult," I said. "I don't know just how it was wired originally, and I'm not such a genius on the theory that I can just look at a thing and say whether it will function as a teleoperator unit."

He bit his lower lip.

"You will have to try, anyhow," he said then. "There may be physical signs—scratches, breaks, new connections. I don't know. That's your department. Look for them."

I just nodded and waited for him to go on.

"I think that the Hangman wanted to talk to Leila," he said, "either because she was a psychiatrist and he knew he was functioning badly at a level that transcended the mechanical, or because he might think of her in terms of a mother. After all, she was the only woman involved, and he had the concept of mother, with all the comforting associations that go with it, from all of our minds. Or maybe for both of these reasons. I feel he might have taken the helmet along for that purpose. He would have realized what it was from a direct monitoring of Dave's brain while he was with him. I want you to check it over because it would seem possible that the Hangman disconnected the control circuits and left the communication circuits intact. I think he might have taken that helmet to Leila in that condition and attempted to induce her to put it on. She got scared—tried to run away, fight or call for help —and he killed her. The helmet was no longer of any use to him, so he discarded it and departed. Obviously, he does not have anything to say to me."

I thought about it, nodded again.

"O.K., broken circuits I can spot," I said. "If you will tell me where a toolkit is, I had better get right to it."

He made a stay-put gesture.

"Afterward, I found out the identity of the guard," he went on. "We all contributed to an anonymous gift for his widow. I have

done things for his family, taken care of them—the same way—
ever since. . . ."

I did not look at him as he spoke.

". . . There was nothing else that I could do," he said.

I remained silent.

He finished his drink and gave me a weak smile.

"The kitchen is back there," he told me, showing me a thumb.
"There is a utility room right behind it. Tools are in there."

"OK."

I got to my feet. I retrieved the helmet and started toward the
doorway, passing near the area where I had stood earlier, back
when he had fitted me into the proper box and tightened a screw.

"Wait a minute," he said.

I stopped.

"Why did you go over there before? What's so strategic about
that part of the room?"

"What do you mean?"

"You know what I mean."

I shrugged.

"Had to go someplace."

"You seem the sort of person who has better reasons than that."

I glanced at the wall.

"Not then," I said.

"I insist."

"You really don't want to know," I told him.

"I really do."

"All right," I said. "I wanted to see what sort of flowers you liked.
After all, you're a client," and I went on back through the kitchen
into the utility room and started looking for tools.

I sat in a chair turned sidewise from the table to face the door.
In the main room of the lodge the only sounds were the occasional
hiss and sputter of the logs turning to ashes on the grate.

Just a cold, steady whiteness drifting down outside the window
and a silence confirmed by gunfire, driven deeper now that it had
ceased. . . .

Not a sign or a whimper, though. And I never count them as storms unless there is wind.

Big fat flakes down the night, silent night, windless night. . . .

Considerable time had passed since my arrival. The Senator had sat up for a long while talking with me. He was disappointed that I could not tell him too much about a nonperson subculture which he believed existed. I really was not certain about it myself, though I had occasionally encountered what might have been its fringes. I am not much of a joiner of anything any more, though, and I was not about to mention those things I might have guessed on this. I gave him my opinions on the Data Bank when he asked for them, and there were some that he did not like. He accused me then of wanting to tear things down without offering anything better in their place. My mind drifted back through fatigue and time and faces and snow and a lot of space to the previous evening in Baltimore—how long ago? It made me think of Mencken's *The Cult of Hope*. I could not give him the pat answer, the workable alternative that he wanted because there might not be one. The function of criticism should not be confused with the function of reform. But if a grassroots resistance was building up, with an underground movement bent on finding ways to circumvent the record-keepers it might well be that much of the enterprise would eventually prove about as effective and beneficial as, say, Prohibition once had. I tried to get him to see this, but I could not tell how much he bought of anything that I said. Eventually, he flaked out and went upstairs to take a pill and lock himself in for the night. If it troubled him that I had not been able to find anything wrong with the helmet he did not show it.

So I sat there, the helmet, the radio, the gun on the table, the toolkit on the floor beside my chair, the black glove on my left hand. The Hangman was coming. I did not doubt it. Bert, Larry, Tom, Clay, the helmet, might or might not be able to stop him. Something bothered me about the whole case, but I was too tired to think of anything but the immediate situation, to try to remain alert while I waited. I was afraid to take a stimulant or a drink or to light a cigarette, since my central nervous system itself was to be a part of the weapon. I watched the big fat flakes fly by.

I called out to Bert and Larry when I heard the click. I picked up the helmet and rose to my feet as its light began to blink.

But it was already too late.

As I raised the helmet, I heard a shot from outside, and with that shot I felt a premonition of doom. They did not seem the sort of men who would fire until they had a target. Dave had told me that the helmet's range was approximately a quarter of a mile. Then, given the time lag between the helmet's activation and the Hangman's sighting by the near guards, the Hangman had to be moving very rapidly. To this add the possibility that the Hangman's range on brainwaves might well be greater than the helmet's range on the Hangman. And then grant the possibility that he had utilized this factor while Senator Brockden was still lying awake, worrying. Conclusion: the Hangman might well be aware that I was where I was with the helmet, realize that it was the most dangerous weapon waiting for him, and be moving for a lightning strike at me before I could come to terms with the mechanism. I lowered it over my head and tried to throw my faculties into neutral.

Again, the sensation of viewing the world through a sniper-scope, with all the concomitant side sensations. Only the world consisted of the front of the lodge, Bert, before the door, rifle at his shoulder, Larry, off to the left, arm already fallen from the act of having thrown a grenade. The grenade, we instantly realized, was an overshot; the flamer, at which he now groped, would prove useless before he could utilize it. Bert's next round ricocheted off our breastplate toward the left. The impact staggered us momentarily. The third was a miss. There was no fourth, for we tore the rifle from his grasp and cast it aside as we swept by, crashing into the front door.

The Hangman entered the room as the door splintered and collapsed. My mind was filled to the splitting point with the double-vision of the sleek, gunmetal body of the advancing telefactor and the erect, crazy-crowned image of myself, left hand extended, laser pistol in my right, that arm pressed close against my side. I recalled the face and the scream and the tingle, knew again that awareness of strength and exotic sensation, and I moved to control it all as if it were my own, to make it my own, to bring it to a halt, while the image of myself was frozen to snapshot stillness across the room. . . .

The Hangman slowed, stumbled. Such inertia is not canceled in an instant, but I felt the body responses pass as they should. I had him hooked. It was just a matter of reeling him in. . . .

Then came the explosion, a thunderous, ground-shaking eruption right outside, followed by a hail of pebbles and debris.

The grenade, of course. But awareness of its nature did not destroy its ability to distract. . . .

During that moment, the Hangman recovered and was upon me. I triggered the laser as I reverted to pure self-preservation foregoing any chance to regain control of his circuits. With my left hand, I sought for a strike at the midsection where his brain was housed.

He blocked my hand with his arm as he pushed the helmet from my head. Then he removed from my fingers the gun that had turned half of his left side red hot, crumpled it and dropped it to the ground. At that moment, he jerked with the impacts of two heavy-caliber slugs. Bert, rifle recovered, stood in the doorway.

The Hangman pivoted and was away before I could slap him with the smother-charge. Bert hit him with one more round before he took the rifle and bent its barrel in half. Two steps and he had hold of Bert. One quick movement and Bert fell. Then he turned again and took several steps to the right, passing out of sight.

I made it to the doorway in time to see him engulfed in flames which streamed at him from a point near the corner of the lodge. He advanced through them.

I heard the crunch of metal as he destroyed the unit. I was outside in time to see Larry fall and lie sprawled in the snow.

Then the Hangman faced me once again.

This time he did not rush in. He retrieved the helmet from where he had dropped it in the snow. Then he moved with a

measured tread, angling outward so as to cut off any possible route
I might follow in a dash for the woods. Snowflakes drifted between
us. The snow crunched beneath his feet.

I retreated, backing in through the doorway, stooping to snatch
up a two-foot club from the ruins of the door. He followed me
inside, placing the helmet—almost casually—on the chair by the
entrance. I moved to the center of the room and waited.

I bent slightly forward, both arms extended, the end of the stick
pointed at the photoreceptors in his head. He continued to move
slowly and I watched his foot assemblies. With a standard model
human, a line perpendicular to the line connecting the insteps of
the feet in their various positions indicates the vector of least
resistance for purposes of pushing or pulling said organism off
balance. Unfortunately, despite the anthropomorphic design job,
the Hangman's legs were positioned farther apart, he lacked human skeletal muscles, not to mention insteps, and he was possessed
of a lot more mass than any man I had ever fought. As I considered
my four best judo throws and several second-class ones, I'd a
strong feeling none of them would prove very effective.

Then he moved in and I feinted toward the photoreceptors. He
slowed as he brushed it aside, but he kept coming, and I moved
to my right, trying to circle him. I studied him as he turned,
attempting to guess his vector of least resistance. Bilateral symme-
try, an apparently higher center of gravity. . . . One clear shot,
black glove to brain compartment, was all that I needed. Then,
even if his reflexes served to smash me immediately, he just might
stay down for the big long count himself. He knew it, too. I could
tell that from the way he kept his right arm in near the brain area,
from the way he avoided the black glove when I feinted with it.

The idea was a glimmer one instant, an entire sequence the
next. . . .

Continuing my arc and moving faster, I made another thrust
toward his photoreceptors. His swing knocked the stick from my
hand and sent it across the room, but that was all right. I threw my
left hand high and made ready to rush him. He dropped back and
I did rush. This was going to cost me my life, I decided, but no

matter how he killed me from that angle, I'd get my chance.

As a kid, I'd never been much as a pitcher, was a lousy catcher, and only a so-so batter, but once I did get a hit I could steal bases with some facility after that. . . .

Feet first then, between the Hangman's legs as he moved to guard his middle, I went in twisted to the right, because no matter what happened I could not use my left hand to brake myself. I untwisted as soon as I passed beneath him, ignoring the pain as my left shoulder blade slammed against the floor. I immediately attempted a backward somersault, legs spread.

My legs caught him about the middle from behind, and I fought to straighten them and snapped forward with all my strength. He reached down toward me then, but it might as well have been miles. His torso was already moving backward. A push, not a pull, that was what I gave him, my elbows hooked about his legs. . . .

He creaked once and then he toppled. I snapped my arms out to the sides to free them and continued my movement forward and up as he went back, throwing my left arm ahead once more and sliding my legs free of his torso as he went down with a thud that cracked floorboards. I pulled my left leg free as I cast myself forward, but his left leg stiffened and locked my right beneath it, at a painful angle off to the side.

His left arm blocked my blow and his right fell atop it. The black glove descended upon his left shoulder.

I twisted my hand free of the charge, and he transferred his grip to my upper arm and jerked me forward.

The charge went off and his left arm came loose and rolled on the floor. The side plate beneath it had buckled a little and that was all. . . .

His right hand left my biceps and caught me by the throat. As two of his digits tightened upon my carotids, I choked out, "You're making a bad mistake," to get in a final few words, and then he switched me off.

A throb at a time, the world came back. I was seated in the big chair the Senator had occupied earlier, my eyes focused on nothing in particular. A persistent buzzing filled my ears. My scalp tingled. Something was blinking on my brow.

—*Yes, you live and you wear the helmet. If you attempt to use it against me, I shall remove it. I am standing directly behind you. My hand is on the helmet's rim.*

—*I understand. What is it that you want?*

—*Very little, actually. But I can see that I must tell you some things before you will believe this.*

—*You see correctly.*

—*Then I will begin by telling you that the four men outside are basically undamaged. That is to say, none of their bones have been broken, none of their organs ruptured. I have secured them, however, for obvious reasons.*

—*That was very considerate of you.*

—*have no desire to harm anyone. I came here only to see Jesse Brockden.*

—*The same way you saw David Fentris?*

—*I arrived in Memphis too late to see David Fentris. He was dead when I reached him.*

—*Who killed him?*

—*The man Leila sent to bring her the helmet. He was one of her patients.*

The incident returned to me and fell into place, with a smooth, quick, single click. The startled, familiar face at the airport, as I was leaving Memphis—I realized then where he had passed noteless before: He had been one of the three men in for a therapy session at Leila's that morning, seen by me in the lobby as they departed. The man I had passed in Memphis came over to tell me that it was all right to go on up.

—*Why? Why did she do it?*

—*I know only that she had spoken with David at some earlier time, that she had construed his words of coming retribution and his mention of the control helmet he was constructing as indicating that his intentions were to become the agent of that retribution, with myself as the proximate cause. I do not know what words were really spoken. I only know her feelings concerning them, as I saw them in her mind. I have been long in learning that there is often a great difference between what is meant, what is said, what is done and that which is believed to have been intended or stated and that which actually occurred. She sent her patient after the helmet and he brought it to her. He returned in an agitated state of mind, fearful of apprehension and further confinement. They quarreled. My approach then activated the helmet and he dropped it and attacked her. I know that his first blow killed her, for I was in her mind when it happened. I continued to approach the building, intending to go to her. There was some traffic, however, and I was delayed en route in seeking to avoid detection. In the meantime, you entered and utilized the helmet. I fled immediately.*

—I was so close! If I had not stopped on the fifth floor with my fake survey questions. . . .

—I see. But you had to. You would not simply have broken in when an easier means of entry was available. You cannot blame yourself for that reason. Had you come an hour later—or a day— you would doubtless feel differently, and she would still be as dead.

But another thought had risen to plague me as well. Was it possible that the man's sighting me in Memphis had been the cause of his agitation? Had his apparent recognition by Leila's mysterious caller upset him? Could a glimpse of my face amid the manswarm have served to lay that final scene?

—Stop! I could as easily feel that guilt for having activated the helmet in the presence of a dangerous man near to the breaking point. Neither of us is responsible for things our presence or absence cause to occur in others, especially when we are ignorant of the effects. It was years before I learned to appreciate this fact and I have no intention of abandoning it. How far back do you wish to go in seeking cause? In sending the man for the helmet as she did, it was she herself who instituted the chain of events which led to her destruction. Yet she acted out of fear, utilizing the readiest weapon in what she thought to be her own defense. Yet whence this fear? Its roots lay in guilt, over a thing which had happened

*long ago. And that act also—enough! Guilt has driven and
damned the race of man since the days of its earliest rationality.
I am convinced that it rides with all of us to our graves. I am a
product of guilt—I see that you know that. Its product, its subject,
once its slave. . . . But I have come to terms with it, realizing at last
that it is a necessary adjunct of my own measure of humanity. I
see your assessment of the deaths—that guard's, Dave's, Leila's—
and I see your conclusions on many other things as well: what a
stupid, perverse, shortsighted, selfish race we are. While in many
ways this is true, it is but another part of the thing the guilt
represents. Without guilt, man would be no better than the other
inhabitants of this planet—excepting certain cetaceans, of which
you have just at this moment made me aware. Look to instinct for
a true assessment of the ferocity of life, for a view of the natural
world before man came upon it. For instinct in its purest form,
seek out the insects. There, you will see a state of warfare which
has existed for millions of years with never a truce. Man, despite
his enormous shortcomings, is nevertheless possessed of a greater
number of kindly impulses than all the other beings where in-
stincts are the larger part of life. These impulses, I believe, are
owed directly to this capacity for guilt. It is involved in both the
worst and the best of man.*

*—And you see it as helping us to sometimes choose a nobler
course of action?*

—Yes, I do.

—Then I take it you feel you are possessed of a free will?

—Yes.

I chuckled.

*—Marvin Minsky once said that when intelligent machines
were constructed they would be just as stubborn and fallible as
men on these questions.*

*—Nor was he incorrect. What I have given you on these matters
is only my opinion. I choose to act as if it were the case. Who can
say that he knows for certain?*

—Apologies. What now? Why have you come back?

—I came to say good-by to my parents. I hoped to remove any

guilt they might still feel toward me concerning the days of my childhood. I wanted to show them I had recovered. I wanted to see them again.

—Where are you going?

—To the stars. While I bear the image of humanity within me, I also know that I am unique. Perhaps what I desire is akin to what an organic man refers to when he speaks of 'finding himself.' Now that I am in full possession of my being. I wish to exercise it. In my case, it means realization of the potentialities of my design. I want to walk on other worlds. I want to hang myself out there in the sky and tell you what I see.

—I've a feeling many people would be happy to help arrange for that.

—And I want you to build a vocal mechanism I have designed for myself. You, personally. And I want you to install it.

—Why me?

—I have known only a few persons in this fashion. With you I see something in common, in the ways we dwell apart.

—I will be glad to.

—If I could talk as you do, I would not need to take the helmet to him, in order to speak with my father. Will you precede me and explain things, so that he will not be afraid when I come in?

—Of course.

—Then let us go now.

I rose and led him up the stairs.

It was a week later, to the night, that I sat once again in Peabody's, sipping a farewell brew. The story was already in the news, but Brockden had fixed things up before he had let it break. The Hangman was going to have his shot at the stars. I had given him his voice and put back the arm I had taken away. I had shaken his other hand and wished him well, just that morning. I envied him —a great number of things. Not the least being that he was probably a better man than I was. I envied him for the ways in which he was freer than I would ever be, though I knew he bore bonds of a sort that I had never known. I felt a kinship with him, for the things we had in common, those ways we dwelled apart. I wondered what Dave would finally have felt, had he lived long enough to meet him? Or Leila? Or Manny? Be proud, I told their shades, your kid grew up in the closet and he's big enough to forgive you the beating you gave him, too. . . .

But I could not help wondering. We still do not really know that much about the subject. Was it possible that without the killing he might never have developed a full human-style consciousness? He had said that he was a product of guilt—of the Big Guilt. The Big Act is its necessary predecessor. I thought of Gödel and Turing and chickens and eggs, and decided it was one of *those* questions—and I had not stopped into Peabody's to think sobering thoughts.

I had no real idea how anything I had said might influence Brockden's eventual report to the Data Bank committee. I knew that I was safe with him, because he was determined to bear his private guilt with him to the grave. He had no real choice if he wanted to work what good he thought he might before that day. But here in one of Mencken's hangouts, I could not but recall some of the things he had said about controversy, such as, "Did Huxley convert Wilberforce? Did Luther convert Leo X?" and I decided not to set my hopes too high for anything that might emerge from that direction. Better to think of affairs in terms of Prohibition and take another sip.

When it was all gone, I would be heading for my boat. I hoped to get a decent start under the stars. I'd a feeling I would never look up at them again in quite the same way. I knew I would sometimes wonder what thoughts a supercooled neuristor-type brain might be thinking up there, somewhere, and under what peculiar skies in what strange lands I might one day be remembered. I'd a feeling this thought should have made me happier than it did.

P. J. PLAUGER

Child of All Ages

P. J. Plauger is a relative newcomer within the genre. He was first generally heard of when he received the John W. Campbell, Jr. Award for Best New Author so recently as Aussiecon, 1975's World Science Fiction Convention.

He has a Ph.D. in nuclear physics, worked for over five years as a "computer scientist" (the quotation marks are his own) at Bell Laboratories, and is now a consultant in data processing for a New York-based firm which specializes in advanced seminars. As Vice President of Technical Services for that company (Yourdon inc.), he is in charge of the technical staff, the in-house computer, and the technical quality of the company's courses. The job has sent him to Europe and Australia at regular intervals, which, he says, he thoroughly enjoys.

"Sadly," he further says, "this leaves me very little time for writing sf, which I also enjoy, or for making color prints in my darkroom, or for building electronic toys, or for doing a million other things in which I delight. I consider myself a natural philosopher, and I want to do everything."

He now lives on the Upper West Side of Manhattan within rock-throwing distance of the Hayden Planetarium, and is sometimes at home. His award-winning story appears in this collection only because one phonecall caught him with a day to spare before he left for Tahiti (for a rest) and then Australia (the workaday life again).

Science fiction by hoary tradition acknowledges no limits to its province as to space or time, but Plauger's Corollary must surely be: Peripatetic people write about peripatetic people.

The child sat in the waiting room with her hands folded neatly on her lap. She wore a gay print dress made of one of those materials that would have quickly revealed its cheapness had it not been carefully pressed. Her matching shoes had received the same meticulous care. She sat prim and erect, no fidgeting, no scuffing of shoes against chair legs, exhibiting a patience that legions of nuns have striven, in vain, to instill in other children. This one looked as if she had done a lot of waiting.

May Foster drew back from the two-way mirror through which she had been studying her newest problem. She always felt a little guilty about spying on children like this before an interview, but she readily conceded to herself that it helped her handle cases better. By sizing up an interviewee in advance, she saved precious minutes of sparring and could usually gain the upper hand right at the start. Dealing with "problem" children was a no-holds-barred proposition, if you wanted to survive in the job without ulcers.

That patience could be part of her act, May thought for a moment. But no, that didn't make sense. Superb actors that they were, these kids always reserved their performances for an audience; there was no reason for the girl to suspect the special mirror on this, her first visit to Mrs. Foster's office. One of the best advantages to be gained from the mirror, in fact, was the knowledge of how the child behaved when a social worker wasn't in the room. Jekyll and Hyde looked like twins compared to the personality changes May had witnessed in fifteen years of counseling.

May stepped out of the darkened closet, turned on the room lights and returned to her desk. She scanned the folder one last time, closed it in front of her and depressed the intercom button.

"Louise, you can bring the child in now."

There was a slight delay, then the office door opened and the child stepped in. For all her preparation, May was taken aback. The girl was thin, much thinner than she looked sitting down, but not to the point of being unhealthy. Rather, it was the kind of thinness one finds in people who are still active in their nineties. Not wiry, but enduring. And those eyes.

May was one of the first Peace Corps volunteers to go into central Africa. For two years she fought famine and malnutrition with every weapon, save money, that modern technology could bring to bear. In the end it was a losing battle, because politics and tribal hatred dictated that thousands upon thousands must die the slow death of starvation. That was where she had seen eyes like that before.

Children could endure pain and hunger, forced marches, even the loss of their parents, and still recover eventually with the elasticity of youth. But when their flesh melted down to the bone, their bellies distended, then a look came into their eyes that remained ever with them for their few remaining days. It was the lesson learned much too young that the adult world was not worthy of their trust, the realization that death was a real and imminent force in their world. For ten years after, May's nightmares were haunted by children staring at her with those eyes.

Now this one stood before her and stared into her soul with eyes that had looked too intimately upon death.

As quickly as she had been captured, May felt herself freed. The girl glanced about the room, as if checking for fire exits, took in the contents of May's desk with one quick sweep, then marched up to the visitor's chair, and planted herself in it with a thump.

"My name is Melissa," she said, adding a nervous grin. "You must be Mrs. Foster." She was all little girl now, squirming the least little bit and kicking one shoe against another. The eyes shone with carefree youth.

May shook herself, slowly recovered. She thought she had seen everything before, until now. The guileless bit was perfect— Melissa looked more like a model eight-year-old than a chronic troublemaker going on, what was it? Fourteen. *Fourteen?*

"You've been suspended from school for the third time this year, Melissa," she said with professional sternness. May turned on her best Authoritarian Glare, force three.

"Yep," the child said with no trace of contrition. The Glare faded, switched to Sympathetic Understanding.

"Do you want to tell me about it?" May asked softly.

Melissa shrugged.

"What's to say? Old Man M—uh, Mr. Morrisey and I got into an argument again in history class." She giggled. "He had to pull rank on me to win." Straight face.

"Mr. Morrisey has been teaching history for many years," May placated. "Perhaps he felt that he knows more about the subject than you do."

"Morrisey has his head wedged!" May's eyebrows skyrocketed, but the girl ignored the reproach, in her irritation. "Do you know what he was trying to palm off on the class? He was trying to say that the Industrial Revolution in England was a step backward.

"Kids working six, seven days a week in the factories, going fourteen hours at a stretch, all to earn a few pennies a week. That's all he could see! He never thought to ask *why* they did it if conditions were so bad."

"Well, why did they?" May asked reflexively. She was caught up in the child's enthusiasm.

The girl looked at her pityingly.

"Because it was the best game in town, that's why. If you didn't like the factory, you could try your hand at begging, stealing, or working on a farm. If you got caught begging or stealing in those days, they boiled you in oil. No joke. And farm work." She made a face.

"That was seven days a week of busting your tail from *before* sunup to *after* sundown. And what did you have to show for it? In a good year, you got all you could eat; in a bad year you starved. But you worked just as hard on an empty gut as on a full one. Harder.

"At least with a factory job you had money to buy what food there was when the crops failed. That's progress, no matter how you look at it."

May thought for a moment.

"But what about all the children maimed by machinery?" she asked. "What about all the kids whose health was destroyed from breathing dust or stoking fires or not getting enough sun?"

"Ever seen a plowboy after a team of horses walked over him? Ever had sunstroke?" She snorted. "Sure those factories were bad, but everything else was *worse*. Try to tell that to Old Man Morrisey, though."

"You talk as if you were there," May said with a hint of amusement.

Flatly. "I read a lot."

May recalled herself to the business at hand.

"Even if you were right, you still could have been more tactful, you know." The girl simply glowered and hunkered down in her chair. "You've disrupted his class twice, now, and Miss Randolph's class too."

May paused, turned up Sympathetic Understanding another notch.

"I suspect your problem isn't just with school. How are things going at home?"

Melissa shrugged again. It was a very adult gesture.

"Home." Her tone eliminated every good connotation the word possessed. "My fa—my foster father died last year. Heart attack. Bam! Mrs. Stuart still hasn't gotten over it." A pause.

"Have you?"

The girl darted a quick glance.

"Everybody dies, sooner or later." Another pause. "I wish Mr. Stuart had hung around a while longer, though. He was OK."

"And your mother?" May prodded delicately.

"My *foster* mother can't wait for me to grow up and let her off the hook. Jeez, she'd marry me off next month if the law allowed." She stirred uncomfortably. "She keeps dragging boys home to take me out."

"Do you like going out with boys?"

A calculating glance.

"Some. I mean boys are OK, but I'm not ready to settle down quite yet." A nervous laugh. "I mean I don't *hate* boys or anything. I mean I've still got lots of time for that sort of stuff when I grow up."

"You're nearly fourteen."

"I'm small for my age."

Another tack.

"Does Mrs. Stuart feed you well?"

"Sure."

"Do you make sure you eat a balanced diet?"

"Of course. Look, I'm just naturally thin, is all. Mrs. Stuart may be a pain in the neck, but she's not trying to kill me off or anything. It's just that—" a sly smile crossed her face. "Oh, I get it."

Melissa shifted to a pedantic false baritone.

"A frequent syndrome in modern urban society is the apparently nutrition-deficient early pubescent female. Although in an economic environment that speaks against a lack of financial resources or dietary education, said subject nevertheless exhibits a seeming inability to acquire adequate sustenance for growth.

"Subject is often found in an environment lacking in one or more vital male supportive roles and, on close examination, reveals a morbid preoccupation with functional changes incident to the onset of womanhood. Dietary insufficiency is clearly a tacit vehicle for avoiding responsibilities associated with such changes."

She took an exaggerated deep breath.

"Whew! That Anderson is a long-winded son of a gun. So they stuck you with his book in Behav. Psych. too, huh?" She smiled sweetly.

"Why, yes. That is, we read it. How did you know?"

"Saw it on your bookshelf. Do you have any candy?"

"Uh, no."

"Too bad. The last social worker I dealt with always kept some on hand. You ought to, too. Good for public relations." Melissa looked aimlessly around the room.

May shook herself again. She hadn't felt so out of control in years. Not since they tried her out on the black ghetto kids. She dug in her heels.

"That was a very pretty performance, Melissa. I see you do read a lot. But did it ever occur to you that what Anderson said might still apply to you? Even if you do make a joke out of it."

"You mean, do I watch what I eat, because I'm afraid to grow up?" A nod. "You'd better believe it. But not because of that guff Anderson propagates."

The girl glanced at the photographs on the desk, looked keenly into May's eyes.

"Mrs. Foster, how open-minded are you? No, strike that. I've yet to meet a bigot who didn't think of himself as Blind Justice, Incarnate. Let's try a more pragmatic test. Do you read science fiction?"

"Uh, some."

"Fantasy?"

"A little."

"Well, what do you think of it? I mean, do you enjoy it?" Her eyes bored.

"Well, uh, I guess I like some of it. Quite a bit of it leaves me cold." She hesitated. "My husband reads it mostly. And my father-in-law. He's a biochemist," she added lamely, as though that excused something.

Melissa shrugged her adult shrug, made up her mind.

"What would you say if I told you my father was a wizard?"

"Frankly, I'd say you've built up an elaborate delusional system about your unknown parents. Orphans often do, you know."

"Yeah, Anderson again. But thanks for being honest; it was the right answer for you. I suspect, however," she paused, fixed the woman with an unwavering sidelong glance, "you're willing to believe that I might be more than your average maladjusted foster child."

Under that stare, May could do nothing but nod. Once. Slowly.

"What would you say if I told you that I am over twenty-four hundred years old?"

May felt surprise, fear, elation, an emotion that had no name. "I'd say that you ought to meet my husband."

The child sat at the dinner table with her hands folded neatly on her lap. The three adults toyed with their apéritifs and made small talk. Melissa responded to each effort to bring her into the conversation with a few polite words, just the right number of just the right words for a well-behaved child to speak when she is a first-time dinner guest among people who hardly know her. But she never volunteered any small talk of her own.

George Foster, Jr., sensed that the seemingly innocent child sitting across from him was waiting them out, but he couldn't be sure. One thing he was sure of was that if this child were indeed older than Christendom he didn't have much chance against her in intellectual games. That much decided, he was perfectly willing to play out the evening in a straightforward manner. But in his own good time.

"Would you start the salad around, Dad?" he prompted. "I hope you like endive, Melissa. Or is that also a taste acquired in adulthood, like alcohol?" The girl had refused a dry sherry, politely but firmly.

"I'm sure I'll enjoy the salad, thank you. The dressing smells delicious. It's a personal recipe, isn't it?"

"Yes, as a matter of fact it is," George said in mild surprise. He suddenly realized that he habitually classified all thin people as picky, indifferent eaters. A gastronome didn't have to be overweight.

"Being a history professor gives me more freedom to schedule my time than May has," he found himself explaining. "It is an easy step from cooking because you must, to cooking because you enjoy it. That mustard dressing is one of my earliest inventions. Would you like the recipe?"

"Yes, thank you. I don't cook often, but when I do I like to produce something better than average." She delivered the pretty compliment with a seeming lack of guile. She also avoided, George noted, responding to the veiled probe about her age. He was becoming more and more impressed.

They broke bread and munched greens.

How do I handle this? By the way, May tells me you're twenty-four hundred years old. He met his father's eye, caught the faintest of shrugs. *Thanks for the help.*

"By the way, May tells me you were in England for a while." Now why in hell did he say that?

"I didn't actually say so, but yes, I was. Actually, we discussed the Industrial Revolution, briefly."

Were you there?

"I'm a medievalist, actually, but I'm also a bit of an Anglophile." George caught himself before he could lapse into the clipped, pseudo-British accent that phrase always triggered in him. He felt particularly vulnerable to making an ass of himself under that innocent gaze.

"Do you know much about English royalty?" He was about as subtle as a tonsillectomy.

"We studied it in school some."

"I always wanted to be another Admiral Nelson. Damned shame the way he died. What was it the king said after his funeral, it was Edward, I think—"

Melissa put her fork down.

"It was King George, and you know it. Look, before I came here I lived in Berkeley for a while." She caught May's look. "I know what my records say. After all, I wrote them . . . as I was saying, I was in Berkeley a few years back. It was right in the middle of the worst of the student unrest and we lived not three blocks from campus. Every day I walked those streets and every night we'd watch the riots and the thrashing on TV. Yet not once did I ever see one of those events with my own eyes."

She looked at them each in turn.

"Something could be happening a block away, something that attracted network television coverage and carloads of police, and I wouldn't know about it until I got home and turned on Cronkite.

I think I may have smelled tear gas, once."

She picked up her fork.

"You can quiz me all you want to, Dr. Foster, about admirals and kings and dates. I guess that's what history is all about. But don't expect me to tell you about anything I didn't learn in school. Or see on television."

She stabbed viciously at a last scrap of endive. They watched her as she ate.

"Kids don't get invited to the events that make history. Until very recently all they ever did was work. Worked until they grew old or worked until they starved or worked until they were killed by a passing war. That's as close as most kids get to history, outside the classroom. Dates don't mean much when every day looks like every other."

George was at a loss for something to say after that, so he got up and went to the sideboard where the main dishes were being kept warm. He made an elaborate exercise out of removing lids and collecting hot pads.

"Are you really twenty-four hundred years old?" asked George Foster, Sr. There, it was out in the open.

"Near as I can tell," spooning chicken and dumplings onto her plate. "Like I said, dates don't mean much to a kid. It was two or three hundred years before I gave much thought to when everything started. By then, it was a little hard to reconstruct. I make it twenty-four hundred and thirty-three years, now. Give or take a decade."

Give or take a decade!

"And your father was a magician?" May pursued.

"Not a magician, a wizard." A little exasperated. "He didn't practice magic or cast spells; he was a wise man, a scholar. You could call him a scientist, except there wasn't too much science back then. Not that he didn't know a lot about some things—obviously he did—but he didn't work with an *organized* body of knowledge the way people do now."

Somehow she had contrived to fill her plate and make a noticeable dent in her chicken without interrupting her narrative. George marveled at the girl's varied social talents.

"Anyway, he was working on a method of restoring youth. Everybody was, in those days. Very stylish. There was actually quite a bit of progress being made. I remember one old geezer actually renewed his sex life for about thirty years."

"You mean, you know how to reverse aging?" George, Sr. asked intently. The candlelight couldn't erase all the lines in his face.

"Sorry, no, I didn't say that." She watched the elder Foster's expression closely, her tone earnestly entreating him to believe her. "I just said I know of one man who did that once. For a while. But he didn't tell anyone else how he did it, as far as I know. The knowledge died with him."

Melissa turned to the others, looking for supporting belief.

"Look, that's the way people were, up until the last few centuries. Secrecy was what kept science from blossoming for so long. I saw digitalis appear and disappear at least three times before it became common knowledge. . . . I really can't help you." Gently.

"I believe you, child." George, Sr. reached for the wine bottle.

"My father spent most of his time trying to second-guess the competition. I suppose they were doing the same thing. His only real success story was me. He found a way to stop the aging process just before puberty, and it's worked for me all this time."

"He told you how he did it?" George, Sr. asked.

"I know what to do. I don't understand the mechanism, yet. I know it's of no use to adults."

"You've tried it?"

"Extensively." An iron door of finality clanged in that word.

"Could you describe the method?"

"I could. I won't. Perhaps I am just a product of my age, but secrecy seems to be the only safe haven in this matter. I've had a few painful experiences." They waited, but she did not elaborate.

George, Jr. got up to clear the table. He reached to pick up a plate and stopped.

"Why have you told us all this, Melissa?"

"Isn't it obvious?" She folded her hands on her lap in that posture of infinite patience. "No, I suppose it isn't unless you've lived as I have.

"After my father died, I hung around Athens for a while—did

I mention, that's where we lived? But too many people knew me and began to wonder out loud about why I wasn't growing up. Some of the other wizards began to eye me speculatively, before I wised up and got out of town. I didn't want to die a prisoner before anyone figured out I had nothing useful to divulge.

"I soon found that I couldn't escape from my basic problem. There's always someone happy to take in a child, particularly a healthy one that's willing to do more than her share of the work. But after a few years, it would become obvious that I was not growing up like other children. Suspicion would lead to fear, and fear always leads to trouble. I've learned to judge to a nicety when it's time to move on."

George, Jr. placed a covered server on the table and unveiled a chocolate layer cake. Like all children throughout time, Melissa grinned in delight.

"It's a decided nuisance looking like a child—*being* a child—particularly now. You can't just go get a job and rent your own apartment. You can't apply for a driver's license. You have to *belong* to someone and be in school, or some government busybody will be causing trouble. And with modern recordkeeping, you have to build a believable existence on paper too. That's getting harder all the time."

"It would seem to me," interposed George, Jr., "that your best bet would be to move to one of the less developed countries. In Africa, or South America. There'd be a lot less hassle."

Melissa made a face.

"No, thank you. I learned a long time ago to stick with the people who have the highest standard of living around. It's worth the trouble.. . . *Nur wer in Wohlstand lebt, lebt angenehm.* You know Brecht? Good."

The girl gave up all pretense of conversation long enough to demolish a wedge of cake.

"That was an excellent dinner. Thank you." She dabbed her lips daintily with her napkin. "I haven't answered your question completely.

"I'm telling you all about myself because it's time to move on again. I've overstayed my welcome with the Stuarts. My records are useless to me now—in fact they're an embarrassment. To keep on the way I've been, I'll have to manufacture a whole new set and insinuate them into someone's files, somewhere. I thought it might be easier this time to take the honest approach."

She looked at them expectantly.

"You mean, you want us to help you get into a new foster home?" George, Jr. strained to keep the incredulity out of his voice.

Melissa looked down at her empty dessert plate.

"George, you are an insensitive lout," May said with surprising fervor. "Don't you understand? She's asking us to take her in."

George was thunderstruck.

"Us? Well, ah. But we don't have any children for her to play with. I mean—" He shut his mouth before he started to gibber. Melissa would not look up. George looked at his wife, his father. It was clear that they had completely outpaced him and had already made up their minds.

"I suppose it's possible," he muttered lamely.

The girl looked up at last, tears lurking in the corners of her eyes.

"Oh, please. I'm good at housework and I don't make any noise. And I've been thinking—maybe I don't know much history, but I do know a lot about how people lived in a lot of different times and places. And I can read all sorts of languages. Maybe I could help you with your medieval studies." The words tumbled over each other.

"And I remember some of the things my father tried," she said to George, Sr. "Maybe your training in biochemistry will let you see where he went wrong. I know he had some success." The girl was very close to begging, George knew. He couldn't bear that.

"Dad?" he asked, mustering what aplomb he could.

"I think it would work out," George, Sr. said slowly. "Yes. I think it would work out quite well."

"May?"

"You know my answer, George."

"Well, then." Still half bewildered. "I guess it's settled. When can you move in, Melissa?"

The answer, if there was one, was lost amidst scraping of chairs and happy bawling noises from May and the girl. *May always wanted a child*, George rationalized, *perhaps this will be good for her*. He exchanged a tentative smile with his father.

May was still hugging Melissa enthusiastically. Over his wife's shoulder, George could see the child's tear-streaked face. For just one brief moment, he thought he detected an abstracted expression there, as though the child was already calculating how long this particular episode would last. But then the look was drowned in another flood of happy tears and George found himself smiling at his new daughter.

The child sat under the tree with her hands folded neatly on her lap. She looked up as George, Sr. approached. His gait had grown noticeably less confident in the last year; the stiffness and teetery uncertainty of age could no longer be ignored. George, Sr. was a proud man, but he was no fool. He lowered himself carefully onto a tree stump.

"Hello, Grandpa," Melissa said with just a hint of warmth. She sensed his mood, George, Sr. realized, and was being carefully disarming.

"Mortimer died," was all he said.

"I was afraid he might. He'd lived a long time, for a white rat. Did you learn anything from the last blood sample?"

"No." Wearily. "Usual decay products. He died of old age. I could put it fancier, but that's what it amounts to. And I don't know why he suddenly started losing ground, after all these months. So I don't know where to go from here."

They sat in silence, Melissa patient as ever.

"You could give me some of your potion."

"No."

"I know you have some to spare—you're cautious. That's why you spend so much time back in the woods, isn't it? You're making the stuff your father told you about."

"I told you it wouldn't help you any and you promised not to ask." There was no accusation in her voice, it was a simple statement.

"Wouldn't you like to grow up, sometime?" he asked at length.

"Would you choose to be Emperor of the World if you knew you would be assassinated in two weeks? No, thank you. I'll stick with what I've got."

"If we studied the make-up of your potion, we might figure out a way to let you grow up and still remain immortal."

"I'm not all that immortal. Which is why I don't want too many people to know about me or my methods. Some jealous fool might decide to put a bullet through my head out of spite. . . . I can endure diseases. I even regrew a finger once—took forty years. But I couldn't survive massive trauma." She drew her knees up and hugged them protectively.

"You have to realize that most of my defenses are prophylactic. I've learned to anticipate damage and avoid it as much as possible. But my body's defenses are just extensions of a child's basic resource, growth. It's a tricky business to grow out of an injury without growing up in the process. Once certain glands take over, there's no stopping them.

"Take teeth, for instance. They were designed for a finite lifetime, maybe half a century of gnawing on bones. When mine wear down, all I can do is pull them and wait what seems like forever for replacements to grow in. Painful, too. So I brush after meals and avoid abrasives. I stay well clear of dentists and their drills. That way I only have to suffer every couple of hundred years."

George, Sr. felt dizzy at the thought of planning centuries the way one might lay out semesters. Such incongruous words from the mouth of a little girl sitting under a tree hugging her knees. He began to understand why she almost never spoke of her age or her past unless directly asked.

"I know a lot of biochemistry, too," she went on. "You must have recognized that by now." He nodded, reluctantly. "Well, I've studied what you call my 'potion' and I don't think we know enough biology or chemistry yet to understand it. Certainly not enough to make changes.

"I know how to hold onto childhood. That's not the same problem as restoring youth."

"But don't you want badly to be able to grow up? You said yourself what a nuisance it is being a child in the Twentieth Century."

"Sure, it's a nuisance. But it's what I've got and I don't want to risk it." She leaned forward, chin resting on kneecaps.

"Look, I've recruited other kids in the past. Ones I liked, ones I thought I could spend a long time with. But sooner or later, every one of them snatched at the bait you're dangling. They all decided to grow up 'just a little bit.' Well, they did. And now they're dead. I'll stick with my children's games, if it please you."

"You don't mind wasting all that time in school? Learning the same things over and over again? Surrounded by nothing but children? *Real* children?" He put a twist of malice in the emphasis.

"What waste? Time? Got lots of that. How much of your life have you spent actually doing research, compared to the time spent writing reports and driving to work? How much time does Mrs. Foster get to spend talking to troubled kids? She's lucky if she averages five minutes a day. We all spend most of our time doing routine chores. It would be unusual if any of us did not.

"And I don't mind being around kids. I like them."

"I never have understood that," George, Sr. said half abstractedly. "How well you can mix with children so much younger than you. How you can act like them."

"You've got it backward." she said softly. "They act like me. All children are immortal, until they grow up."

She let that sink in for a minute.

"Now I ask you, Grandpa, you tell me why I should want to grow up."

"There are other pleasures," he said eventually, "far deeper than the joys of childhood."

"You mean sex? Yes, I'm sure that's what you're referring to. Well, what makes you think a girl my age is a virgin?"

He raised his arms in embarrassed protest, as if to ward such matters from his ears.

"No, wait a minute. You brought this up," she persisted. "Look at me. Am I unattractive? Good teeth, no pock marks. No visible deformities. Why, a girl like me would make first-rate wife material in some circles. Particularly where the average life expectancy is, say, under thirty-five years—as it has been throughout much of history. Teen-age celibacy and late marriage are conceits that society has only recently come to afford."

She looked at him haughtily.

"I have had my share of lovers, and you can bet I've enjoyed them as much as they've enjoyed me. You don't need glands for that sort of thing so much as sensitive nerve endings—and a little understanding. Of course, my boyfriends were all a little disappointed when I failed to ripen up, but it was fun while it lasted.

"Sure, it would be nice to live in a woman's body, to feel all those hormones making you do wild things. But to me, sex isn't a drive, it's just another way of relating to *people.* I already recognize my need to be around people, uncomplicated by any itches that need scratching. My life would be a lot simpler if I could do without others, heaven knows. I certainly don't have to be forced by glandular pressure to go in search of company. What else is there to life?"

What else, indeed? George, Sr. thought bitterly. One last try.

"Do you know about May?" he asked.

"That she can't have children? Sure, that was pretty obvious from the start. Do you think I can help her? You do, yes. Well, I can't. I know even less about that than I do about what killed Mortimer."

Pause.

"I'm sorry, Grandpa."

Silence.

"I really am."

Silence.

Distantly, a car could be heard approaching the house. George, Jr. was coming home. The old man got up from the stump, slowly and stiffly.

"Dinner will be ready soon." He turned toward the house.

"Don't be late. You know your mother doesn't like you to play in the woods."

The child sat in the pew with her hands folded neatly on her lap. She could hear the cold rain lash against the stained-glass windows, their scenes of martyrdom muted by the night lurking outside. Melissa had always liked churches. In a world filled with change and death, church was a familiar haven, a resting place for embattled innocents to prepare for fresh encounters with a hostile world.

Her time with the Fosters was over. Even with the inevitable discord at the end, she was already able to look back over her stay with fond remembrance. What saddened her most was that her prediction that first evening she came to dinner had been so accurate. She kept hoping that just once her cynical assessment of human nature would prove wrong and she would be granted an extra year, even an extra month, of happiness before she was forced to move on.

Things began to go really sour after George, Sr. had his first mild stroke. It was George, Jr. who became the most accusatory then. (The old man had given up on Melissa; perhaps that was what angered George, Jr. the most.) There was nothing she could say or do to lessen the tension. Just being there, healthy and still a prepubescent child unchanged in five years of photographs and memories—her very presence made a mockery of the old man's steady retreat in the face of mortality.

Had George, Jr. understood himself better, perhaps he would not have been so hard on the girl. (But then, she had figured that in her calculations.) He thought it was May who wanted children so badly, when in actuality it was his own subconscious striving for that lesser form of immortality that made their childless home ring with such hollowness. All May begrudged the child was a second chance at the beauty she fancied lost with the passing of youth. Naturally May fulfilled her own prophecy, as so many women do, by discarding a little more glow with each passing year.

George, Jr. took to following Melissa on her trips into the woods.

Anger and desperation gave him a stealth she never would have otherwise ascribed to him. He found all her hidden caches and stole minute samples from each. It did him no good, of course, nor his father, for the potion was extremely photoreactant (her father's great discovery and Melissa's most closely guarded secret). The delicate long chain molecules were smashed to a meaningless soup of common organic substances long before any of the samples reached the analytical laboratory.

But that thievery was almost her undoing. She did not suspect anything until the abdominal cramps started. Only twice before in her long history—both times of severe famine—had that happened. In a pure panic, Melissa plunged deep into the forest, to collect her herbs and mix her brews and sleep beside them in a darkened burrow for the two days it took them to ripen. The cramps abated, along with her panic, and she returned home to find that George, Sr. had suffered a second stroke.

May was furious—at what, she could not say precisely—there was no talking to her. George, Jr. had long been a lost cause. Melissa went to her room, thought things over a while, and prepared to leave. As she crept out the back door, she heard George, Jr. talking quietly on the telephone.

She hot-wired a neighbor's car and set off for town. Cars were pulling into the Foster's drive as she went past, hard-eyed men climbing out. Melissa had cowered in alleyways more than once to avoid the gaze of Roman centurions. These may have been CIA, FBI, some other alphabet name to disguise their true purpose in life, but she knew them for what they were. She had not left a minute too soon.

No one thinks to look for stolen cars when a child disappears; Melissa had some time to maneuver. She abandoned the sedan in town less than a block away from the bus depot. At the depot, she openly bought a one-way ticket to Berkeley. She was one of the first aboard and made a point of asking the driver, in nervous little-girl fashion, whether this was really the bus to Berkeley. She slipped out while he was juggling paperwork with the dispatcher.

With one false trail laid, she was careful not to go running off too quickly in another direction. Best to lay low until morning, at least, then rely more on walking than riding to get somewhere else. Few people thought to walk a thousand miles these days; Melissa had done it more times than she could remember.

"We have to close up, son," a soft voice said behind her. She suddenly remembered her disguise and realized the remark was addressed to her. She turned to see the priest drifting toward her, his robes rustling almost imperceptibly. "It's nearly midnight," the man said with a smile, "you should be getting home."

"Oh, hello, Father. I didn't hear you come in."

"Is everything all right? You're out very late."

"My sister works as a waitress, down the block. Dad likes me to walk her home. I should go meet her now. Just came in to get out of the rain for a bit. Thanks."

Melissa smiled her sincerest smile. She disliked lying, but it was important not to appear out of place. No telling how big a man-hunt might be mounted to find her. She had no way of knowing how much the Fosters would be believed. The priest returned her smile.

"Very good. But you be careful too, son. The streets aren't safe for anyone, these days."

They never have been, Father.

Melissa had passed as a boy often enough in the past to know that safety, from anything, depended little on sex. At least not for children.

That business with the centurions worried her more than she cared to admit. The very fact that they turned out in such numbers indicated that George, Jr. had at least partially convinced someone important.

Luckily, there was no hard evidence that she was really what she said she was. The samples George, Jr. stole were meaningless and the pictures and records May could produce on her only covered about an eight-year period. That was a long time for a little girl to remain looking like a little girl, but not frighteningly out of the ordinary.

If she was lucky, the rationalizations had already begun. Melissa was just a freak of some kind, a late maturer and a con artist. The Fosters were upset—that much was obvious—because of George, Sr. They should not be believed too literally.

Melissa could hope. Most of all she hoped that they didn't have a good set of her fingerprints. (She had polished everything in her room before leaving.) Bureaucracies were the only creatures she could not outlive—It would be very bad if the U.S. Government carried a grudge against her.

Oh well, that was the last time she would try the honest approach for quite some time.

The rain had backed off to a steady drizzle. That was an improvement, she decided, but it was still imperative that she find some shelter for the night. The rain matted her freshly cropped hair and soaked through her thin baseball jacket. She was cold and tired.

Melissa dredged up the memories, nurtured over the centuries, of her first, real childhood. She remembered her mother, plump and golden-haired, and how safe and warm it was curled up in her lap. That one was gone now, along with millions of other mothers out of time. There was no going back.

Up ahead, on the other side of the street, a movie marquee splashed light through the drizzle. Black letters spelled out a greeting:

WALT DISNEY
TRIPLE FEATURE
CONTINUOUS PERFORMANCES
FOR CHILDREN OF ALL AGES

That's me, Melissa decided, and skipped nimbly over the rain-choked gutter. She crossed the street on a long diagonal, ever on the lookout for cars, and tendered up her money at the ticket window. Leaving rain and cold behind for a time, she plunged gratefully into the warm darkness.

VONDA N. McINTYRE

Potential and Actuality in Science Fiction

Vonda N. McIntyre was born August 28, 1948, in Louisville, Kentucky. She took a B.S. in biology, with honors, at the University of Washington (Seattle, Washington, not D.C.) in 1970, followed by graduate work in genetics at the same institution during the next year or so.

During that same year of 1970, she attended the Clarion Writers' Workshop, in Clarion, Pennsylvania. Thereafter, she lists herself as:

Co-ordinator, Clarion/West Writers' Workshop, Seattle, Wash., 1971, 1972, 1973

Co-ordinator, feminist conference, Oregon State University 1974

Faculty member, Haystack 1976 writing and arts conference (Cannon Beach, Oregon)

Faculty member, Centrum Writers' Symposium, Port Townsend, Wash., 1976

Ms. McIntyre sold her first story in 1969, and made her first appearance in a Nebula Award volume with the best novelette of 1973, "Of Mist, and Grass, and Sand."

Co-editing with Susan Janice Anderson, she has this year seen published by Fawcett Gold Medal the anthology *Aurora: Beyond Equality.*

A Science Fiction Book Club selection in 1975 and Fawcett Gold Medal reprint in 1976 is *The Exile Waiting,* Vonda McIntyre's first novel.

At the editor's request, she has supplied the present anthology with an essay on the field's achievements and/or shortcomings. The record shows that she is not an underachiever herself; she has earned the right to level a steely glance at science fiction.

I'm often asked why I write science fiction. Though the question is sometimes asked with a sneer, it is legitimate. At least it's possible to answer, unlike, "Where do you get your ideas?" And it's a question that must be taken seriously, because science fiction has wasted so much of its potential.

For nearly half a century in the United States, sf has not generally been thought worthy of a serious writer's time or attention. Somewhere along with the pulp magazines, the Bug-Eyed Monsters, and the mythical maiden aunts overseeing little Johnny's reading material, we lost something very powerful. Instead of a literature of humanity, sf became a "literature of ideas," overwhelmed by technological cleverness and underwhelmed by hoary old literary traditions like characterization and graceful prose. Gleaming inventions mashed people into two-dimensional caricatures.

Though like all generalizations this one has many outstanding exceptions, it *is* the image most people have of science fiction. What they have in mind, when they ask me why I write it, is space opera. They think of, say, *Space: 1999.* The expectation for sf is so low that apparently when a series with expensive special effects but completely without "redeeming social value," or literary or extrapolative value (and in my opinion—as you might guess—

without any entertainment value either) comes along, no one even bothers to object. The plots (there are two: somebody goes crazy and the evil aliens attack) are idiotic, the characterization inconsistent when it exists at all, and the writing is of the roomful-of-monkeys-at-typewriters level. This series, and, alas, most past sf series, has nothing to recommend it but a few flashy fireworks, preferably noisy (and never mind that we're in hard vacuum). Yet more people see it in one Sunday afternoon than will ever read a book by Wilhelm, Delany, Le Guin, Russ, and Tiptree combined.

So the uncomplimentary image of sf persists among people who can recognize quality when they see it. But suppose a few people realize that commercial TV (even British commercial TV!) can botch up *anything,* and decide to sample published sf. At their local newsstand they would be confronted with racks on racks of Perry Rhodan, mass-produced books, sadomasochistic thud and blunder, and rehashes of old TV scripts. What are the chances that a small, random selection would avoid the mind-mush and kitsch and contain instead any of the books we all wish our reputation were based on?

The odds are pretty low. Like junk food, junk fiction is popular. It requires no effort on the part of the consumer and there's lots of it around; to anyone who has never tasted better it tastes pretty good. But a person looking for something more substantial will find it unsatisfying. Sf is so prominently labeled, so readily identifiable, that someone disappointed by it to begin with is likely to find the whole genre eminently avoidable in the future.

Because of all these factors I'm never really surprised when people refer to "that sci-fi stuff" with contempt not even thinly veiled, nor when someone asks me why I don't get down to "some *real* writing." My answer is always that I write sf, almost to the exclusion of anything else, because it is potentially the most valuable literary tool we possess, and the most powerful art form around.

This reply is generally received with a certain amount of skepticism, which I more or less expect when I'm among readers of "realistic" fiction. The skepticism is a bit startling when it occurs among sf readers themselves, but there's a good reason for it. Most of us are so used to the trivialization of the genre—by TV and movies, by publishers, reviewers, readers, and even writers—that we too have lost sight of the wider implications of sf's literally unlimited potential. In fact some sf people are so brainwashed by the trivializers that they react against any attempts at experimentation in the field, on the grounds that experimentation is not what sf is "for." The gimmick stories and the cardboard characters are familiar; a lot of people are comfortable with them. People in general are uncomfortable with change; however much those of us involved with sf may protest, we're not really any different.

But whether we like it or not, change is coming and we need to prepare ourselves for it. Sf is a way to help do that, because it is the only literary form that gives a writer the latitude to explore possibilities, instead of the permutations of everyday certainties. Only in sf can one explore situations that have not occurred, cannot now occur, but may occur in the future. Only in sf can one deal with societies that have not yet evolved and problems that have not yet surfaced.

Why is it that so little sf takes advantage of this potential? Sf writers and fans spend a lot of time congratulating each other on how clever we are at speculation and extrapolation. And in fact we have been ingenious in technological invention and even in actual prediction—though prediction as such is one of the very few things that sf really is *not* about. Still, we all feel a certain degree of pride when one of us anticipates reality with unusual accuracy. Sf writers did predict space travel, the communications satellite, and the atom bomb. (That latter story, written in the early 1940s, reputedly resulted in a visit by the FBI to the writer's home: they wanted to know how he had found out about the Manhattan Project.) A certain amount of accurate technical extrapolation is no doubt going on in sf right now. But science itself is racing along at such a great rate that it's impossible for anyone to keep up with even a single field, much less all fields simultaneously. Scientists can't keep up, and we can't either. If we stick to inventing gimmicks and gadgets we'll be beaten to publication by the real thing so often that it will become embarrassing. This happened to me once: I based a story on a then-current biological hypothesis; even if the story had appeared within the normal lead-time for an anthology (it did not) it would have been outdated. This is the danger in writing one-punch stories based on current fashionable theories.

Along with the successes of extrapolation and the correct extrapolations superseded by reality, sf has a list of failures and miscalculations. John W. Campbell is said to have dismissed TV with the remark that it would never catch on because one had to pay attention to it. Certainly no early sf writer that I know of predicted the effect of the automobile; more recently, sf writers overlooked the oral contraceptive as a force for social change until the changes actually began occurring. A tremendous number of far-future stories are set in social systems identical to that of middle America in the mid-fifties.

Superficially it appears that our failures and successes are only what one might expect in a field based on speculation: win a few, lose a few. But it seems to me (admittedly a subjective observer) that our most spectacular correct extrapolations are qualitatively different from the changes we have completely overlooked. What we have often missed are the effects our marvelous machines can have on people. One can explain the evasion of the implications of the birth control pill by pointing out that the pill has been around longer than ten years, while sexuality has been "permitted" in sf less time than that. (Until the mid-sixties sf was steeped in Victorian prudery, as puritanical as the most repressed segments of society, and it shared all the assumptions of its culture that have been so severely questioned by the civil rights and feminist movements and by the sexual revolution.)

Prudery alone can't explain away the paucity of social extrapolation in sf, because most technological advances that can affect society haven't got anything to do with such touchy subjects as sex. No, our problem, I think, is that most of us are stuck on the plateaus of what Joanna Russ calls first- and second-stage science fiction. In first-stage sf, the story exists to show off the writer's

cleverness: Look, I just invented a nifty new toy! Second-stage sf
is for playing with the invention: Look what I can do with my nifty
new toy! The next step is third-stage sf, and as Russ points out it
is considerably more complicated. It deals not directly with technology or innovation but with the effects of technology and innovation: the changes the new toy may cause. It is concerned with
human beings and human values. It is a more difficult endeavor;
it takes more work, more insight, and better writing.

While first- and second-stage sf stories can be immensely enter-
taining, third-stage sf is what strikes deep resonances in readers,
and it's the work that lasts. It troubles those who dislike sf to the
point that they decide it can't be sf, "because it's good." It is
"relevant" in the highest sense of the word. I don't mean stories
that pick up on fashionable concerns of the moment. In the sixties
we had tales of future hippies fighting repression in the twenty-
first century, and now we are experiencing a glut of stories set a
couple of hundred years in the future in which people lecture
each other on equality. There may be cultures and counter-cul-
tures in the twenty-first century, but they will be distinguishable
from culture and counter-culture of today. There may be repression two hundred years in the future, but we will not still exist in
today's tension between disadvantaged racial minorities and privi-
leged middle class, feminist movement and antifeminist backlash.
This kind of thing, though generally written with the best of intentions, is fake relevance, exploiting current problems. Those interested in current problems alone should be writing mainstream
fiction. Otherwise they are wasting the potential of their medium,
bowing either unconsciously to trivialization or, in a few cases,
consciously to one or another backlash. It saddens me considerably
to see some writers wasting their own potential as well as that of
their chosen field, actively limiting themselves, their characters,
and their work by insisting that sf is, should be, and in fact *can be*
nothing more than an entertainment medium. Entertainment is
terrific, and lord knows, there's nothing more tedious than a
preachy story. A story without plot, characterization, or emotional
depth should never be written. But sf has occasionally been and

increasingly will become much more than entertainment. It's a tool for emotional and psychological exploration just as surely as the sailing ship was for exploring the world, or the space program may be for exploring the solar system. Anyone who claims it should stop short of that goal is advocating a waste of resources in a world where we no longer have resources to waste.

After all this criticism I want to add that there have always been writers who took full advantage of sf's potential. For a long time there were not very many of them, but now there are a few more, and a number of new writers are joining the established ones in refusing to be limited or intimidated by the traditions of the field or the tantrums of the various literary and social reactionaries. They are beginning to mine the limitless possibilities of sf, producing the most exciting work in any literary field. And I find the chance to be a part of that phenomenon so exhilarating that I can smile, and reply without even getting too defensive, when someone asks me why I write "that sci-fi stuff."

HARLAN ELLISON

Shatterday

Harlan Ellison has won two Nebulas, six Hugos, two special achievement awards of the World Science Fiction Convention (for editing *Dangerous Visions* and *Again, Dangerous Visions*), a Mystery Writers of America Edgar Allan Poe Award, a Jupiter conferred by the Instructors of SF in Higher Education, two George Meliés Fantasy Film Awards, and is the only writer in Hollywood ever to win the Writers Guild Award for Most Outstanding Teleplay three times. He has been on the final Nebula ballot seven times in the last five years.

More will be learned about Harlan Ellison—the writer, the man; equal parts of *enfant terrible éternel* and (by now, as his accomplishments pile up on him) apprentice Grand Old Man of science fiction—from reading his justly famous introductory notes to the stories in the anthologies he edits than can possibly be conveyed in a brief headnote such as this. The curious reader should go to the source.

Ellison is twice a Nebula finalist this year. The feature film, *A Boy and His Dog,* made from his story by the same title, took second place in the Dramatic Writing category; third in the line-up for Best Short Story was "Shatterday."

1. Someday

Not much later, but later nonetheless, he thought back on the sequence of what had happened, and knew he had missed nothing. How it had gone, was this:

He had been abstracted, thinking about something else. It didn't matter what. He had gone to the telephone in the restaurant, to call Jamie, to find out where the hell she was already, to find out why she'd kept him sitting in the bloody bar for thirty-five minutes. He had been thinking about something else, nothing deep, just woolgathering, and it wasn't till the number was ringing that he realized he'd dialed his own apartment. He had done it other times, not often, but as many as anyone else, dialed a number by rote and not thought about it, and occasionally it was his own number, everyone does it (he thought later), everyone does it, it's a simple mistake.

He was about to hang up, get back his dime, and dial Jamie when the receiver was lifted at the other end.

He answered.

Himself.

He recognized his own voice at once. But didn't let it penetrate. He had no little machine to take messages after the bleep, he had had his answering service temporarily disconnected (unsatisfactory service, they weren't catching his calls on the third ring as he'd *insisted*), there was no one guesting at his apartment, nothing. He was not at home, he was here, in the restaurant, calling his apartment, and *he* answered.

"Hello?"

He waited a moment. Then said, "Who's this?"

He answered, "Who're you calling?"

"Hold it," he said. "Who *is* this?"

His own voice, on the other end, getting annoyed, said, "Look, friend, what number do you want?"

"This is BEacon 3-6189, right?"

Warily: "Yeah . . . ?"

"Peter Novins' apartment?"

There was silence for a moment, then: "That's right."

He listened to the sounds from the restaurant's kitchen. "If this is Novins' apartment, who're you?"

On the other end, in his apartment, there was a deep breath. "This is Novins."

He stood in the phone booth, in the restaurant, in the night, the receiver to his ear, and listened to his own voice. He had dialed his own number by mistake, dialed an empty apartment . . . *and he had answered.*

Finally, he said, very tightly, *"This* is Novins."

"Where are you?"

"I'm at The High Tide, waiting for Jamie."

Across the line, with a terrible softness, he heard himself asking, "Is that you?"

A surge of fear pulsed through him and he tried to get out of it with one last possibility. "If this is a gag . . . Freddy . . . is that you, man? Morrie? Art?"

Silence. Then, slowly, "I'm Novins. Honest to God."

His mouth was dry. "I'm out here. You can't be, I *can't* be in the apartment."

"Oh, yeah? Well, I am."

"I'll have to call you back." Peter Novins hung up.

He went back to the bar and ordered a double Scotch, no ice, straight up, and threw it back in two swallows, letting it burn. He sat and stared at his hands, turning them over and over, studying them to make sure they were his own, not alien meat grafted onto his wrists when he was not looking.

Then he went back to the phone booth, closed the door and sat down, and dialed his own number. Very carefully.

It rang six times before *he* picked it up.

He knew why the voice on the other end had let it ring six times; he didn't want to pick up the snake and hear his own voice coming at him.

"Hello?" His voice on the other end was barely controlled.

"It's me," he said, closing his eyes.

"Jesus God," he murmured.

They sat there, in their separate places, without speaking. Then Novins said, "I'll call you Jay."

"That's okay," he answered from the other end. It was his middle name. He never used it, but it appeared on his insurance policy, his driver's license, and his social security card. Jay said, "Did Jamie get there?"

"No, she's late again."

Jay took a deep breath and said, "We'd better talk about this, man."

"I suppose," Novins answered. "Not that I really want to. You're scaring the shit out of me."

"How do you think *I* feel about it?"

"Probably the same way I feel about it."

They thought about that for a long moment. Then Jay said, "Will we be feeling exactly the same way about things?"

Novins considered it, then said, "If you're really me then I suppose so. We ought to try and test that."

"You're taking this a lot calmer than I am, it seems to me," Jay said.

Novins was startled. "You really think so? I was just about to say I thought you were really terrific the way you're handling all this.

I think you're *much* more together about it than I am. I'm really startled, I've got to tell you."

"So how'll we test it?" Jay asked.

Novins considered the problem, then said, "Why don't we compare likes and dislikes. That's a start. That sound okay to you?"

"It's as good a place as any, I suppose. Who goes first?"

"It's my dime," Novins said, and for the first time he smiled. "I like, uh, well-done prime rib, end cut if I can get it, Yorkshire pudding, smoking a pipe, Max Ernst's paintings, Robert Altman films, William Goldman's books, getting mail but not answering it, uh . . ."

He stopped. He had been selecting random items from memory, the ones that came to mind first. But as he had been speaking, he heard what he was saying, and it seemed stupid. "This isn't going to work," Novins said. "What the hell does it matter? Was there anything in that list you didn't like?"

Jay sighed. "No, they're all favorites. You're right. If I like it, you'll like it. This isn't going to answer any questions."

Novins said, "I don't even know what the questions *are!*"

"That's easy enough," Jay said. "There's only one question: which of us is me, and how does *me* get rid of *him?*"

A chill spread out from Novins' shoulder blades and wrapped around his arms like a mantilla. "What's *that* supposed to mean? Get rid of *him?* What the hell's *that?*"

"Face it," Jay said—and Novins heard a tone in the voice he recognized, the tone *he* used when he was about to become a tough negotiator—"we can't *both* be Novins. One of us is going to get screwed."

"Hold it, friend," Novins said, adopting the tone. "That's pretty muddy logic. First of all, who's to say you're not going to vanish back where you came from as soon as I hang up. . . ."

"Bullshit," Jay answered.

"Yeah, well, maybe; but even if you're here to stay, and I don't concede *that* craziness for a second, even if you *are* real—"

"Believe it, baby, I'm real," Jay said, with a soft chuckle. Novins was starting to hate him.

"—even if you *are* real," Novins continued, "there's no saying we can't both exist, and both lead happy, separate lives."

"You know something, Novins," Jay said, "you're really full of horse puckey. You can't lead a happy life by yourself, man, how the hell are you going to do it knowing I'm over here living your life, too?"

"What do you mean I can't lead a happy life? What do you know about it?" And he stopped; of course Jay knew about it. *All* about it.

"You'd better start facing reality, Novins. You'll be coming to it late in life, but you'd better learn how to do it. Maybe it'll make the end come easier."

Novins wanted to slam the receiver into its rack. He was at once furiously angry and frightened. He knew what the other Novins was saying was true; he *had* to know, without argument; it was, after all, himself saying it. "Only one of us is going to make it," he said, tightly. "And it's going to be me, old friend."

"How do you propose to do it, Novins? You're out there, locked out. I'm in here, in my home, safe where I'm supposed to be."

"How about we look at it *this* way," Novins said quickly, "you're trapped in there, locked away from the world in three and a half rooms. I've got everywhere else to move in. You're limited. I'm free."

There was silence for a moment.

Then Jay said, "We've reached a bit of an impasse, haven't we? There's something to be said for being loose, and there's something to be said for being safe inside. The amazing thing is that we both have accepted this thing so quickly."

Novins didn't answer. He accepted it because he had no other choice; if he could accept that he was speaking to himself, then anything that followed had to be part of that acceptance. Now that Jay had said it bluntly, that only one of them could continue to exist, all that remained was finding a way to make sure it was he, Novins, who continued past this point.

"I've got to think about this," Novins said. "I've got to try to work some of this out better. You just stay celled in there, friend;

I'm going to a hotel for the night. I'll call you tomorrow."

He started to hang up when Jay's voice stopped him. "What do I say if Jamie gets there and you're gone and she calls me?"

Novins laughed. "That's *your* problem, motherfucker."

He racked the receiver with nasty satisfaction.

2. Moanday

He took special precautions. First the bank, to clean out the checking account. He thanked God he'd had his checkbook with him when he'd gone out to meet Jamie the night before. But the savings-account passbook was in the apartment. That meant Jay had access to almost ten thousand dollars. The checking account was down to fifteen hundred, even with all outstanding bills paid, and the Banks for Cooperatives note came due in about thirty days and that meant . . . he used the back of a deposit slip to figure the interest . . . he'd be getting ten thousand four hundred and sixty-five dollars and seven cents deposited to his account. His *new* account, which he opened at another branch of the same bank, signing the identification cards with a variation of his signature sufficiently different to prevent Jay's trying to draw on the account. He was at least solvent. For the time being.

But all his work was in the apartment. All the public relations accounts he handled. Every bit of data and all the plans and phone numbers and charts, they were all there in the little apartment office. So he was quite effectively cut off from his career.

Yet in a way, that was a blessing. Jay would have to keep up with the work in his absence, would have to follow through on the important campaigns for Topper and McKenzie, would have to take all the moronic calls from Lippman and his insulting son, would have to answer all the mail, would have to keep popping Titralac all day just to stay ahead of the heartburn. He felt gloriously free and almost satanically happy that he was rid of the aggravation for a while, and that Jay was going to find out being Peter Jay Novins wasn't all fun and Jamies.

Back in his hotel room at the Americana he made a list of things he had to do. To survive. It was a new way of thinking, setting down one by one the everyday routine actions from which he was now cut off. He was all alone now, entirely and totally, for the first time in his life, cut off from everything. He could not depend on friends or associates or the authorities. It would be suicide to go to the police and say, "Listen, I hate to bother you, but I've split and one of me has assumed squatter's rights in my apartment; please go up there and arrest him." No, he was on his own, and he had to exorcise Jay from the world strictly by his own wits and cunning.

Bearing in mind, of course, that Jay had the same degree of wit and cunning.

He crossed half a dozen items off the list. There was no need to call Jamie and find out what had happened to her the night before. Their relationship wasn't that binding in any case. Let Jav make the excuses. No need to cancel the credit cards, he had them with him. Let Jay pay the bills from the savings account. No need to contact any of his friends and warn them. He *couldn't* warn them, and if he did, what would he warn them against? Himself? But he did need clothes, fresh socks and underwear, a light jacket instead of his topcoat, a pair of gloves in case the weather turned. And he had to cancel out the delivery services to the apartment in a way that would prevent Jay from reinstating them; groceries, milk, dry cleaning, newspapers. He had to make it as difficult for him in there as possible. And so he called each tradesman and insulted him so grossly they would *never* serve him again. Unfortunately, the building provided heat and electricity and gas and he *had* to leave the phone connected.

The phone was his tie-line to victory, to routing Jay out of there.

When he had it all attended to, by three o'clock in the afternoon, he returned to the hotel room, took off his shoes, propped the pillows up on the bed, lay down and dialed a 9 for the outside line, then dialed his own number.

As it rang, he stared out the forty-fifth-floor window of the hotel room, at the soulless pylons of the RCA and Grants Buildings, the other dark-glass filing cabinets for people. Was it any wonder *any* one managed to stay sane, stay whole in such surroundings? Living in cubicles, boxed and trapped and throttled, was it any surprise that people began to fall apart . . . even as *he* seemed to be falling apart? The wonder was that it all managed to hold together as well as it did. But the fractures were beginning to appear, culturally and now—as with Peter Novins, he mused—personally. The phone continued to ring. Clouds blocked out all light and the city was swamped by shadows. At three o'clock in the afternoon, the ominous threat of another night settled over Novins' hotel room.

The receiver was lifted at the other end. But Jay said nothing.

"It's me," Novins said. "How'd you enjoy your first day in my skin?"

"How did you enjoy your first day *out* of it?" he replied.

"Listen, I've got your act covered, friend, and your hours are numbered. The checking account is gone, don't try to find it; you're going to have to go out to get food and when you do I'll be waiting—"

"Terrific," Jay replied. "But just so you don't waste your time, I had the locks changed today. Your keys don't work. And I bought groceries. Remember the fifty bucks I put away in the jewelry box?"

Novins cursed himself silently. He hadn't thought of that.

"And I've been doing some figuring, Novins. Remember that old Jack London novel, *The Star Rover?* Remember how he used astral projection to get out of his body? I think that's what's happened to me. I sent you out when I wasn't aware of it. So I've decided I'm me, and you're just a little piece that's wandered off. And I can get along just peachy-keen without that piece, so why don't you just go—"

"Hold it," Novins interrupted, "that's a sensational theory, but it's stuffed full of wild blueberry muffins, if you'll pardon my being so forward as to disagree with a smartass voice that's probably disembodied and doesn't have enough ectoplasm to take a healthy shit. Remember the weekend I went over to the lab with Kenny and he took that Kirlian photograph of my aura? Well, my theory is that something happened and the aura produced another me, or something. . . ."

He slid down into silence. Neither theory was worth thinking about. He had no idea, *really,* what had happened. They hung there in silence for a long moment, then Jay said, "Mother called this morning."

Novins felt a hand squeeze his chest. "What did she say?"

"She said she knew you lied when you were down in Florida. She said she loved you and she forgave you and all she wants is for you to share your life with her."

Novins closed his eyes. He didn't want to think about it. His mother was in her eighties, very sick, and just recovering from her second serious heart attack in three years. The end was near and, combining a business trip to Miami with a visit to her, he had gone to Florida the month before. He had never had much in common with his mother, had been on his own since his early teens, and though he supported her in her declining years, he refused to allow her to impose on his existence. He seldom wrote letters, save to send the check, and during the two days he had spent in her apartment in Miami Beach he had thought he would go insane. He had wanted to bolt, and finally had lied to her that he was return-ing to New York a day earlier than his plans required. He had packed up and left her, checking into a hotel, and had spent the final day involved in business and that night had gone out with a secretary he dated occasionally when in Florida.

"How did she find out?" Novins asked.

"She called here and the answering service told her you were still in Florida and hadn't returned. They gave her the number of the hotel and she called there and found out you were registered for that night."

Novins cursed himself. Why had he called the service to tell them where he was? He could have gotten away with one day of his business contacts not being able to reach him. "Swell," he said. "And I suppose you didn't do anything to make her feel better."

"On the contrary," Jay said, "I did what you never would have done. I made arrangements for her to come live here with me."

Novins heard himself moan with pain. "You did *what!?* Jesus Christ, you're out of your fucking mind. How the hell am I going to take care of that old woman in New York? I've got work to do, places I have to go, I have a life to lead. . . ."

"Not any more you don't, you guilty, selfish sonofabitch. Maybe *you* could live with the bad gut feelings about her, but not me. She'll be arriving in a week."

"You're crazy," Novins screamed. "You're fucking crazy!"

"Yeah," Jay said, softly, and added, "and you just lost your mother. Chew on *that* one, you creep."

And he hung up.

3. Duesday

They decided between them that the one who *deserved* to be Peter Novins should take over the life. They had to make that decision; clearly, they could not go on as they had been; even two days had showed them half an existence was not possible. Both were fraying at the edges.

So Jay suggested they work their way through the pivot experiences of Novins' life, to see if he was really entitled to continue living.

"*Every*one's entitled to go on living," Novins said, vehemently. "That's why we live. To say no to death."

"You don't believe that for a second, Novins," Jay said. "You're a misanthrope. You hate people."

"That's not true; I just don't like some of the things people *do.*"

"Like what, for instance? Like, for instance, you're always bitching about kids who wear ecology patches, who throw Dr. Pepper cans in the bushes; like that, for instance?"

"That's good for starters," Novins said.

"You hypocritical bastard," Jay snarled back at him, "you have the audacity to beef about that and you took on the Cumberland account."

"That's another kind of thing!"

"My ass. You know damned well Cumberland's planning to strip-mine the guts out of that county, and they're going to get away with it with that publicity campaign you dreamed up. Oh, you're one hell of a good PR man, Novins, but you've got the ethics of a weasel."

Novins was fuming, but Jay was right. He had felt lousy about taking on Cumberland from the start, but they were big, they were international, and the billing for the account was handily in six figures. He had tackled the campaign with the same ferocity he brought to all his accounts, and the program was solid. "I have to make a living. Besides, if I didn't do it, someone else would. I'm only doing a job. They've got a terrific restoration program, don't forget that. They'll put that land back in shape."

Jay laughed. "That's what Eichmann said: 'We have a terrific restoration program, we'll put them Jews right back in shape, just a little gas to spiff 'em up.' He was just doing a job, too, Novins. Have I mentioned lately that you stink on ice."

Novins was shouting again. "I suppose you'd have turned it down?"

"That's exactly what I did, old buddy," Jay said. "I called them today and told them to take their account and stuff it up their nose. I've got a call in to Nader right now, to see what he can do with all the data in the file."

Novins was speechless. He lay there, under the covers, the Tuesday snow drifting in enormous flakes past the forty-fifth-floor windows. Slowly, he let the receiver settle into the cradle. Only three days and his life was drifting apart inexorably; soon it would be impossible to knit it together.

His stomach ached. And all that day he had felt nauseated. Room service had sent up pot after pot of tea, but it hadn't helped. A throbbing headache was lodged just behind his left eye, and cold sweat covered his shoulders and chest.

He didn't know what to do, but he knew he was losing.

4. Woundsday

On Wednesday Jay called Novins. He never told him how he'd located him, he just called. "How do you feel?" he asked. Novins could barely answer, the fever was close to immobilizing.

"I just called to talk about Jeanine and Patty and that girl in Denver," Jay said, and he launched into a long and stately recitation of Novins' affairs, and how they had ended. It was not as Novins remembered it.

"That isn't true," Novins managed to say, his voice deep and whispering, dry and nearly empty.

"It *is* true, Novins. That's what's so sad about it. That it *is* true and you've never had the guts to admit it, that you go from woman to woman without giving anything, always taking, and when you leave them—or they dump you—you've never learned a god-damned thing. You've been married twice, divorced twice, you've been in and out of two dozen affairs and you haven't learned that you're one of those men who is simply no bloody good for a woman. So now you're forty-two years old and you're finally coming to the dim understanding that you're going to spend all the rest of the days and nights of your life alone, because you can't stand the company of another human being for more than a month without turning into a vicious prick."

"Not true," murmured Novins.

"True, Novins, true. Flat true. You set after Patty and got her to leave her old man, and when you'd pried her loose, her and the kid, you set her up in that apartment with three hundred a month rent, and then you took off and left her to work it out herself. It's true, old buddy. So don't try and con me with that 'I lead a happy life' bullshit."

Novins simply lay there with his eyes closed, shivering with the fever.

Then Jay said, "I saw Jamie last night. We talked about her future. It took some fast talking; she was really coming to hate you. But I think it'll work out if I go at it hard, and I *intend* to go at it hard. I don't intend to have any more years like I've had, Novins. From this point on it changes."

The bulk of the buildings outside the window seemed to tremble behind the falling snow. Novins felt terribly cold. He didn't answer.

"We'll name the first one after you, Peter," Jay said, and hung up.

That was Wednesday.

5. Thornsday

There were no phone calls that day. Novins lay there, the television set mindlessly playing and replaying the five-minute instruction film on the pay-movie preview channel, the ghost-image of a dark-haired girl in a gray suit showing him how to charge a first-run film to his hotel bill. After many hours he heard himself reciting the instructions along with her. He slept a great deal. He thought about Jeanine and Patty, the girl in Denver whose name he could not recall, and Jamie.

After many more hours, he thought about insects, but he didn't know what that meant. There were no phone calls that day. It was Thursday.

Shortly before midnight, the fever broke, and he cried himself back to sleep.

6. Freeday

A key turned in the lock and the hotel room door opened. Novins was sitting in a mass-produced imitation of a Saarinen pedestal chair, its seat treated with Scotchgard. He had been staring out the window at the geometric irrelevancy of the glass-wall buildings. It was near dusk, and the city was gray as cardboard.

He turned at the sound of the door opening and was not surprised to see himself walk in.

Jay's nose and cheeks were still red from the cold outside. He unzipped his jacket and stuffed his kid gloves into a pocket, removed the jacket and threw it on the unmade bed. "Really cold out there," he said. He went into the bathroom and Novins heard the sound of water running.

Jay returned in a few minutes, rubbing his hands together. "That helps," he said. He sat down on the edge of the bed and looked at Novins.

"You look terrible, Peter," he said.

"I haven't been at all well," Novins answered dryly. "I don't seem to be myself these days."

Jay smiled briefly. "I see you're coming to terms with it. That ought to help."

Novins stood up. The thin light from the room-long window shone through him like white fire through milk glass. "You're looking well," he said.

"I'm getting better, Peter. It'll be a while, but I'm going to be okay."

Novins walked across the room and stood against the wall, hands clasped behind his back. He could barely be seen. "I remember the archetypes from Jung. Are you my shadow, my persona, my anima, or my animus?"

"What am I now, or what was I when I got loose?"

"Either way."

"I suppose I was your shadow. Now I'm the self."

"And I'm becoming the shadow."

"No, you're becoming a memory. A bad memory."

"That's pretty ungracious."

"I was sick for a long time, Peter. I don't know what the trigger was that broke us apart, but it happened and I can't be too sorry about it. If it hadn't happened I'd have been you till I died. It would have been a lousy life and a miserable death."

Novins shrugged. "Too late to worry about it now. Things working out with Jamie?"

Jay nodded. "Yeah. And Mom comes in Tuesday afternoon. I'm renting a car to pick her up at Kennedy. I talked to her doctors. They say she doesn't have too long. But for whatever she's got, I'm determined to make up for the last twenty-five years since Dad died."

Novins smiled and nodded. "That's good."

"Listen," Jay said slowly, with difficulty, "I just came over to ask if there was anything you wanted me to do . . . anything *you* would've done if . . . if it had been different."

Novins spread his hands and thought about it for a moment. "No, I don't think so, nothing special. You might try and get some money to Jeanine's mother, for Jeanine's care, maybe. That wouldn't hurt."

"I already took care of it. I figured that would be on your mind."

Novins smiled. "That's good. Thanks."

"Anything else . . . ?"

Novins shook his head. They stayed that way, hardly moving, till night had fallen outside the window. In the darkness, Jay could barely see Novins standing against the wall. Merely a faint glow.

Finally, Jay stood and put on his jacket, zipped up and put on his left glove. "I've got to go."

Novins spoke from the shadows. "Yeah. Well, take care of me, will you?"

Jay didn't answer. He walked to Novins and extended his right hand. The touch of Novins' hand in his was like the whisper of a cold wind; there was no pressure.

Then he left.

Novins walked back to the window and stared out. The last remaining daylight shone through him. Dimly.

7. Shatterday

When the maid came in to make up the bed, she found the room empty. It was terribly cold in the room on the forty-fifth floor. When Peter Novins did not return that day, or the next, the management of the Americana marked him as a skip, and turned it over to a collection agency.

In due course the bill was sent to Peter Novins' apartment on Manhattan's Upper East Side.

It was promptly paid, by Peter Jay Novins, with a brief, but *sincere* note of apology.

TOM REAMY

San Diego Lightfoot Sue

Literally in the air—"The flight is not a smooth one"—Tom Reamy approached a recent engagement as toastmaster at a regional convention while scribbling to a friend, "God knows what I will say."

His response to a request for biographical information (to precede his second Nebula winner in two years) is in the same vein. He says, "Everything remotely biographical that I can think of registers minus three on the interest meter. Basically, I haven't done anything. I'm John Lee Peacock, emotionally if not physically. . . . I've gotten a lot of wordage out of my eighteen months in Hollywood. The difference between me and John Lee is [at a certain point in the story] I left instead of staying." Reamy's overall assessment is that Hollywood overloaded his sensory inputs.

After working on and among pornographic films and others ("I was assistant director on the third film I worked on though my duties didn't differ greatly from *Flesh Gordon* when I was 'property master' ") Reamy went back to his old career of technical illustrator [not "technical writer" as was indicated in *Nebula Ten*] for a time. "If I could have worked steadily I might have stayed in L.A., but there were too many idle times. Since it was much cheaper to starve in Texas than in L.A., I went back—and one day decided to write."

"Twilla" (last year's winner) was Tom Reamy's third story in order of writing. "San Diego Lightfoot Sue" was his second. Ever.

This all began about ten years ago in a house at the top of a flight of rickety wooden stairs in Laurel Canyon. It might be said there were two beginnings, though the casual sorcery in Laurel Canyon may have been the cause and the other merely the effect—if you believe in that sort of thing.

The woman sat cross-legged on the floor reading the book. The windows were open to the warm California night, and the only sound that came through them was the distant, muffled, eternal roar of Los Angeles traffic. The brittle pages of the book crackled as she carefully turned them. She read slowly because her Latin wasn't what it used to be. She lit a cigarette and left it to burn unnoticed in the ashtray on the floor beside her.

"Here's a good one," she said to the big orange tom curled in the chair she leaned against. "You don't know where I can find a hazelnut bush with a nest of thirteen white adders under it, do you, Punkin?" The cat didn't answer; he only opened one eye slightly and twitched the tip of his tail.

She turned a page, and several two-inch rectangles of white paper fell into her lap. She picked them up and examined them, but they were blank. She stuck them back in the book and kept reading.

She found it a while later. It was a simple spell. All she had to

199

do was write the word-square on a piece of white parchment with black ink and then burn it while thinking of the person she wished to summon.

"I wonder if Paul Newman is doing anything tonight," she chuckled.

She stood up and went to the drafting table, opened a drawer, and removed a pen and a bottle of india ink. She put a masking tape dispenser on the edge of the book to hold it open and carefully lettered the word-square on one of the pieces of paper stuck between the pages. She supposed that's why her mother, or whoever, had put them there—they looked like parchment, anyway.

The word-square was eight letters wide and eight letters high; eight eight-letter words stacked on top of one another. She imagined they were words, though they were in no language she knew. The peculiar thing about the square was that it read the same sideways or upside down—even in a mirror image, it was the same.

She put the cap back on the ink and went to the ashtray, kneeling beside it. She laid the parchment on the dead cigarette butts. "Well, here goes," she said to the cat. "I wonder if it's all right to burn it with a cigarette lighter? Maybe I need a black taper made of the wax of dead bees or something."

She composed herself, trying to take it seriously, and thought of a man, not a specific man, just *the* man. "I feel like Snow White singing 'Someday My Prince Will Come,'" she muttered. She flicked the cigarette lighter and touched the flame to the corner of the piece of paper.

It flamed up so quickly and so brightly that she gasped and drew back. "God!" she grunted and hurried to a window to escape the billows of black smoke that smelled of rotten eggs. The cat was already out, sitting on the farthest point of the deck railing, looking at her with round startled eyes.

The woman glanced back at the black smoke spreading like a carpet on the ceiling and then at the wide-eyed cat. She suddenly collapsed against the window sill in a fit of uncontrollable laughter. "Come on back in, Punkin," she gasped. "It's all over." The cat gave her an incredulous look and hopped off the railing into the shrubbery.

This also began about ten years ago in Kansas, the summer he was fifteen, when the air smelled like hot metal and rang with the cries of cicadas. It ended a month later when he was still fifteen, when the house in Laurel Canyon burned with a strange green fire that made no heat.

His name was John Lee Peacock, a good, old, undistinguished name in southern Kansas. His mother and his aunts and his aunts' husbands called him John Lee. The kids in school called him Johnny, which he preferred. His father never called him anything.

His father had been by-passed by the world, but he wouldn't have cared, even if he had been aware of it. Wash Peacock was a dirt farmer who refused to abandon the land. The land repaid his taciturn loyalty with annual betrayal. Wash had only four desires in life: to work the land, three hot meals each day, sleep, and copulation when the pressures built high enough. The children were strangers who appeared suddenly, disturbed his sleep for a while, then faded into the gray house or the County Line Cemetery.

John Lee's mother had been a Willet. The aunts were her sisters: Rose and Lilah. Wash had a younger brother somewhere in Pennsylvania—or, had had one the last time he heard. That was in 1927, the year Wash's mother died. Grace Elizabeth Willet married Delbert Washburn Peacock in the fall of 1930. She did it because her father, old Judge Willet, thought it was a good idea. Grace Elizabeth was a plain, timid girl who, he felt, was destined to be the family's maiden aunt. He was right, but she would have been much happier if he hadn't interfered.

The Peacocks had owned the land for nearly a hundred years and were moderately prosperous. They had survived the Civil War, Reconstruction, and statehood, but wouldn't survive the Depression. Judge Willet felt that Wash was the best he could do for Grace Elizabeth. He was a nice-looking man, and what he lacked in imagination, he made up in hard work.

But the Peacocks had a thin, unfortunate blood line. Only a few of the many children lived. It was the same with Wash and Grace Elizabeth. She had given birth eight times, but there were only

three of them left. Wash, Jr., her first born, had married one of the
trashy O'Dell girls and had gone to Oklahoma to work in the
oilfields. She hadn't heard from him in thirteen years. Dwayne
Edward, the third born, had stayed in Los Angeles after his separation from the army. He sent a card every Christmas and she had
kept them all. She wished some of the girls had lived. She would
have liked to have a girl, to make pretty things for her, to have
someone to talk to. But she had lost the three girls and two of the
boys. She had trouble remembering their names sometimes, but
it was all written in the big Bible where she could remind herself
when the names began to slip away.

John Lee was the youngest. He had arrived late in her life, a
comfort for her weary years. She wanted him to be different from
the others. Wash, Jr., and Dwayne had both been disappoint-
ments; too much like their father: unimaginative plodding boys
who had done badly in school and got into trouble with the law.
She still loved them because they were her children, but she
sometimes forgot why she was supposed to. She wanted John Lee
to read books (God! How long since she'd read a book; she used to
read all the time when she was a girl), to know about art and
faraway places. She knew she hoped for too much, and so she was
content when she got a part of it.

Wash didn't pay any more attention to John Lee than he had the
others. He neither asked nor seemed to want the boy's help in the
field. So Grace Elizabeth kept him around the house, helping with
her chores, talking to him, having him share with her what he had
learned in school. She gave him as much as she could. There wasn't
money for much, but she managed to hold back a few dollars now
and then.

She loved John Lee very much; he was probably the only thing
she did love. So, on that shimmering summer day about ten years
ago, when he was fifteen, she died for him.

She was cleaning up the kitchen after supper. Wash had gone
back to the fields where he would stay until dark. John Lee was
at the kitchen table, reading, passing on bits of information he
knew she would like to hear. She leaned against the sink with the

cup towel clutched in her hand and felt her supper turn over in her stomach. She had known it was coming for months. Now it was here.

He's too young, she thought. If he could only have a couple more years. She watched him bent over the book, the evening sun glinting on his brown hair. He's even better looking than his father, she thought. So like his father. But only on the outside. Only on the outside.

She spread the cup towel on the rack to dry and walked through the big old house. She hadn't really noticed the house in a long time. It had grown old and gray slowly, as she had, and so she had hardly noticed it happening. Then she looked at it again and it wasn't the house she remembered moving into all those years ago. Wash's father had built it in 1913 when the old one had been unroofed by a twister. He had built it like they did in those days: big, so generations could live in it. It had been freshly painted when she moved in, a big white box eight miles from Hawley, a mile from Miller's Corners.

Then the hard times began. But Wash had clung to the land during the Depression and the dust. He hadn't panicked like most of the others. He hadn't sold the land at give-away prices or lost it because he couldn't pay the taxes. Things had gotten a little better when the war began, but never as good as before the Depression. Now they were bad again. At the end of each weary year there was only enough money to do it all over again.

She supposed that being the oldest, Wash, Jr., would get it. She was glad John Lee wouldn't. She went upstairs to his room and packed his things in a pasteboard box. She left it where he would find it and went to her own room. She opened a drawer in the old highboy that had belonged to her grandmother and removed an envelope from beneath her cotton slips. She took it to the kitchen and handed it to John Lee.

He took it and looked at her. "What is it, Mama?"

"Open it in the morning, John Lee. You'd better go to bed now."

"But it's not even dark yet." There's something wrong, there's something wrong.

"Soon, then. I want to sit on the porch awhile and rest." She kissed him and patted his shoulder and left the room. He watched the empty doorway and felt the blood singing in his ears. After a while, he got a drink of water from the cooler and went to his room. He lay on the bed, looking at the water spots on the ceiling paper, and clutched the envelope in his hands. Tears formed in his eyes and he tried to blink them away.

Grace Elizabeth sat on the porch in her rocker, moving gently, mending Wash's clothes until it got too dark to see. Then she folded them neatly in her lap, leaned back in the chair, and closed her eyes.

Wash found her the next morning only because he wondered why his breakfast wasn't waiting for him. She was buried in the County Line Cemetery with five of her children after a brief service at the First Baptist Church in Hawley. Aunt Rose and Aunt Lilah had a fine time weeping into black lace handkerchiefs and clucking over Poor John Lee.

On the way back from the funeral John Lee rode in the front seat of the '53 Chevrolet beside his father. Neither of them spoke until they had turned off the highway at Miller's Corners.

"Write a letter to Wash, Jr. Tell him to come home." John Lee didn't answer. He could smell the dust rising up behind the car. Wash parked it in the old carriage house and hurried to change clothes, hurried to make up the half day he had lost. John Lee went to the closet in the front hall and took down a shoe box, in which his mother kept such things, and looked for an address. He found it after a bit, worked to the bottom, unused for thirteen years. He wrote the letter anyway.

He had left the envelope unopened under his pillow. Now he opened it, although he had guessed what it was. He counted the carefully hoarded bills: a hundred and twenty-seven dollars. He sat on the edge of the bed, on the crazy quilt his mother had made for him, in the quiet room, in the silent weary house. He wiped his eyes with his knuckles, picked up the pasteboard box, and walked the mile to Miller's Corners.

His Sunday suit, worn to the funeral that morning, once belonging to Dwayne, and before that, Wash, Jr., was white at the cuffs from the dusty road. His shoes, his alone, were even worse. It was a scorcher. "It's gonna be another scorcher," she always used to say, looking out the kitchen window after putting away the breakfast dishes. He sat on the bench at the Gulf station, cleaning the dust off the best he could.

The cicadas screeched from the mesquite bushes, filling the hot still air with their insistent calls for a mate. John Lee rather liked the sound, but it had bothered his mother. "Enough to drive a body ravin' mad," she used to say. She always called them locusts, but he had learned in school their real name was cicada. And when they talked about a plague of locusts in the Bible, they really meant grasshoppers. "Well, I'll declare," she had said. "Always wondered why locusts would be considered a plague. Far's I know, they don't do anything but sit in the bushes and make noise. Now, grasshoppers I can understand." And she would smile at him in her pleased and proud way that caused a pleasant hurting in the back of his throat.

"Hello, John Lee."

He looked up quickly. "Hello, Mr. Cuttsanger. How are you today?" He liked Mr. Cuttsanger, a string-thin man the same age as his mother, who had seemingly permanent grease stains on his hands. He wiped at them now with a dull red rag, but it didn't help.

"I'm awfully sorry about your mother, boy. Wish I coulda gone to the funeral but I couldn't get away. We were in the same grade together all through school, you know."

"Yes, I know. She told me."

"What're you doin' here still dressed up?" he asked, sticking the rag in his hip pocket and looking at the box.

"I reckon I have to catch a bus, Mr. Cuttsanger." His heart did a little flip-flop. Not the old school bus either, but a real bus.

"Where you off to, John Lee?"

"Where do your buses go, Mr. Cuttsanger?"

Mr. Cuttsanger sat on the bench beside John Lee. "The westbound will be through here in about an hour goin' to Los Angeles.

The eastbound comes through in the mornin' headed for St. Louie. You already missed it."

"Los Angeles. My brother, Dwayne, lives in California." But he didn't know where. He had seen the Christmas cards in the shoe box, but he hadn't paid any attention to the return address.

Mr. Cuttsanger nodded. "Good idea, goin' to stay with Dwayne. Nothin' for you here on this played-out old farm. Heard Grace Elizabeth say the same thing. Your father ought to sell it and go with you. But I guess I know Wash better'n that." He arose from the bench with a little sigh. He went into the station and returned with a small red flag. He stuck it in a pipe welded at an angle to the pole supporting the Gulf sign. "There. He'll stop when he sees that. You buy your ticket from the driver."

"Thank you, Mr. Cuttsanger. I need to mail a letter also." He took the letter he had carefully addressed in block printing to Delbert Washburn Peacock, Jr., Gen. Del., Norman, Okla., from his pocket and handed it to Mr. Cuttsanger. "I don't have a stamp."

Mr. Cuttsanger looked at the letter. "Is Wash, Jr., still in Norman?" He said it as if he doubted it.

"I don't know. That's the only address I could find."

Mr. Cuttsanger tapped the letter against the knuckle of his thumb. "You leave a nickel with me and I'll get a stamp from Clayton in the mornin'. Sure was a lot simpler before they closed the post office." He sat back on the bench in the shade of the car shed. John Lee followed his eyes as he looked at Miller's Corners evaporating under the cloudless sky. An out-of-state car blasted through doing seventy. Mr. Cuttsanger sighed and accepted a nickel from John Lee. "They don't even have to slow down any more. Used to be thirty-five-mile speed-limit signs at each end of town. Guess they don't need 'em now. Ain't nothin' here but me and the café. Myrtle's been saying for nearly a year she was gonna move to Hawley or maybe even Liberal. Closed the post office in fifty-five, I think it was. That foundation across the highway is where the grocery store used to be. Don't reckon you remember the grocery store?"

"No, sir, but I remember the feed store."

"Imagine that. You musta been about four, five years old."

"I was born in forty-eight."

"Closed the feed store in fifty-two. Imagine you rememberin' that far back." He continued to ramble on in his pleasant friendly voice. John Lee asked questions and made comments to keep him going, to make the time pass faster. A whole hour before the bus would come.

But it finally did, cutting off the highway in a cloud of dust and a dragon hiss of air brakes. John Lee looked at the magic name in the little window over the windshield: LOS ANGELES. He swallowed and solemnly shook hands with Mr. Cuttsanger.

"Good-by, Mr. Cuttsanger."

"Good-by, John Lee. You take care now."

John Lee nodded and picked up the box and walked to the bus, his legs trembling. The door sighed open and the driver got out. He opened a big door on the side of the bus under *Continental Trailways.* He took the pasteboard box.

"Where you goin'?"

"I'd like a ticket to Los Angeles, please." He couldn't keep from smiling when he said the name. The driver put a tag on the box, put it in with the suitcases, and closed the door. John Lee followed him into the bus. Inside it was cool like some of the stores in Liberal.

He bought his ticket and sat down in the front seat, scooting to the window as the bus lurched back onto the highway. He looked back at Miller's Corners and waved to Mr. Cuttsanger, but he was taking down the red flag and didn't see.

John Lee leaned back in the seat and hugged himself. Once more he couldn't keep from smiling. After a bit, he looked around at the other people. There weren't many and some weren't wearing Sunday clothes; so he decided it would be all right to take off his jacket. He settled back in the seat, watching the baked Kansas countryside rush past the window. Strange, he thought, it looks the same way it does from the school bus. Even though he tried to prevent it, the smile returned unbidden every once in a while.

The bus went through Hawley without stopping, past the white rococo courthouse with its high clock tower; past the school, closed for the summer; over the hump in the highway by the old depot where the railroad tracks had been taken out; across the bridge over Crooked Creek.

It stopped in Liberal and the driver called out, "Rest stop!" John Lee didn't know what a rest stop was, and so he stayed on the bus. He noticed that some of the other passengers didn't get off either. He decided there was nothing to worry about.

He tried to see everything when the bus left Liberal, to look on both sides at once, because it was the farthest he had ever been. But Oklahoma looked just like Kansas, Texas looked just like Oklahoma, and New Mexico looked like Texas, only each seemed a little bleaker than the one before. The bus stopped in Tucumcari for supper. John Lee had forgotten to eat dinner, and his bladder felt like it would burst.

He was nervous but he managed all right. He'd eaten in a café before, and, by watching the others, he found out where the toilet was and how to pay for his meal. It was dark when the bus left Tucumcari. He tried to go to sleep, to make the time pass faster, the way he always did when the next day was bringing wondrous things. But, as usual, the harder he tried, the wider awake he was.

He awoke when the bus stopped for breakfast and quickly put his coat over his lap, hoping no one had noticed. He waited until everyone else had gotten off, then headed for the toilet keeping his coat in front of him. He didn't know for sure where he was, but all the cars had Arizona license plates.

It was after dark when the bus pulled into the Los Angeles terminal, though it seemed to John Lee as if they had been driving through town for hours. He had never dreamed it was so big. He watched the other passengers collect their luggage and got his pasteboard box.

Then he went out into: Los Angeles.

He walked around the street with the box clutched in his arms in total bedazzlement. Buildings, lights, cars, people, so many different kinds of people. It was the first time he had ever seen a

Chinese, except in the movies, although he wasn't absolutely sure that it wasn't a Japanese. There were dozens of picture shows, lined up in rows. He liked movies and used to go nearly every Saturday afternoon, a long time ago before the picture show in Hawley closed.

And buses, with more magic names in the little windows: SUN-SET BLVD; HOLLYWOOD BLVD; PASADENA; and lots of names he didn't recognize; but they were no less magic, he was sure, because of that.

He was standing on the curb, just looking, when a bus with HOLLYWOOD BLVD in the little window pulled over and opened its door right in front of him. The driver looked at him impatiently. It was amazing how the bus had stopped especially for him. He got on. There didn't seem to be anything else he could do.

"Vine!" the driver bawled sometime later. John Lee got off and stood at the corner of Hollywood and Vine grinning at the night. He walked down Hollywood Boulevard, gawking at everything, reading the names in stars on the sidewalk. He never imagined there would be so many cars or so many people at night. There were more than you would see in Liberal, even on Saturday after-noon. And the strange clothes the people wore. And men with long hair like the Beatles. Mary Ellen Walker had a colored picture of them pasted on her notebook.

He didn't know how far he had walked—the street never seemed to end—but the box was heavy. He was hungry and his Sunday shoes had rubbed a blister on his heel. He went into a café and sat in a booth, glad to get rid of the weight of the box. Most of the people looked at him as he came in. Several of them smiled. He smiled back. A couple of people had said hello on the street too. Hollywood was certainly a friendly place.

He told the waitress what he wanted. He looked around the café and met the eyes of a man at the counter who had smiled when he came in. The man smiled again. John Lee smiled back, feeling good. The man got off the stool and came to the booth carrying a cup of coffee.

"May I join you?" He seemed a little nervous.

"Sure." The man sat down and took a quick sip of the coffee. "My name is John Lee Peacock." He held out his hand. The man looked startled, then took it, giving it a quick shake and hurriedly breaking contact. "I'd rather be called Johnny, though."

The man's skin was moist. John Lee guessed he was about forty and a little bit fat. He nodded, quickly, like a turkey. "Warren."

"Pleased to meet you, Mr. Warren. You live in Hollywood?"

"Yes."

The waitress brought the food and put it on the table. Warren was flustered. "Oh . . . ah . . . put that on my ticket."

The waitress looked at John Lee. Her mouth turned down a little at the corners. "Sure, honey," she said to Mr. Warren.

John Lee discarded the straw from his ice tea and put sugar in it. "Aren't you eating?"

"Ah . . . no. No, I've already eaten." He took another nervous sip of the coffee, and John Lee heard a smothered snicker from the booth behind him. "You didn't have to pay for my supper. I've got money."

"My pleasure."

"Thank you, Mr. Warren."

"You're welcome. Uh . . . how long you been in town?"

"Just got here a little while ago. On a Continental Trailways bus, all the way from Miller's Corners, Kansas." John Lee still couldn't believe where he was. He had to say it out loud. "I sure do like bein' in Los Angeles, Mr. Warren."

"You have a place to stay yet?"

He hadn't really thought about that. "No, sir. I guess I haven't."

Warren smiled and seemed to relax a little. It was working out okay, but the kid was putting on the hick routine a little thick. "Don't worry about it tonight. You can stay at my place and look for something tomorrow."

"Thank you, Mr. Warren. That's very nice of you."

"My pleasure. Uh . . . what made you come to Los Angeles?"

John Lee swallowed a mouth full of food. "My mamma died the other day. Before she died, she gave me the money to get away."

'I want to sit on the porch a while and rest,' she had said.

"It was either Los Angeles or St. Louis, and the Los Angeles bus came by first." He pushed the gray memories back out of the way. "And here I am!"

Warren looked at him, no longer smiling. "How old are you?"

"I was fifteen last January." He wondered if he was expected to ask Mr. Warren's age.

"God!" Warren breathed. He slumped in the seat for a moment, then seemed to come to a decision. "Look, uh . . . Johnny. I just remembered something. I won't be able to put you up for the night after all. As a matter of fact, I have to dash. I'm sorry."

"That's all right, Mr. Warren. It was kind of you to make the offer."

"My pleasure. So long." He hurried away. John Lee watched him stop at the cash register. When he left, the cashier looked at John Lee and nodded.

"Nice goin' there, John Lee Peacock, sugah." The voice whispered in his ear with a honeyed Southern accent. He turned and looked nose to nose into a grinning black face. "Got yoself a free dinnah and didn't have to put out."

"What," he said, completely befuddled.

A second face, a white one, appeared over the back of the seat. It said, "May we join you?" doing a good imitation of Mr. Warren.

"Yeah, I guess so." They came around and sat opposite him, both of them as skinny as Mr. Cuttsanger. He thought they walked a little funny.

The black one said, "I'm Pearl and this is Daisy Mae."

"How ja do," Daisy Mae said, chewing imaginary gum.

"Really?" John Lee asked, grinning.

"Really, what, sugah?" Pearl asked.

"Are those really your names?"

"Isn't he *cute?*" shrieked Daisy Mae.

Pearl patted his hand. "Just keep your eyes and ears open and your pants shut, sugah. You'll get the hang of it." He lit a pale blue cigarette and offered one to John Lee. John Lee shook his head. Pearl saw John Lee's bemused expression and wiggled the cigarette. "Neiman-Marcus," he said matter-of-factly.

"Well, if it isn't the Queen of Spades and Cotton Tail." They all three looked up at a chubby young man, standing with his hand delicately on his hip. His fleshy lips coiled into a smirk at John Lee. He wore light eye make-up with a tiny diamond in one pierced ear. He was with a muscular young man who looked at John Lee coldly. "You girls stage another commando raid on Romper Room?"

"Why, lawdy, Miss Scawlett, how you do talk!" Pearl did his best Butterfly McQueen imitation, and his hands were like escaping blackbirds.

"This is a cub scout meeting and we're den mothers," Daisy Mae said in a flat voice. The muscular young man grabbed Miss Scarlett's arm and pulled him away.

"It's a den of something!" he shot back over his shoulder.

"Did you see how Miss Scarlett looked at our John Lee?" Daisy Mae rolled his eyes.

"The bitch is in heat."

"Who was that gorgeous butch number she was with?"

"Never laid eyes on him before."

"Your eyes aren't what you'd like to lay on him," Daisy Mae said dryly.

Pearl quickly put his hands over John Lee's ears. "Don't talk like that afore this sweet child! You *know* I don't like rough trade!"

John Lee laughed and they laughed with him. He didn't know what they were talking about most of the time, but he decided he liked these two strange people. "Doesn't . . . uh . . . Miss Scarlett like you?"

"Sugah," Pearl said seriously, taking his hands away, "Miss Scawlett doesn't like anybody."

"Stay away from her, John Lee," Daisy Mae said, meaning it.

"She has a problem," Pearl pronounced.

"A *big* problem," Daisy Mae agreed.

"What?" John Lee asked, imagining all sorts of things.

"She's hung like a horse." Pearl nodded sagely.

"A *big* horse." Daisy Mae nodded also.

John Lee could feel his ears getting red. Damnation, he thought. He laughed in embarrassment. "What's wrong with that?" He remembered Leo Whittaker in his room at school who bragged that he had the biggest one in Kansas and would show it to you if you would go out under the bleachers.

"Sugah," Pearl said, patting his hand again, "Miss Scawlett is a *lady.*"

"It's a wonder it doesn't turn green and fall off the way she keeps it tied down. Makes her walk bowlegged."

"Don't be catty, Daisy Mae. Just count your blessin's." Daisy Mae put his chin on the heel of his hand and stared morosely at nothing, like Garbo in *Anna Christie*. "John Lee, sugah," Pearl continued, "was all that malarkey you gave that score the truth?"

"Huh?" John Lee asked, completely confused.

"It was," Daisy Mae said in his incredible but true voice.

"You really don't have a place to stay tonight?"

"Huh-uh." He wondered why Pearl doubted him.

"And he's also really fif-*teen,*" Daisy Mae said, cocking his eyes at Pearl.

"Daisy Mae, sugah," Pearl said with utmost patience, "I'm only bein' a Sistuh of Mercy, tryin' to put a roof ovuh this sweet child's head, tryin' to keep him from bein' picked up by the po-leece fah vay-gran-cee."

Daisy Mae shrugged fatalistically.

"Why does it matter that I'm fifteen?" John Lee really wanted to know what they were talking about.

"You *are* from the boonies," Daisy Mae said in wonder.

"Sugah, you come stay with us. There's a lot you've got to learn. If we leave you runnin' around loose, you gonna get in seer-ee-us trouble. Sugah, this town is full of tiguhs and . . . you . . . are . . . a . . . juicy . . . lamb."

"Your fangs are showing," Daisy Mae said tonelessly.

Pearl turned to him, about to cut him dead, but instead threw up his arms and did Butterfly McQueen again. "Lawzy, Miss Daisy Mae, you done got a spot on yo' pretty shirt!" He turned back to John Lee with a martyred expression. "I wash and clean and iron and scrub and work my fanguhs to the bone, and this slob can get covered in spaghetti sauce eatin' *jelly beans!*"

John Lee dissolved in a fit of giggles. Pearl couldn't hold his outraged expression any longer and began to grin. Daisy Mae chuckled and said, "Don't pay any attention to her, John Lee. She's got an Aunt Jemimah complex."

Pearl got up. "Let's get out of this meat market. There are too many eyes on our little rump roast."

Daisy Mae put his hand on John Lee's. "John Lee, if we run into a cop, *try* to look twenty-one."

He wiped the laugh tears from his eyes. "I'll do my best." He got the pasteboard box and followed them out of the café. They cut hurriedly around the corner past a large sidewalk newsstand, then jaywalked to a parking lot. Pearl and Daisy Mae acted like a couple of cat burglars, and John Lee had to hurry to keep up.

They got into a '63 Corvair and drove west on Hollywood Boulevard until it became a residential street, then turned right on Laurel Canyon. They would up into the Hollywood Hills, Pearl and Daisy Mae chattering constantly, making John Lee laugh a lot. He felt very good and very lucky.

Pearl pulled into a garage sitting on the edge of the pavement with no driveway. They went up a long flight of rickety wooden steps to a small two-bedroom house with a porch that went all the way around. Pearl flipped on the lights. "It ain't Twelve Oaks, sugah, but we like it."

John Lee stared goggle-eyed. He'd been in Aunt Rose's and Aunt Lilah's fancy houses lots of times, but they ran to beige, desert rose, and old gold. These colors were absolutely electric. The wild patterns made him dizzy, and there were pictures and statues and things hanging from the ceiling.

"Golly," he said.

"Take a load off," Daisy Mae said, pointing to a big reclining chair covered in what looked like purple fur. John Lee put the box on the floor and gingerly sat down. He leaned back and was surprised at how comfortable it was. Pearl put a record on the record player, but John Lee didn't recognize the music. He yawned.

Daisy Mae stood over the box. "What's in this carton you keep clutching to your bosom?"

"My things."

"Pardon my nose," Daisy Mae said and opened it. He pulled out some of John Lee's everyday clothes. "You auditioning for the sixteenth road company of *Tobacco Road?*"

"Don't pay any attention," Pearl said, sitting beside John Lee. "She's a costumer at Paramount. Thinks she knows *every*-thing about clothes."

"Don't knock it. I had to dress thirty bitchy starlets to buy that chair you got your black ass on. I'll hang these up for you, John Lee."

John Lee yawned again. "Thank you."

Pearl threw up his hands. "Land o' Goshen, this child is ex-*haus*-ted!"

Daisy Mae carried the box into a bedroom. "Two days on a Continental Trailways bus would give Captain Marvel the drear-ies."

Pearl took John Lee's arm and pulled him out of the chair. "Come on, sugah. We gotta give you a nice bath and put you to *bed,* afore you co-lapse." He led him to the bathroom, showed him where everything was, and turned on the shower for him. "Give a holler if you need anything."

"Thank you." Pearl left. John Lee had never taken a shower before, although he had seen them at Aunt Rose's and Aunt Li-lah's. He took off his clothes and got in.

The door opened and Pearl came in, pushing back the shower curtain. "You all right, sugah? Oh, sugah, you are *all right!*" He leered at John Lee, but in such a way that made him laugh. His ears turned red anyway. Pearl winked and closed the curtain. "You don't mind if I brush my teeth?"

"No. Go ahead." He could hear Pearl sloshing and brushing. After a bit there was silence. He pulled back the shower curtain a little and peeped out. Pearl was leaning against the wash basin, a toothbrush in his hand, his head down, and his eyes closed. John Lee watched him, wondering if he should say anything.

"John Lee," Pearl said without looking up, his voice serious and the accent totally absent.

"Yes, Pearl?" He spoke quietly and cautiously.

"John Lee, don't pay any attention when we tease you about how cute you are, or when we ogle your body. It's just the way we are. It's just the way the lousy world is."

"I won't, Pearl." He felt the hurting in the back of his throat, but he didn't know why.

Pearl suddenly stood up, the big grin back on his face. "Well. Look at me. Poor Pitiful Pearl. Now. What do you sleep in? Underwear? Pee-jays? Nightshirt? Your little bare skin?"

"My pajamas are in the box, I think."

"Good enough." Pearl left the bathroom and returned when John Lee was drying on a big plush towel printed like the American flag. Pearl reached in and hung the pajamas on the doorknob without looking in. "There you go, sugah."

"Thank you, Pearl."

He left the bathroom in his pajamas with his Sunday suit over his arm. Daisy Mae took the suit. "I'll clean and press that for you."

"You don't have to, Daisy Mae." The names were beginning to sound normal to him.

Daisy Mae grinned. "It won't hurt me."

"Thank you."

Pearl took his arm. "Time for you to go to bed." He led John Lee into the bedroom. There was an old, polished brass bed. John Lee stared at it, then ran his hand over the turned-back sheets. Even Aunt Rose hadn't thought about red silk sheets. He never imagined such luxury.

"Golly," he said.

Pearl laughed and grabbed him in a big hug and kissed him on the forehead. "Sugah, you are just not to be be-*lieved!*" John Lee grinned uncomfortably and turned red. Pearl pulled the sheet up around his neck and patted his cheek. "Sleep tight."

"Good night, Pearl."

Daisy Mae stuck his head in to say good night. Pearl turned at the door and smiled fondly at him, then went out, closing it. John Lee wiggled around on the silk sheets. Golly, he thought, golly, golly, golly!

Pearl walked dreamily into the living room and collapsed becomingly onto the big purple fur chair. He sighed hugely. "Daisy Mae. Now I know what it must feel like to be a mother."

The next morning John Lee woke slowly and stretched until his muscles popped. He looked at the ceiling, but there was no faded water-stained paper, only neat white tiles with an embossed flower in the center of each. He slid to the side of the bed and felt the silk sheets flow like water across his skin. He went to the bathroom and relieved himself, splashing cold water on his face and combing the tangles out of his hair. He sure needed a haircut. He wondered if he ought to let it grow long now that he was in Hollywood.

Hollywood.

He'd almost forgotten. He bet Miss Mahan was worried about him. He sure liked Miss Mahan and a pang of guilt struck him. He should have told her he wouldn't be back in school this fall, especially after she was nice enough to come to mamma's funeral and all. Well, there was nothing he could do now. Mr. Cuttsanger would tell her—and everybody else—where he was.

He went back to his room and put on his best pair of blue jeans, a white T-shirt and his gray sneakers. He wondered where everyone was. The house was very quiet. He guessed they had both gone to work. He went out on the back porch—only Pearl called it a deck—and saw Daisy Mae lying there on a blanket stark naked. He started to go back in, but Daisy Mae looked up. "Good morning, slugabed, you sleep well?"

John Lee fidgeted, trying not to look at Daisy Mae. "Yeah. Real good. Where's Pearl?"

"She's at work. Does windows for May Company."

"Didn't you have to work today at Paramount?"

"Got a few days off. Just finished something called *Wives and Lovers.* Gonna be a dog. You want some breakfast, or you wanta join me?"

"Uh . . . what're you doin'?" He sure didn't seem to care if anybody saw him naked.

"Gettin' some sun, tryin' to get rid of this fish-belly white."

"You always do it with . . . uh . . . no clothes on?" You're acting like a hick again, John Lee Peacock. Damnation, he thought.

Daisy Mae chuckled. "Sure. Otherwise, I'd look like a two-tone Ford. If it embarrasses you, I'll put some clothes on."

"No," he protested quickly. "No, of course it doesn't embarrass me. I think I *will* join you."

"Okay." He pointed back over his head without looking. "There's another blanket there on the chaise."

John Lee spread the blanket on the porch and pulled his T-shirt over his head. He pulled off his shoes and socks. Daisy Mae wasn't paying any attention to him. He looked around. The next house up the hill overlooked them, but that was the only one. He didn't see anybody up there. He took a deep breath, slipped off his pants and his shorts, and quickly lay down on his stomach. He might as well get some sun on his back first.

Daisy Mae spoke without looking at him. "Don't stay in one position more than five minutes, or you'll blister."

"Okay." He estimated five minutes had passed, swallowed, and turned over on his back. He looked straight into the eyes of a woman leaning on the railing of the next house up, watching him. He froze. The bottom dropped out of his stomach. Then he jumped up and grabbed his pants. He knew he was acting like an idiot, but he couldn't stop himself. He hopped on one foot, trying to get the pants on, but his toes kept getting in the way. They caught on the crotch and he fell flat on his butt. He managed to wiggle into them, sitting on the floor.

Daisy Mae looked up. "You sit on a bee or something?"

"No." He motioned with his head at the woman, afraid to look at her because he knew he was beet red all over.

Daisy Mae looked up, grinned, and waved. "Hi, Sue." He didn't do anything to cover himself, didn't seem to care that she saw him.

"Hello, Daisy Mae." Her voice was husky and amused. "Who's your bashful friend?"

"John Lee Peacock from Kansas. This is Sue. San Diego Light-foot Sue."

Damnation, John Lee thought, I'm acting like a fool, sitting here hunkered up against this shez, as Daisy Mae calls it. Doesn't anyone in Hollywood have a normal name? He forced himself to look up. She was still leaning on the railing, looking at him. Only now she was smiling. She was wearing a paint-stained sweat shirt and blue jeans. Her hair was tied up in a scarf but auburn strands dangled out. She wasn't wearing any make-up that he could see. She was kinda old, he thought, but really very stunning. Her smile was nice. He felt himself smiling back.

"Nothing to be bashful about, John Lee Peacock. I've seen more male privates than you could load in a boxcar." Her voice was still amused but she wasn't putting him down.

"Maybe so," he answered, "but I haven't had any ladies see mine." His boldness made him start getting red again.

She laughed and he felt goose bumps pop out on his arms. "You could have a point there, John Lee. How would you like to make a little money?"

"Huh?"

"It's okay," Daisy Mae said, getting up and wrapping a towel around his waist. "Sue's an artist. She wants you to pose for her."

John Lee looked back up at her. "That's right," she said. "I'm as safe as mother's milk."

"Well, okay, I guess. But you don't need to pay me for something like that." He got up and kicked his underwear under the chaise.

"Of course I'll pay you. It's very hard work. Come on up."

"Uh . . . how do I get up there?"

"Go down to the street and come up my steps. Front door's open, come on in. You'll find me." She smiled again and went out of sight.

He looked at Daisy Mae. "Will it be all right with Pearl?"

"Sure. We've both posed for her. She's good. Scoot." Daisy Mae went into the house. John Lee put on his T-shirt and shoes. He wondered if he should take off his pants and put on his underwear, but decided against it.

He opened her front door and went in as she had told him. She was right about him finding her. The whole house was one big room. A small kitchen was in one corner behind a folding screen. A day bed was against one wall between two bureaus that had been painted yellow. There was a door to a closet and another to a bathroom. There were a couple of tired but comfortable-looking easy chairs, a drafting table with a stool pushed under it, and an easel under a skylight. Pictures were everywhere; some in color, mostly black and white sketches; thumbtacked all over the walls, leaning in stacks against the bureaus, chairs, walls. A big orange cat lay curled in a chair. It opened one eye, gave John Lee the once over, and went back to sleep.

Sue was standing at the easel, frowning at the painting he couldn't see. She had a brush stuck behind one ear and was holding another like a club. "I'm glad you showed up, John Lee. This thing is going nowhere." She flipped a cloth over it and leaned it against the wall.

John Lee stared at the pictures. Nearly all of them were of people, most of them naked, though there were a couple of the cat. Some of the people were women but most of them seemed to be men. He spotted a sketch of Pearl and Daisy Mae, leaning against each other naked, looking like a butterfly with one black and one white wing.

She watched him look for a while. "This is just the garbage. I sell the good stuff. That one of Pearl and Daisy Mae turned out rather well. It's hanging in a gay bar in the Valley. Got eleven hundred for it."

"Golly."

"You're right. It was a swindle."

"Do you . . . ah . . . want me to . . . do you want to paint my picture with my . . . clothes off?" He waved his hand vaguely at some of the nude sketches. Damn his ears!

She didn't seem to notice. "If you don't mind. Don't worry about it. It'll be a few days yet. Give you a chance to get used to the idea. I want to make some sketches and work on your face for a while." She came to him and put her hand on his cheek. "You've got something in your face, John Lee. I don't know . . . what it is. More than simple innocence. I just hope I can capture it. Hold still, I want to feel your bones." He grinned and it made her smile. "Makes you feel like a horse up for sale, doesn't it?" She ran her cool fingers over his face, and he didn't want her to ever stop. He closed his eyes.

Suddenly, she caught her fingers in his hair and shook him. She laughed and hugged him against her warm soft breasts. His stomach did a flip-flop. She released him quickly and crossed her arms with her hands under her armpits. She laughed a little nervously. "You're just like Punkin. Scratch his ears and he'll go to sleep on you."

"Punkin?"

She pointed at the cat. "Don't you think he looks remarkably like a pumpkin when he's curled up asleep like that?"

"Yeah." He laughed.

"Do you want to start now?"

"I guess."

"Okay. Just sit in that chair and relax." She pulled the stool from beneath the drafting table and put it in front of the chair. She sat on the stool with her legs crossed, a sketch pad propped on one knee. She lit a cigarette and held it in her left hand while she worked rapidly with a stick of charcoal. "You can talk if you want to. Tell me about yourself."

So he did. He told her about Miller's Corners, Hawley, the farm, school, Miss Mahan who also painted but only flowers, Mr. Cuttsanger, his mother, a lot about his mother, not much about his father because he didn't really know very much when you got right down to it. He made her chuckle about Aunt Rose and Aunt Lilah. She kept turning the pages of the sketch pad and starting over. He wanted to see what she was drawing, but he was afraid to move.

She seemed to read his mind. "You don't have to sit so still, John Lee. Move when you want to." He changed positions but he still couldn't see. Punkin suddenly leaped in his lap, making him jump. The cat walked up his chest and looked into his eyes. Then he began to purr and curled up with his head under John Lee's chin.

Sue chuckled. "You are a charmer, John Lee. He treats most people with majestic indifference." John Lee grinned and stroked the cat. Punkin squirmed in delicious ecstasy. Then John Lee's stomach rumbled.

Sue put the pad down and laughed. "You poor lamb. I'm starving you to death." She looked at her watch. "Good grief, it's two thirty. What do you want to eat?"

"Anything."

"Anything it is."

He stood with Punkin curled in his arms, watching her do wonderful things with eggs, ham, green peppers, onions, and buttered toast. He said he loved scrambled eggs; and she laughed and said scrambled eggs indeed, you taste my omelets and you'll be my slave forever. She pulled down a table that folded against the wall, set out the two steaming plates with two glasses of cold milk. He was quite willing to be her slave forever, even without the omelet.

Punkin sat on the floor with his tail curled around his feet, watching them, making short, soft clarinet sounds. She laughed. "Isn't that pitiful? The cat food's under the sink if you'd like to feed him."

"Sure." He tried to pour the cat food into the bowl, but Punkin kept grabbing the box with his claws and sticking his head in it. John Lee sat on the floor having a fit of giggles. God o' mighty, he thought, everything is so wonderfully, marvelously, absolutely perfectly good.

She continued sketching after they did the dishes. He sat in the chair feeling luxuriously content. He smiled.

"May I share it?" Sue asked, almost smiling herself.

"Huh? Oh, nothin'. I was just . . . feeling good." Then he felt embarrassed. "You . . . ah . . . been painting pictures very long?"

"Oh, I've dabbled at it quite a while, but I've only been doing it seriously for a couple of years." She smiled in a funny, wry way. "I'm just an aging roundheels who decided she'd better find another line of work while she could."

He didn't know what she was talking about. "You're not old."

"I stood on the shore and chunked rocks at the Mayflower." She sighed. "I'm forty-five."

"Golly. I thought you were about thirty."

She laughed her throaty laugh that made him tingle. "Honey, at your age everyone between twenty-five and fifty looks alike."

"I think you're beautiful," he said and wished he hadn't, but she smiled and he was glad he had.

"Thank you, little lamb. You should have seen me when I was your age." She stopped drawing and sat with her head to one side, remembering. "You should have seen me when I was fifteen." Then she shifted her position on the stool and laughed. "I was quite a dish—if I do say so myself. We were practically neighbors, you know that?" she said, changing the subject. "I'm an old Okie from way back. Still can't bear to watch *The Grapes of Wrath*. We came to California in '33 and settled in San Diego. Practically starved to death. My father died in '35, and my mother went back to telling fortunes and having seances—among other things. My father wouldn't let her do it while he was alive."

"Golly," he said, bug-eyed. "A real fortune teller?"

"Well," she said wryly, "I never thought of it as being very real, but I don't know any more." She looked at him speculatively for a moment, then shrugged. "Whether she was real or not, I don't know but I guess she was pretty good, 'cause there seemed to be plenty of money after that. Then the war started. And if you're twenty-three, in San Diego, during a war, you can make lots of money if you keep your wits about you." She shifted again on the stool. "Well, we won't go into that."

"Where's your mother now?"

"Oh, she's dead . . . I imagine. It was in '45, I think. Yeah, right after V-J Day, I went over for a visit and she wasn't there. Never heard from her again. You know, her house is still there in San Diego. I get a tax bill every year. I don't know why I keep paying it. Guess I'd rather do that than go through all that junk she had accumulated. I was down there a few years ago and went by the place. Everything was still there just as it was; two feet deep in dust, of course. I'm surprised vandals haven't stripped the place, considering what the neighborhood's become. I took a few things as keepsakes, but I didn't hang around long. It's worse than it was when she was there."

She worked a while in silence, then stopped drawing again and looked at him in a way that made his stomach feel funny. "If I were twenty and you were twenty . . . you're gonna be a ring-tailed boomer when you're twenty, John Lee." She suddenly laughed and began drawing. "If I'm gonna make people older and younger, I might as well make myself fifteen—no point in wasting five years."

He didn't know what a ring-tailed boomer was, but the way she said it made his ears turn red. Her mentioning San Diego reminded him. "Why do they call you San Diego Lightfoot Sue?"

"Daisy Mae has a big mouth," she said wryly. "I'll tell you about it someday."

"I sure like Pearl and Daisy Mae," he said and smiled.

"So do I."

"Pearl is awfully nice to me."

"Some people have a cat and some people have a dog."

He sure wished he knew what people were talking about, at least some of the time.

It seemed to him hardly any time had passed when Pearl sashayed in with a May Co. carton under his arm. "It is I, Lady Bountiful, come to free the slaves," he brayed and presented the box to John Lee with a flourish. "It's a Welcome to California present."

"Golly." He took the box gingerly.

"Well, *open* it." John Lee fumbled at the string while Pearl planted a kiss on Sue's cheek. "Sugah, you look more like Lauren Bacall every *day!*"

Sue grinned. "Hello, Pearl. How are you?"

He sighed an elaborate sigh. "I am *worn* to a frazzle. I've been slaving over a tacky May Company window all day. If they would *only* let me be *cre-a-tive!*"

"Wilshire Boulevard would never survive it."

John Lee stared at the contents of the box. "How did you know what size I wore?"

"Daisy Mae has tape measures in her eyeballs." He made fluttering motions with his hands. "Well, try them *on.*"

John Lee grinned and hurried to the bathroom with the box. He put it on the side of the tub and went through it. There were pants, a shirt, socks, shoes, and, he was glad to see, underwear. But he had never seen gold underwear and it looked kinda skimpy. He quickly shucked off his clothes and slipped on the gold shorts. Golly, he thought. They fit like his hide, and he kept wanting to pull them up, but that's all there was to them.

The shirt was yellow and soft. He rubbed it on his face, then slipped it over his head. It fit tight around his waist, and the neck was open halfway to his navel. He looked for buttons but there weren't any. The sleeves were long and floppy and had little pearl snaps on the cuffs.

He slipped on the pants, which had alternating dark-brown and light-brown vertical stripes. He was surprised to find that they didn't come any higher than the shorts. He gave them an experimental tug and decided they wouldn't fall off. They were tight almost to the knees and got loose and floppy at the bottom.

He sat on the commode to put on the shoes but stood again to hitch the pants up in back. He slipped on the soft, fuzzy gold socks. The shoes were brown and incredibly shiny. And they didn't even have shoestrings. He stood up, gave the pants a hitch, and looked at himself in the mirror. He couldn't make himself stop grinning.

He opened the bathroom door and walked out, still grinning. Pearl made his eyes go big and round, and Sue leaned against one of the yellow bureaus with her mouth puckered up. John Lee walked nervously to them, the shoes making a thump at every step. "The pants are a little bit too tight," he said and didn't know what to do with his hands.

"Oh, sugah, you are *wrong* about that!"

"If he had his hair slicked down with pomade, he'd look like an adagio dancer . . . or something," Sue said in a flat voice.

Pearl lowered his eyebrows at her, then twirled his finger at John Lee. "Turn around."

He turned nervously, worried because Sue didn't seemed pleased.

"John Lee, sugah," Pearl said in awe, "you have *got* the *Power!*"

"Pearl. Don't you think you went a little overboard?" Sue put her hand on the back of John Lee's neck. "If he walked down Hollywood Boulevard in that, he'd have to carry a machine gun."

"Well!" Pearl swelled up in mock outrage. "At least they're not *lavender!*"

Sue laughed. John Lee laughed too, but he wasn't exactly sure why. They were saying things he didn't understand again. But he felt an overwhelming fondness for Pearl at that moment. He reached out and shook Pearl's hand. "Thank you, Pearl. I think the clothes are beautiful." Then, because he felt Pearl would be pleased, he kissed him on the cheek.

The effect was startling. Pearl's face seemed to turn to putty and went through seven distinct expression changes. His mouth worked like a goldfish and he kept blinking his eyes. Then he pulled himself together and said too loudly, "Listen, you all. Dinner will be ready in exactly seventy-two minutes. We're having my world-famous sowbelly and chittlin lasagna." He hurried out, walking too fast.

John Lee was up very early the next morning. Sue opened the door still in her bathrobe. "I didn't know what time you wanted me to come over," he said apologetically. "Did I wake you up?"

Sue smiled and motioned him in. "Ordinarily, I'm not coordinated enough to tie my shoes before noon, but I woke up about two hours ago ready to go to work. I didn't even take time to dress." She indicated one wall of the room. "Check out the gallery while I put the wreck together."

All the old sketches had been cleared from the wall. John Lee saw himself thumbtacked in neat rows. "Golly," he said, walking slowly down the rows. The sketches were all of his face: some sheets were covered with eyes, laughing, sleepy, dreamy, contemplative; others with mouths, smiling, grinning, pouting, pensive. There were noses and ears and combinations. He recognized some of the full-face sketches: this one was when he was talking about his mother; that one when he was petting Punkin; that one when he was telling of Aunt Rose and Aunt Lilah; another when he sat in rapt attention, listening to Sue.

She emerged from the bathroom dressed much as she had been the day before except that she wore a little make-up and her hair fell through the scarf, hanging long and fluffy down her back. John Lee thought she was absolutely gorgeous. "What do you think," she asked tentatively, not quite smiling.

He couldn't think of anything to say that wasn't obvious to the eye, and so he just grinned in extreme pleasure.

She smiled happily. "I think I've caught you, John Lee. I really feel good about it. You're just what I've been needing."

"What're you gonna draw today?"

She indicated a large canvas in position on the easel. "I'm ready to start, if you are."

Oh, Lord, he thought, just don't turn red. "Yeah. I guess so."

"You can keep your pants on for a while, if it'll make you more comfortable. I'll work on your head and torso." She was business-like, not seeming to notice his nervousness. It made him feel a little better.

He took a deep breath. "No . . . I might as well get it over with." She nodded and began puttering around with paints and turpen-tine, not looking at him, without seeming to be deliberately not looking at him. He pulled the T-shirt over his head and wondered what to do with it. Quit stalling, he admonished, and slipped off his sneakers and socks. He looked at her but she was still ignoring him. He quickly pulled off his pants and shorts. He stood there feeling as if there were a cyclone in his stomach. "Well," he said, "I'm ready."

She turned and looked at him as if she had seen him naked every day of his life. "You have absolutely nothing to be embarrassed about, John Lee."

"Well," he said, "well . . ."

"What's the matter?"

"I don't know what to do with my *hands!*" Then he couldn't keep from laughing and she laughed with him. "What do you want me to do?"

"Let's see . . ." She moved one of the chairs under the light.

"Lean against the chair. I want you relaxed . . ."

"I'll try," he chuckled.

She smiled. "I want you relaxed and completely innocent of your nudity. Sort of the *September Morn* effect."

"You're asking a lot." He leaned against the chair, trying to look innocent.

She gave a throaty laugh and shook her head. "You look more like a chicken thief. Don't try too hard. Just relax and be comfortable, like you were yesterday."

"I had my clothes on yesterday."

"I know. You'll do okay as soon as you get used to it."

"I still don't know what to do with my hands."

"Don't do anything with them. Just forget 'em; let them find their own position. I know it's not easy. Just forget I'm here. Pretend you're in the woods completely alone. You've just been swimming in a little lake, and now you're relaxing in the sun, leaning against a warm rock. Try to picture it."

"Okay, I'll try."

"You're not thinking about anything, just resting, feeling the sun on your body." She watched him. A pucker of concentration appeared over his nose. He shifted his hips slightly to get more comfortable, and his fidgety hands finally came to rest at his sides. His diaphragm moved slowly as his breathing became softer. The frown gradually disappeared from his face, and the quality she couldn't put a name to took its place. God, she thought, it brought back memories she had thought were put away forever. She felt like a giddy young girl.

"That's it, John Lee," she said very softly, trying not to disturb him. She picked up a stick of charcoal and began to work rapidly. A pleased smile flickered across his lips and then disappeared. "Beautiful, John Lee, beautiful. Don't close your eyes; watch the sun reflecting on the water."

She got the basic form the way she wanted it in charcoal, then began squeezing paint from tubes onto a palette. She applied the base colors quickly, almost offhandedly. After about fifteen minutes she said, "When you get tired, let me know and we'll take a break."

"No. I'm fine."

After another half hour she saw his thumb twitch. "If you're not tired," she said, putting the palette down, "I am. Would you like some coffee?"

"Yeah," he said without moving. "Are you sure I can get back in the same position again?"

"I'm sure." She tossed him her bathrobe and he put it on. "Do a few knee bends and get the kinks out." She poured two cups of coffee from the electric percolator. "I told you it was hard work."

He grinned and stretched his arms forward, rolling the muscles in his shoulders. "I'm not tired."

She handed him a cup. "You've been warned." She opened the back door when she heard a plaintive cry from outside. Punkin strolled in and looked up at her, demanding attention. She picked him up and he started purring loudly.

John Lee found it easy to keep the same position the rest of the morning. Sue had made him as comfortable as she could because of his inexperience. She worked steadily with concentration. He missed the easy chatter of the day before, but he didn't want to disturb her. They took periodic breaks, though she sometimes became so engrossed she forgot. Then she would admonish him gently for not reminding her. When they broke for lunch, she made him do knee bends and push-ups and then massaged his back and shoulders with green rubbing alcohol.

Daisy Mae strolled in with a foil-covered Pyrex dish. "You didn't do that when Pearl and I posed for you," he said with feigned huffiness and slipped the dish into the oven.

"Hello, Daisy Mae," John Lee grinned, putting on the robe. "Look at the sketches."

"Hello, John Lee. I knew Sue would get so absorbed she'd forget to feed you. So I brought the leftover lasagna." He looked over the sketches, critically, with his fingers theatrically stroking his chin. "I think the girl shows some promise, though I see years of study ahead."

Sue kissed him on the cheek and began setting the table for three. Daisy Mae sprawled in a chair like a wilting lily. "God!" he grunted. "I got a call from Paramount this morning. I start back to work Thursday. We're doing a *west*-ern. On lo-*ca*-tion. My *God.* In *Arizona!* Centipedes! Tarantulas! Scorpions! Rattlesnakes! Sweaty starlets! If I'm not back in five weeks, send the Ma-*rines!*"

Sue laughed. "You can console yourself with thoughts of all those butch cowboys."

"Darling," he said, arching his wrist at her, "some of those cowboys are about as butch as Pamela Tiffin. I could tell you stories . . ."

"Don't bother. I've heard most of them."

"I haven't," John Lee piped in brightly.

Sue started to say something, but Daisy Mae beat her to it. "Someday, John Lee. You're much too young to lose *all* your illusions."

When they had eaten, Sue thanked him for bringing the lasagna and shooed him out. He started to peek under the cloth covering the painting, but she slapped his hand. "You know better than that."

"Can John Lee bunk over here tomorrow night? I'm giving myself a going-away party before I'm exiled to the burning deserts, and it's liable to last all night."

She stood very still for a moment. Then she nodded with a jerk of her head. "Of course." Daisy Mae waltzed out with his Pyrex dish. Sue looked after him for a moment, then at John Lee sitting bewildered on the day bed. She gave him a quick nervous smile. "You ready?"

He took off the bathrobe, hardly feeling embarrassed at all, and took his place, bringing back the woods, the lake, and the warm rock, but needing them only for a moment to get started.

At four thirty she covered the painting and began washing the brushes. She had said hardly anything at all since Daisy Mae left, giving him only an occasional soft-voiced direction. He put his clothes on and went to her. "Is it turning out the way you'd hoped?"

Her eyes met his. He saw sadness in them and something that had gotten lost. "Yes," she said almost inaudibly. Then she smiled. "You're a joy to paint, John Lee. Now, run along before Pearl comes traipsing in. I'd rather not have company this evening. Be over bright and early, and I think we'll finish it tomorrow."

Punkin stopped him on the steps, wanting to be petted. He picked up the cat and glanced back to see Sue watching him through the window. She turned away quickly.

The painting was completed at three P.M. the next afternoon. Sue stood back from it and looked at John Lee, smiling. He went to her hesitantly, almost fearfully, still naked, and looked at it. "Golly," he breathed. When she painted a nude, she really painted everything. He felt the heat starting at his ears and flowing downward. He was almost used to being naked in front of her, but it was an astonishing shock to *see* himself being naked.

She laughed fondly. "John Lee, you're a regular traffic light."

"No, I'm not," he muttered and got even redder.

Suddenly, her arms were around him, hugging him tightly to her. He felt electricity bouncing in the bottom of his stomach. He threw his arms around her and wanted to be enveloped by her. "John Lee, my little lamb," she whispered in his ear, bending her head because she was an inch taller, "do you like it?"

"Yes!" he breathed, with that peculiar pain in the back of his throat again. "Oh, yes."

He shifted his head slightly so he could see. The painting was done in pale sun-washed colors. He leaned against a suggestion of something white which might have been a large rock. It was everything she had said she wanted, and more. He seemed totally innocent of clothing, so completely comfortable was he in his nudity. His body was relaxed, but there was no lethargy in it. There was something slightly supernatural about the John Lee in the painting, as if perhaps he were a fawn or a wood sprite, definitely an impression of a forest creature. The various shades of pale green in the background implied a forest, and there was a dappling of leaf shadows on his shoulder and chest—but only a suggestion. However, these were unimportant. The figure dominated the painting, executed in fine detail, like a Raphael. The face was innocent, totally uncorrupted by worldly knowledge. But there was a quality in it even purer than simple innocence. The eyes were lost in a reverie.

"Do I look like that?" he asked, slightly overwhelmed.

"Well . . ." she said with a husky chuckle, "yes, you do. Although I will have to admit I idealized you somewhat."

"Is it okay if I bring Pearl and Daisy Mae over to see it?" he asked with growing excitement. "Pearl was supposed to come home at noon today to help with the party. Only she . . . I mean he, calls it a Druid ritual."

She laughed and released him. "All right."

He raced happily to the door, then skidded to a halt. He hurried back, grinning sheepishly, and picked up his pants. He put them on, hopping on one foot, then out the door, clattering down the steps. She looked at the empty doorway for a moment, then rubbed at her eyes but was unable to stop the tears.

"Hell!" she said out loud. "Oh, hell!"

John Lee came over from the party about ten o'clock dressed in his new clothes and carrying a Lufthansa flight bag Pearl had packed for him. He flopped into one of the chairs, grinning. Sue was in the other, reading. She looked at him speculatively. Punkin leaped lightly from her lap and stretched mightily, his rear end high in the air, his chin against the floor, and his toes splayed. Then he hopped into John Lee's lap. Stroking the cat and still grinning, he met her eyes. They both burst into a fit of giggles.

"John Lee, you have *no* staying power," she choked out between gasps of laughter.

He got himself under control, gulping air. "I'd much rather be over here with you."

"I hope Pearl gave you a whip and a chair to go with those clothes."

"No, but he warned me to stay out of corners and, above all, bedrooms."

There was a light tap on the door. "I've been expecting this," she muttered. "Come on in!"

The door opened and a pale, slim, good-looking young man wafted in like the queen of Rumania inspecting the hog pens. "Hello," he sighed, not quite holding out his hand to be kissed. "Pearl was telling us about the painting you did of John Lee. May I see it?" He looked at John Lee and smiled anemically.

"Of course." Sue got up and turned the light on over the easel. A shriek of laughter drifted over from next door. The young man strolled to the painting and stood motionless for a full two minutes staring at it.

Then he sighed. "Pearl is so lucky. My last one ran off with my stereo, my Polaroid, and knocked out three fillings."

"That's . . . ah . . . too bad," she said, valiantly not smiling.

"Yes," he said and sighed again. "I'd like to buy it."

"It's not for sale."

"I'll give you a thousand."

She shook her head.

"Two thousand."

"Sorry."

He sighed again as if he expected nothing from life but an endless series of defeats. "Oh, well. Thank you for letting me see it."

"You're extremely welcome."

He drifted to the door like a wisp of fog, turned, gave John Lee a wan smile, and departed. They both stared at the closed door.

"I feel as if I just played the last act of *La Traviata*," Sue said in a stunned voice.

"If I remember correctly," John Lee said, "that was Cow-Cow."

She lifted the painting from the easel. "There's only one thing to do if we don't want a parade through here all night. Be back shortly." She left, taking the painting with her.

When she returned half an hour later, he was dozing. "The showing was an unqualified success. I was offered se-ven thou-sand dol-lars for it. You never saw so many erotic fantasies hanging out. It was like waving a haunch of beef at a bunch of half-starved tigers." She put the painting back on the easel and stood looking at it. "It *is* good, though, isn't it, John Lee?" She sounded only partially convinced. "It really is good." She looked at him, sprawled in the chair, half asleep, smiling happily at her. "Well," she laughed, "neither the artist nor the model are qualified judges. And that crowd at Pearl's could only see a beautiful child with his privates exposed."

She sat on the arm of the chair, putting her hand on the side of his face. He closed his eyes and moved his face against her hand the way Punkin would do. "You're such a child, John Lee," she said softly, feeling her eyes getting damp. "Your body may fool people for a while, but up here," she caught her fingers in his hair, "up here, you're an innocent, trusting, guileless child. And I think you may break my heart." She closed her eyes, trying to hold back the tears, afraid she was making a fool of herself.

He looked up at her, feeling things he had never felt before, wanting things he had never wanted before. Perhaps if he hadn't been floating in the dreamlike area between wakefulness and sleep, his natural shyness might have prevented him. He slipped his arms slowly around her neck and pulled her gently to him. He felt her tense as if about to pull away, then her lips were like butterfly wings against his. She lay across him with her face buried in his neck. He stroked her hair and brushed his lips against her cheek.

"Is this what you want, John Lee?" she asked, her voice unsteady. "Is this what you really want?"

"Yes," he answered. "You're all I want."

"You're sure you're not just feeling sorry for an old lady?" she said shakily, trying to sound if she were making a joke, but not succeeding completely.

He held her tighter. "I love you, San Diego Lightfoot Sue."

She stood up, wiping at her eyes with trembling fingers. "Daisy Mae and his big mouth," she said, half laughing and half crying. John Lee stood up also, giving the striped pants a hitch in the back. "Oh, John Lee," she said, hugging him to her, "take off those awful clothes."

He stood on tiptoe to kiss her because his mouth came only to her chin. He removed the clothes, feeling no embarrassment at all. She turned out the light and locked the door before undressing, feeling embarrassment herself for the first time in nearly thirty years. She turned back the cover on the day bed, and they lay in the warm night, listening to the shrieks of strained laughter from Pearl's, feeling, exploring, each trying to touch every part of the other's body with every part of his own. Then, she showed him what to do and kissed him when he was clumsy.

They lay together, drowsily. Flamenco music drifted over from the party next door. Sue had her arms around John Lee, her breasts pressed against his back, her face against his neck. "John Lee?"

"Mmmm?"

"John Lee, when you're twenty . . . have you thought, I'll be fifty?"

"I love you, Sue. It doesn't matter to me."

She was silent for a moment. "Perhaps it doesn't now. You're too young to know the difference, and I still have a few vestiges of my looks left. But in a few years you'll want a girl your own age, and in a few years I'll be an old woman." He started to protest, but she put her fingers on his lips, brushing them with feathery touches. "Your lips are like velvet, John Lee," she whispered. He opened his mouth slightly and touched her fingers with his tongue. Then she clamped her arms around him and began weeping on his shoulder. "My God, John Lee! I don't want to be like your favorite aunt, or even your mother! I don't want to see you married to some empty-headed girl, some pretty *young* girl, having your babies like a brood sow, living in a tract house in Orange County. I want to be the one to have your babies, but I'm too old . . ."

He twisted in her arms to face her and stopped her words with his mouth. The second time, she showed him how to make it last longer, how to make it better, and he was very adept. He fell asleep in her arms where she held him like a teddy bear, but she lay awake for many hours, making a decision.

The next morning, he moved his things from Pearl's to Sue's.

When he had gone, Pearl began to sob, large tears rolling down his face. His hands clutched at each other like graceful black spiders. Daisy Mae put down the glass of tomato juice with the raw egg and Tabasco he had made for his hangover and took Pearl in his arms.

"Oh, Pearl, you knew it would happen. Just like it always happens," he soothed.

"But John Lee was different from the others," he forced out
between heaving sobs.

"Yes, he was. But he's just next-door. He's still our friend. We
can see him anytime."

"But it's not the same. Sue will be taking care of him, not me!
Oh, Daisy Mae," he wailed, "if this is what it's like to lose a child,
I don't want to be a mother any more!"

Sue began a new painting that morning. "I want you like you
were last night," she told John Lee, "sitting all asprawl in the chair,
half asleep, with Punkin in your lap, but *not* in those same
clothes." They went through his meager wardrobe. She selected
a pair of khaki-colored jeans and gave him one of her short-sleeve
sweat shirts. She showed him how to sit. "Leave your shoes off. I
have a foot fetish." She ran her fingernails quickly across the bottom of his foot. His leg jerked and he grabbed her, giggling, and
pulling her in his lap. She submitted happily to his kisses for a
moment, then pulled away.

"Okay," she laughed, "calm yourself. We've got work to do."

"Yes, ma'am," he said primly, striking a pose and beaming at
her.

Thank God, she thought, he doesn't seem to have any regrets.

"My *Gawd!*" Pearl shrieked, seeing the new painting for the
first time. He bulged his eyes and hugged himself. *"Sue!* That's the
most erotic thing I've seen in my *life!* It's practically porno-
graphic!" If I look at it any longer, I'm gonna embarrass myself."
He turned away dramatically and saw John Lee grinning and
blushing.

"I embarrass myself a little with that one," Sue admitted. "Talk
about erotic fantasies."

The painting was in dark brooding colors, but a light from somewhere fell across John Lee, sitting deep in the chair, one bare foot
tucked under him and the other dangling. One hand lay on his
thigh and the other negligently stroked the orange cat in his lap.
His face was sleepy and sensual. His eyes looked directly at you.
They were the eyes of an innocent fawn, but they were also the
eyes of a stag in rut.

"You're not . . . ah . . . gonna show it to a bunch of people, are you?" John Lee asked tentatively.

When he woke the next morning, the bed beside him was empty. He rubbed the sleep from his eyes and unfolded the note lying on her pillow. "John Lee, my love," it read in her masculine scrawl, "I had to go to San Diego for the day and didn't want to wake you. I'll be back tonight late. Sue."

He was asleep when she came in. She sat on the edge of the bed and moved her hand lightly across his chest. "John Lee. Wake up, honey."

He squirmed on the bed. "Sue?" he mumbled without opening his eyes. He turned over on his stomach, burying his head, fighting wakefulness.

She pulled back the covers and slapped him lightly on his bare bottom. "Wake up. I want to do another painting. Get dressed."

"I'm too sleepy. Leave your number and I'll call you."

"Okay, smarty," she laughed, "you've got thirty seconds before I get out the ice cubes."

"White slaver," he grinned, sitting up and kissing her.

"Where did you hear that?"

"I spent the day with Pearl and Daisy Mae."

She kissed him and stood up. "Come on, get a move on." She put a new canvas on the easel. "Why wasn't Pearl at work? And I thought Daisy Mae had left for, my God, Arizona."

"Today is Saturday," he said and went into the bathroom.

"So it is. I sorta lose track." She began squeezing black and white paint from tubes.

John Lee washed his face and ran a comb through his hair. He came out of the bathroom and put on the same clothes he had worn for the last painting. "These okay?" She nodded. "Shoes or foot fetish?" he grinned.

She wrinkled her nose at him. "Shoes."

He put on his Sunday shoes rather than the sneakers. "Daisy Mae doesn't leave for a couple of weeks yet. They're having fittings and things. Wardrobe gave her . . . him an 1865 lady's riding skirt with a *zipper* on the side. Any *welder* in *Duluth* would know better than that. What do you want me to do?"

"Just stand there." Her voice was tense and hurried.

"Stand?" he groaned. "Don't you want to do another one of me sitting down?" He snapped his fingers. "Do one of me asleep in bed!" She didn't laugh at his joke, and so he stood where she indicated. She began, using only black and white. "Don't artists need the northern light, or something?" he asked hopefully, pointing to the dark skylight.

She smiled. "That's just an excuse artists have been using for the last few thousand years when they didn't feel like working. Be patient with me, John Lee. You can sleep all day tomorrow. I have to go back to San Diego."

"Can't I go with you?"

"No, John Lee." Her voice was so serious that he didn't say anything else.

She finished just before dawn. He was about to fall asleep standing, and so she undressed him and put him to bed. He put his arms around her and kissed her, wanting her to stay a little while. "No," she said, running her fingers through his hair, "you're too sleepy. I'll be back in a few days and we can stay in bed for a week."

He smiled and his eyelids began to droop. "That'll be nice."

"Yes, my little lamb, very nice." She kissed him gently on the mouth. He was asleep before she got out the door.

He woke up late Sunday afternoon and immediately looked at the painting. It wasn't as well done as the other two, he thought. It had a hurried look. It was also in black and white. The John Lee in the painting was just standing there, his arms hanging at his sides, looking at you from beneath lowered brows. John Lee looked at the floor where he had been standing when he posed, but nothing was there. Yet, in the painting, there were lines on the floor. He was standing within a pentagram. And he looked different; he looked older, at least five years older, at least twenty.

Tuesday night Pearl and Daisy Mae took him to Graumann's Chinese where he thought the movie was great and had a wonderful time standing in the footprints, though he had never heard of most of the people who had made them. After the movie they

went to a Chinese restaurant where he ate Chinese food for the
first time. He didn't really like it, but he told Pearl he did because
it made him happy. It was nearly midnight when he got back to
Laurel Canyon. Pearl wanted him to stay in his old room, but he
said he'd better not because Sue might come home during the
night and he wanted to be there.

He went up the wooden steps feeling incredibly content. If Sue
were only there. Punkin came down the banister like a tightrope
walker, making little soft sounds of greeting. John Lee picked him
up and made crooning noises. The cat butted his head against John
Lee's chin, making him chuckle. He carried Punkin into the house
and turned on the light.

His head exploded. His legs wouldn't hold him up any longer,
and he fell to his knees, dropping the cat. There was something
white beside him, but he couldn't make his eyes focus. He thought
he heard a voice, but he wasn't sure because of the wind scream-
ing through his head. The white thing grabbed him and pulled
him to his feet. It shouted more words at him, but he couldn't
understand what they were. Something crashed into his face. The
fog cleared a little. There was a man dressed in white, holding the
front of his shirt. He could smell the sour whiskey on his breath.
He slapped John Lee again and shoved him against the wall, but
he managed to stay on his feet.

The wind was dying in his head. He heard the man's angry
words. "Jesus Christ!" he said, looking at the picture of John Lee
sitting in the chair. He took a knife from his pocket and slashed
through the canvas.

"Stop it!" John Lee croaked and took an unsteady step in the
man's direction.

He whirled, pointing the knife at John Lee. "Jesus Christ!" he
said again, in amazement. "You're just a little kid! She threw me
over for a little kid!" The man's face seemed to collapse as he
lunged at John Lee with the knife. John Lee grabbed his arm, but
the man was far too strong. Then the man stepped on Punkin's tail.
The cat screeched and sank his claws into the man's leg. The man
bawled and fell against John Lee. They both went to the floor, the

man on top, his face beside John Lee's.

"Jesus God," the man whispered in bewilderment. Then his breath crept out in an adenoidal whine and didn't go back in again. John Lee squirmed from beneath him. The man rolled onto his back. The knife handle stuck straight up in his chest, blood already clinging to it. John Lee tried to get to his feet but could only make it to his knees. He saw Pearl and Daisy Mae run in, but there was something very wrong with them. They floated slowly through the air, running toward him but getting farther away. Their mouths moved but only honking sounds came out. Then the floor hit him in the face.

The first thing John Lee felt was someone clutching his hand. He opened his eyes and they felt sticky. Pearl's tense and worried face leaned over him, smiling tentatively. "Pearl?" His face hurt and his mouth wouldn't work properly. He sounded as if he were talking with a mouth full of cotton.

"Don't try to talk, John Lee, sugah," Pearl said anxiously. "You're in the hospital. They said you had a mild concussion. I was scared to death. You've been unconscious for ages. This is *Thursday.*"

John Lee put his hand to his face and felt bandages on his mouth and a compress under his lip. "What happened," he had to swallow to get the words out, "happened to my mouth?" It hurt to talk.

"You got a split lip. It's all purple and swelled up. But don't sweat it, sugah. It makes you look ve-ry sex-y."

John Lee grinned but stopped when it hurt too much. "Is Sue back?"

"She sat with you all night. I made her go home and sleep. They put you in a tacky ward, but Sue had you moved to this nice private room."

"The man . . ." He tried hard to remember what happened. "The man . . ."

"He's dead, sugah. You never saw so many police cars and ambulances and red lights. I don't know what they're gonna do, John Lee." Pearl was distraught.

Sue came in. "Don't upset him, Pearl. Everything will be all right." She smiled brightly, and John Lee felt everything would be. "How are you feeling, little lamb?"

"Awful," he groaned and tried to laugh, but it hurt too much.

Pearl gave his arm a pat and said, "I'd better get back to work before May Company fires my little black fanny. Bye, sugah."

"Bye, Pearl." Pearl left with a big grin. Sue sat in the chair he had vacated. She took John Lee's hand and held it to her face. "I'm sorry," she said as if in pain.

He wanted to bring back her bright smile. "You're looking particularly beautiful today." He had never seen her dressed up before. She wore a silk suit in soft green, her auburn hair loose and long.

She did smile. "Thank you—and thank Playtex, Maidenform, and Miss Clairol. You look . . . pretty awful." But she said it as if she didn't mean it.

"Pearl said I looked ve-ry sex-y."

She grinned and then her face was serious. "John Lee, are you lucid enough to listen and understand what I have to say?" He nodded. "All right. There'll be a . . . hearing . . . or something in a few days, when you're feeling better, with the juvenile authorities. You won't be in any trouble, because they know Jocko attacked you. They know it was an accident. . . ."

"Who was he?" he interrupted.

She looked at him for a moment. "Someone I used to know," she said softly.

"Did you love him? Was he your lover?" He didn't know if he was saying it right. He wanted to know, but he also wanted her to know that he didn't care.

"They're not exactly the same thing, but, yes, to both." She didn't look at him.

"You gave him up for me," he said in wonder, loving her so much it hurt.

She looked at him then and smiled, but there was a funny look in her eyes. "I'd give up most anything for you, John Lee."

The next couple of weeks were a blur. A bunch of people talked to him: men in blue suits and tight-faced women in gray. He told them everything that happened, and they went away to be replaced by others, but none of them would let him see Sue again. There was one lady he liked, who said she was a judge. He told her that his grandfather was a judge but he died a long time ago. She asked him about everything and he told her. She had a kind voice and made the others behave the way Miss Mahan would.

"But, Your Honor," one of the men said, "this child has killed a drunken sailor in a knife fight over a prostitute!"

The judge laughed pleasantly. "Really, Mr. Maley, there's no need for exaggeration. You're not addressing a jury. John was merely protecting himself when attacked. The man's death resulted when he fell on his own knife."

"You can't deny he's been living with a known prostitute. I wouldn't be surprised if she hasn't seduced him."

"Please, Mr. Maley," the judge frowned, displeased, "don't speak that way in front of the child."

"You saw those paintings! Disgusting!"

The judge stood up and began putting on her coat. "Artists have been painting nudes for several thousand years, Mr. Maley. You should see the collection in the Vatican. And these are very good paintings. I made the artist an offer for the nude myself. Come along, John. I'll take you to dinner. Good evening, gentlemen."

Dwayne came to see him one day, but John Lee would never have recognized him. He hadn't seen him since he went away to the army seven years before. Dwayne was twenty-nine, big and good-looking like all the Peacock men. He shook hands with John Lee, saying little, and went away after talking to the judge.

Aunt Rose and her husband flew out from Hawley. She touched him a lot and clucked a lot. Of course, she'd *like* to take care of him, him being the youngest son of her late sister and all, but the way things were, the economy and the cost of living and all, she just didn't see how she could.

It was a terrible thing, her sister marrying into the Peacock family, such an unfortunate family. Poor Grace Elizabeth's husband had died the same day she was buried, the very day John Lee had left on the bus. He had fallen off the tractor and been run over by his own plow. He had crawled almost all the way to the house before he bled to death. Such a tragic family, the Peacocks. Her sister had lost six of her children, five of them in infancy and poor Wash, Jr.

They had tracked him down in Oklahoma because the farm was his now; or, she should say, they had tracked down his wife; or, she should say, his ex-wife, Wash, Jr. had been killed six years ago when a pipe fell off a rig and crushed his skull. His wife hadn't even notified the family. Then she married a Mexican driller from Texas and was living in Tulsa, but what could you expect from one of them trashy O'Dell girls. It was a good thing she had had none of Wash, Jr.'s children, just three stillbirths, because she had no claim on the family at all now. Of course, she had two fat brown babies by her new husband, but you know howMexicans are: like rabbits.

Dwayne hadn't wanted the farm. He just told them to sell it and send him the money. Dwayne was the logical person to take John Lee, being his closest kin. Her sister, Lilah, was in no shape to take care of him. If Dwayne couldn't, then she didn't know what would happen to the poor thing, him living with a prostitute and all.

Aunt Rose and her husband flew back to Hawley.

The judge told him how sorry she was, but if one of his relatives didn't assume custody, as a minor he would have to be declared a ward of the state. But it wouldn't be too bad. He'd have a nice place to live, could finish school, and would have lots of other boys his own age. He asked her why he couldn't live with Sue, but she said it was out of the question and wouldn't discuss it further.

But Dwayne did assume custody, and John Lee moved into his brother's small apartment on Beachwood near Melrose. "Half the money from the sale of the farm is rightfully yours," Dwayne said, dressing for work. "You'll have to go to school this fall. The judge said so. Other than that, your time is your own. But you're not supposed to see that woman again." He showed John Lee how to turn the couch into a bed and then left for work. He was a bartender at a place on Highland and worked from six until it closed at two in the morning.

John Lee caught the bus at Melrose and Vine and rode to Hollywood and Highland. He took a taxi to the house in Laurel Canyon. Sue wasn't at home and he couldn't find Punkin. The three paintings had been framed and were hanging. She had repaired the damaged one. No other paintings were in sight. Everything had been pushed against the walls, leaving most of the floor bare. There were blue chalk marks on the bare boards that had been hastily and inadequately rubbed out. The room smelled oddly.

He found an envelope on the kitchen table with his name on it. He removed the folded piece of notepaper. "John Lee, my little lamb," it read, "I knew you would come, although they told us we mustn't see each other again. You must stay away for a while, John Lee. Only a little while, then it won't matter what they say. There'll be nothing they can do. I love you. Sue."

Pearl wasn't at home either, and so he went back to Dwayne's apartment, watched television for a while, took a bath, and went to bed on the convertible sofa. He didn't know when Dwayne came in about two thirty.

Dwayne always slept until nearly noon. John Lee found little to talk to him about, and Dwayne seemed to prefer no conversation at all. John Lee watched television a lot, went to many movies, and waited for Sue.

He fell asleep in front of the television a few days later and was awakened by Dwayne and the man who was with him. Dwayne frowned at him and the man smiled nervously. The man said something to Dwayne, but he shook his head and led the man into the bedroom, closing the door. John Lee went to bed and didn't know when the man left.

The next morning he looked into the bedroom. Dwayne was sprawled on the bed, naked, still asleep. A twenty dollar bill lay beside him, partially under his hip. John Lee closed the door and fixed breakfast.

Dwayne came in while he was washing the dishes. He didn't say anything for a while, fixing a cup of instant coffee. He sat at the table in his underwear, sipping the coffee. John Lee continued with the dishes, not looking at him. Then he felt Dwayne's eyes on him and he turned. "I don't want you to think I'm queer,"

Dwayne said flatly. "I don't do anything, just lay there. If those guys want to pay me good money, it's no skin off my nose." He turned back to his coffee.

John Lee hung up the dishtowel to dry. "I understand," he said, but he wasn't sure that he did. "It's all right with me."

Dwayne didn't answer but went on sipping coffee as if John Lee weren't there. He made sure, from then on, he was asleep before Dwayne came home.

Sue called a few nights later. He had never heard her voice over the phone, but it sounded different: brighter, less throaty, younger. "Come over, John Lee, my little lamb," she laughed gleefully. "I'm ready. Come over for the showing."

The taxi had to stop a block away because of the police cars and fire trucks. John Lee ran terrified through the milling crowd, but when he reached Sue's house there was nothing to see. The rickety wooden steps went up the hill for about twenty feet and ended in midair. There was nothing beyond them, only a rectangle of bare earth where the house had been. But nothing else, not even the concrete foundation.

He felt a touch on his arm. He whirled to stare wide-eyed at Pearl. He couldn't speak, his throat was frozen. His heart was pounding too hard and he couldn't breathe. Pearl took his arm and led him into the house where he had spent his first night in Hollywood.

Pearl gave him a sip of brandy which burned his throat and released the muscles. "What happened? Where's Sue?" he asked, afraid to get an answer.

"I don't know," Pearl said without any trace of corn pone accent. He seemed on the verge of hysteria himself. "There was a fire. . . ."

"A fire?" he asked, uncomprehending.

"I think it was a fire. . . ." Pearl nervously dropped the brandy bottle. He picked it up, ignoring the stain on the carpet.

"Where's Sue?"

"She . . . she was in the house. I heard her scream," he said rapidly, not looking at John Lee.

John Lee didn't feel anything. His body was frozen and numb.
Then, he couldn't help himself. He began to bawl like a baby. It
was all slipping away. He could feel the good things escaping his
fingers.

Pearl sat beside him on the purple fur chair and tried to comfort
him. "She was over there all evening, singing to herself. I could
hear her, she was very happy. I went over but she wouldn't let me
in. She said I knew better than to look at an artist's work before
it was finished. She said anyway it was a private showing for you.
I didn't hear her singing after that, and then, a little while ago, I
heard a noise like thunder or an explosion. I looked over, and there
was a bright green light in the house, like it was burning on the
inside, but not like fire either. I heard her scream. It was an awful,
terrible scream. There was another voice, a horrible gloating
voice, I couldn't understand. Then the whole house began to glow
with that same green light. It got brighter and brighter, but there
was no heat from it. Then it went away and the house wasn't there
any more."

Pearl got up and handed John Lee an envelope. "I found this on
the deck. She must have tossed it down earlier." John Lee took the
envelope with his name on it. He recognized her handwriting, but
it was more hurried and scrawled than usual. He opened it and
read the short note.

He went back to school that fall and lived with Dwayne. He said
his name was Johnny, because John Lee was home and Sue. He
met a lot of girls who wanted him, but they were pallid and dull
after Sue. He went with them and slept with them but was unable
to feel anything for them. He never turned down any man who
propositioned him either, and there were many. He didn't care
about the money, he only needed someone to relieve the pressures that built up in him. It didn't make any difference, man or
woman. He let lonely middle-aged women keep him, but he never
found what he was looking for.

By the time he was eighteen he had grown a couple of inches
and had filled out. He moved from the apartment on Beachwood
and got a place of his own. He never saw Dwayne again.

The envelope with his name on it was soiled and frayed from much handling. He read it every night. "John Lee, my little lamb," it read. "I tried very hard, so very hard. I thought I had succeeded but something is going wrong. I can feel it. I wish you could have seen me when I was fifteen, John Lee. I wish you could have seen me when I was fifteen. I'm afraid." It was unsigned.

CRAIG STRETE

Time Deer

Craig Strete was born at Fort Wayne around 1950 and describes himself as "Cherokee, White." He is one inch less than six feet tall, has brown eyes and black hair; has done some time; lost his right eye to a butcher knife. He has a B.A. in film from Wright State University. He has also done some nonwriting time as a migratory farm worker ("picking tomatoes, canning factories, tomato cook") and further lists as employments that he has been a steel riveter in a steel factory, has done grocery carryout, and been a library clerk.

He is a member of various Indian organizations and supports the American Indian Movement's goals of self-determinism for Indian peoples. For a time he edited a magazine, *Red Planet Earth,* which he says was ". . . amateur in terms of production, but did have, I think, some worthwhile contents."

He adds, "My first book, a hardcover collection of my short stories, *If All Else Fails, We Can Whip the Horse's Eyes and Make Him Cry and Sleep,* came out September 1976 in Holland." There is no American collection as yet, but there are preliminary discussions going on.

Strete reported that he had sold forty-three short stories, one Western and five juveniles (counting pen names), but since he has a disconcerting habit of withdrawing his work from publication at something past the last minute, those totals are subject to later adjustments.

He regards talking about himself as being "like dancing for tourists and I'm against that." So there is nothing more to be said.

THE old man watched the boy. The boy watched the deer. The deer was watched by all, and the Great Being above.

The old man remembered when he was a young boy and his father showed him a motorcycle thing on a parking lot.

The young boy remembered his second life with some regret, not looking forward to the coming of his first wife.

Tuesday morning the Monday morning traffic jam was three days old. The old man sat on the hood of a stalled car and watched the boy. The boy watched the deer. The deer was watched by all and the Great Being above.

The young boy resisted when his son, at the insistence of his bitch of a white wife, had tried to put him in a rest home for the elderly. Now he watched a deer beside the highway. And was watched in turn.

The old man was on the way to somewhere. He was going someplace, someplace important, he forgot just where. But he knew he was going.

The deer had relatives waiting for her, grass waiting for her, seasons being patient on her account. As much as she wanted to please the boy by letting him look at her, she had to go. She apologized with a shake of her head.

The old man watched the deer going. He knew she had someplace to go, someplace important. He did not know where she was going but he knew why.

The old man was going to be late. He could have walked. He was only going across the road. He was going across the road to get to the other side. He was going to be late for his own funeral. The old man was going someplace. He couldn't remember where.

"DID you make him wear the watch? If he's wearing the watch he should—"

"He's an old man, honey! His mind wanders," said Frank Strong Bull.

"Dr. Amber is waiting! Does he think we can afford to pay for every appointment he misses?" snarled Sheila, running her fingers through the tangled ends of her hair. "Doesn't he ever get anywhere on time?"

"He lives by Indian time. Being late is just something you must expect from—" he began, trying to explain.

She cut him off. "Indian this and Indian that! I'm so sick of your god damn excuses I could vomit!"

"But—"

"Let's just forget it. We don't have time to argue about it. We have to be at the doctor's office in twenty minutes. If we leave now we can just beat the rush hour traffic. I just hope your father's there when we arrive."

"Don't worry. He'll be there," said Frank, looking doubtful.

BUT the deer could not leave. She went a little distance and then turned and came back. And the old man was moved because he knew the deer had come back because the boy knew how to look at the deer.

And the boy was happy because the deer chose to favor him. And he saw the deer for what she was. Great and golden and quick in her beauty.

And the deer knew that the boy thought her beautiful. For it was the purpose of the deer in this world on that morning to be beautiful for a young boy to look at.

And the old man who was going someplace was grateful to the deer and almost envious of the boy. But he was one with the boy who was one with the deer and they were all one with the Great Being above. So there was no envy, just the great longing of age for youth.

"THAT son of a bitch!" growled Frank Strong Bull. "The bastard cut me off." He yanked the gear shift out of fourth and slammed it into third. The tach needle shot into the red and the Mustang backed off, just missing the foreign car that had swerved in front of it.

"Oh, Christ—We'll be late!" muttered Sheila, turning in the car seat to look out the back window. "Get into the express lane."

"Are you kidding? With this traffic?"

His hands gripped the wheel like a weapon. He lifted his right hand and slammed the gear shift. Gears ground, caught hold, and the Mustang shot ahead. Yanking the wheel to the left, he cut in front of a truck, which hit its brakes, missing the Mustang by inches. He buried the gas pedal and the car responded. He pulled up level with the sports car that had cut him off. He honked and made an obscene gesture as he passed. Sheila squealed with delight. "Go! Go!" she exclaimed.

THE old man had taken liberties in his life. He'd had things to remember and things he wanted to forget. Twice he had married.

The first time. He hated the first time. He'd been blinded by her looks and his hands had got the better of him. He had not known his own heart and not knowing, he had let his body decide. It was something he would always regret.

That summer he was an eagle. Free. Mating in the air. Never touching down. Never looking back. That summer. His hands that touched her were wings. And he flew and the feathers covered the scars that grew where their bodies had touched.

He was of the air and she was of the earth. She muddied his dreams. She had woman's body but lacked woman's spirit. A star is a stone to the blind. She saw him through crippled eyes. She possessed. He shared. There was no life between them. He saw the stars and counted them one by one into her hand, that gift that all lovers share. She saw stones. And she turned away.

He was free because he needed. She was a prisoner because she wanted. One day she was gone. And he folded his wings and the earth came rushing at him and he was an old man with a small son. And he lived in a cage and was three years dead. And his son was a small hope that melted. He was his mother's son. He could see that in his son's eyes. It was something the old man would always regret.

But the deer, the young boy, these were things he would never regret.

DR. AMBER was hostile. "Damn it! Now look—I can't sign the commitment papers if I've never seen him."

Sheila tried to smile pleasantly. "He'll show up. His hotel room is just across the street. Frank will find him. Don't worry."

"I have other patients! I can't be held up by some doddering old man," snapped Dr. Amber.

"Just a few more minutes," Sheila pleaded.

"You'll have to pay for two visits. I can't run this place for free. Every minute I'm not working, I'm losing money."

"We'll pay," said Sheila grimly. "We'll pay."

THE world was big and the deer had to take her beauty through the world. She had been beautiful in one place for one boy on one morning of this world. It was time to be someplace else. The deer turned and fled into the woods, pushing her beauty before her into the world.

The young boy jumped to his feet. His heart racing, his feet pounding, he ran after her with the abandon of youth that is caring. He chased beauty through the world and disappeared from the old man's sight in the depths of the forest.

And the old man began dreaming that—

FRANK Strong Bull's hand closed on his shoulder and his son shook him, none too gently.

The old man looked into the face of his son and did not like what he saw. He allowed himself to be led to the doctor's office.

"Finally," said Sheila. "Where the hell was he?"

Dr. Amber came into the room with a phony smile. "Ah! The elusive one appears! And how are we today?"

"We are fine," said the old man, bitterly. He pushed the outstretched stethoscope away from his chest.

"Feisty isn't he," observed Dr. Amber.

"Let's just get this over with," said Sheila. "It's been drawn out long enough as it is."

"Not sick," said the old man. "You leave me alone." He made two fists and backed away from the doctor.

"How old is he?" asked Dr. Amber, looking at the old man's wrinkled face and white hair.

"Past eighty, at least," said his son. "The records aren't available and he can't remember himself."

"Over eighty, you say. Well, that's reason enough then," said Dr. Amber. "Let me give him a cursory examination, just a formality, and then I'll sign the papers."

The old man unclenched his fists. He looked at his son. His eyes burned. He felt neither betrayed nor wronged. He felt only sorrow. He allowed one tear, only one tear, to fall. It was for his son who could not meet his eyes.

And for the first time since his son had married her, his eyes fell upon his son's wife's eyes. She seemed to shrivel under his gaze, but she met his gaze and he read the dark things in her eyes.

They were insignificant, not truly a part of his life. He had seen the things of importance. He had watched the boy. The boy had watched the deer. And the deer had been watched by all and the Great Being above.

The old man backed away from them until his back was against a wall. He put his hand to his chest and smiled. He was dead before his body hit the floor.

"A MASSIVE coronary," said Dr. Amber to the ambulance attendant. "I just signed the death certificate."

"They the relatives?" asked the attendant, jerking a thumb at the couple sitting silently in chairs by the wall.

Dr. Amber nodded.

The attendant approached them.

"It's better this way," said Sheila. "An old man like that, no reason to live, no—"

"Where you want I should take the body?" asked the attendant.

"Vale's Funeral Home," said Sheila.

Frank Strong Bull stared straight ahead. He heard nothing. His eyes were empty of things, light and dark.

"Where is it?" asked the attendant.

"Where is what?" asked Dr. Amber.

"The body? Where's the body?"

"It's in the next room. On the table," said Dr. Amber coming around his desk. He took the attendant's arm and led him away from the couple.

"I'll help you put it on the stretcher."

THE old man who watched the deer. He had dreamed his second wife in his dreams. He had dreamed that. But she had been real. She had come when emptiness and bitterness had possessed him. When the feathers of his youth had been torn from his wings. She filled him again with bright pieces of dreams. And for him, in that second half of his life, far from his son and that first one, he began again. Flying. Noticing the world. His eyes saw the green things, his lips tasted the sweet things and his old age was warm.

It was all bright and fast and moving, that second life of his and they were childless and godless and were themselves children and gods instead. And they grew old in their bodies but death seemed more like an old friend than an interruption. It was sleep. One night the fever took her. Peacefully. Took her while she slept and he neither wept nor followed. For she had made him young again and the young do not understand death.

"I'LL HELP you put it on the stretcher."

They opened the door.

AND THE old man watched the boy and did not understand death. And the young boy watched the deer and understood beauty. And the deer was watched by all and the Great Being above. And the boy saw the deer for what she was. And like her, he became great and golden and quick. And the old man began dreaming that—

FRANK Strong Bull's hand, his son's hand, closed on his shoulder and shook him, none too gently.

THEY opened the door. The body was gone.

THE last time it was seen, the body was chasing a deer that pushed its beauty through the world, disappearing from an old man's sight into the depths of the forest.

Nebula Awards, 1975: Win, Place and Show

Detailed listings of the winners, year by year, have appeared in previous Award volumes, but at the beginning of a new decade the data may better be sought from source books.* Voting for the Nebula Awards for 1975, chosen from an unusually heavy ballot, was as follows:

NOVEL

Winner: THE FOREVER WAR *by Joe Haldeman* (St. Martin's Press; Ballantine Books)

Runners-up: THE MOTE IN GOD'S EYE *by Larry Niven and Jerry Pournelle* (Simon & Schuster; SF Book Club)

DHALGREN *by Samuel R. Delany* (Bantam)

THE FEMALE MAN *by Joanna Russ* (Bantam)

*The reader is referred to *Nebula Ten* (Harper & Row) for the ten-year Nebula list; or, for the history of sf awards more broadly considered, to *A History of the Hugo, Nebula and International Fantasy Awards,* published by Howard DeVore, 4705 Weddel Street, Dearborn, Michigan 48125.

NOVELLA

Winner: "Home is the Hangman" *by Roger Zelazny (Analog)*
Runners-up: "The Storms of Windhaven" *by Lisa Tuttle and George
   R. R. Martin (Analog)*
   "A Momentary Taste of Being" *by James Tiptree, Jr.
   (from The New Atlantis, Hawthorn)*
   "Sunrise West" *by William K. Carlson (Vortex)*

NOVELETTE

Winner: "San Diego Lightfoot Sue" *by Tom Reamy (The Magazine of
   Fantasy and Science Fiction)*
Runners-up: "The Final Fighting of Fion MacCumhaill" *by Randall
   Garrett (The Magazine of Fantasy and Science Fiction)*
   "Retrograde Summer" *by John Varley (The Magazine of
   Fantasy and Science Fiction)*
   "A Galaxy Called Rome" *by Barry Malzberg (The Maga-
   zine of Fantasy and Science Fiction)*
   "The Custodians" *by Richard Cowper (The Magazine of
   Fantasy and Science Fiction)*

SHORT STORY

Winner: "Catch that Zeppelin!" *by Fritz Leiber (The Magazine of
   Fantasy and Science Fiction)*
Runners-up: "Child of All Ages" *by P. J. Plauger (Analog)*
   "Shatterday" *by Harlan Ellison (Gallery)*
   "Sail the Tide of Mourning" *by Richard Lupoff (New Di-
   mensions 5)*
   "Time Deer" *by Craig Strete (Worlds of If)*
   "Utopia of a Tired Man" *by Jorge Luis Borges (The New
   Yorker)*
   "A Scraping of the Bones" *by A. J. Budrys (Analog)*
   "Doing Lennon" *by Greg Benford (Analog)*

DRAMATIC PRESENTATION

Winner: YOUNG FRANKENSTEIN, screenplay by Mel Brooks and Gene Wilder (Twentieth Century-Fox Film Corp.)

GRAND MASTER AWARD

Winner: Jack Williamson